A FINE LINE

KEN GROSS

A FINE LINE

A TOM DOHERTY ASSOCIATES BOOK
NEW YORK

This is a work of fiction. All the characters and events portrayed in this book are fictitious, and any resemblance to real people or events is purely coincidental.

A FINE LINE

A TOR BOOK
Published by Tom Doherty Associates, Inc.
49 West 24 Street
New York, NY 10010

Library of Congress Cataloging-in-Publication Data

Gross, Kenneth G.
A fine line
A Tom Doherty Associates book.
ISBN 0-312-93139-5
I. Title.
PS3557.R583F5 1989 88-29168
813 .54—dc19

0 9 8 7 6 5 4 3 2

For Max and Andy

A FINE LINE

1

Monday, November 2, 9:45 P.M., 132 Hours and Counting

That was the third time the Whitestone Bridge had passed under Jack Mann's window. He thought, Can I make it home? An airport delay was no big deal, ordinarily. But Jack was so damned tired. He had counted out his stamina like pennies, and now, when they were just about all spent, here he was still circling the airport!

It's a gift, he told himself. I have a rare talent in the bad timing department.

The man beside him in the aisle seat was braced stiff for the landing and Jack was tempted to tell him, Relax, we're only going around a few times, but something made him stop. The thing that stopped him was his own foot, which happened to be crossed over his knee. He noticed with a heavy-hearted sigh that he was displaying a nice blue sock. A moment ago, just before he switched feet, he had been admiring a very attractive black sock.

He felt a flame in his cheeks as he uncrossed his feet and tried to push the legs of his pants lower to cover his embarrassment. A rare talent for bad timing and mismatched socks, he muttered miserably.

Jack didn't exactly blame the man next to him for the fact that he was wearing two different-colored socks, but when it came to public humiliation he blamed everyone. When you feel your cheeks go up in flames, he firmly believed, there are no innocent bystanders. Besides, it did not escape his notice that the guy in the aisle seat was gripping the armrest with beautifully manicured nails. And he was wearing a gold watch. Jack would bet his life that the man was wearing matching silk socks.

Well, that's what happens when economy is full and you get stuck in first class. You find yourself in unsavory company, sitting next to guys who don't wrinkle and who smell of expensive cologne and are well equipped with hose. Jack was definitely not at home flying first-class haberdashery. He felt suffocated, stuffed into a tight, overpriced suit.

But the thing that continued to depress him was the undigested memory of Chicago. Chicago, he told himself, as he had told himself at each new low point in his downwardly mobile life, was the worst.

It wasn't bad enough to spend the night in a seedy hotel room, watching roaches crawling across the floor, listening to mean fights through thin walls between shrill hookers and heartless pimps; it wasn't bad enough to have to pinch the expense account by eating a greasy breakfast that kept bubbling acid back into his throat.

All that wasn't bad enough. He had to endure a crucial insult to his almost broken pride.

He could feel it coming when he stepped off the hushed elevator into the thickly carpeted offices of the insurance company where he was to deliver a sealed envelope to a lawyer. Jack felt dirty and unshaven and dangerously insolent. I will not explode, he warned himself, again and again, no matter what the provocation. And there were subtle provocations. Like the authentic French impressionist paintings that glared down from the walls like cops, reminding Jack of his place. And the woman behind the bulletproof window in the reception area was one of those iron beauties who wore a brittle, insincere smile. When Jack announced himself, she offered to take the envelope herself, as if he was nothing more than an intercity messenger, rather than a courier, which he tried to convince himself was his true role.

No, said Jack, pulling back the envelope, trying to draw this cold fish into eye contact. But she was a pro at this game. In a voice crisp with contempt, she told Jack to be seated. Even the "please" managed to convey the sense that she could see exactly where he had spent the night. Jack was impressed but undaunted.

She'll smile, he thought, when the boss comes out and makes a fuss over me. She'll smile one of those apology smiles, when people realize that they've misjudged the situation.

Still, as he waited in the spotless reception area, restrained by the Muzak and genuine artwork, Jack was conscious of the stains and creases in his suit. Any second, he thought, a roach will crawl out of my cuff. He sat there for an hour on the edge of the leather couch, leafing blind through *Business Week* and the *Law Journal*, feeling that itchy premonition.

Finally the lawyer came out, took the envelope and signed the receipt where Jack told him to sign, then turned away without a word. Without a handshake. Without a human glance of recognition. All he ever showed Jack was the back of his manicured hand.

The receptionist smiled at Jack. It wasn't the apology smile; it was the cold I-told-you-so smile.

And so, Jack thought on the plane circling New York City, why shouldn't I feel a little retaliatory malice toward my fellowman? Maybe this guy on the aisle hadn't been directly responsible for the abuse to his dignity in Chicago, but since when was life fair? Why wasn't he entitled to a little unfair revenge? Everybody else seemed to savor getting even with an innocent bystander. Wasn't that the way it worked nowadays? Cabdrivers took it out on pedestrians; pedestrians took it out on waitresses; waitresses took it out on customers; and customers took it out on cabdrivers. As far as Jack could see, the world spun on a vicious cycle of spite.

A man wearing a custom-made suit and a gold watch and matching silk hosiery could probably stand a little undeserved blame. It would improve his character.

But when he glanced sideways, all Jack saw was a poor, miserable son of a bitch who was gripping the armrest so hard that he was about to break one of the pampered fingernails. He didn't have the heart to let the man sweat like that. It just wasn't in his nature. And so he leaned over and whispered, "Relax, pal, we're only circling."

The man in the aisle seat shut his eyes and remained

rigid with fear. He didn't believe Jack. Not with the stench of champagne and beer on Jack's breath.

So, fuck you; suffer, Jack said under his breath, feeling stupid.

Then Jack heard the crackle of the intercom, followed by the lazy, liquid official voice: "Ladies and gentlemen, this is the captain speaking. Seems we have run into a little bit of traffic. We're just gonna hafta sit up here a bit, but we'll be down on the ground before you know it. Meanwhile, enjoy the view and the cabin attendants will take your order for beverages. It's on the house."

The man beside Jack deflated, then unbuckled his seat belt. He looked over and, with his eyes, delivered a sheepish apology.

Jack smiled back thinly, then turned away to admire the advertised view. However, the famous view was spoiled by a spittle of rain. Rain, he said to himself with resignation. What else could possibly go wrong? He held his hand up and the cabin attendant came by with that cocked eyebrow. "Champagne," he said, although his brain was already swimming in the sour soup of two small splits that they served in first class. She stood there for a moment, hesitating, deciding whether or not to draw the line. Then she asked the manicure if he wanted anything, and he gave her a tight shake of his head. Jack sat back and swallowed the champagne and wished it were beer. He saw the cabin attendant watching him, waiting for a confirming sign that he was riding the wrong class seat into New York.

On the ground, life returned to the natural order of inequality. He was no longer a first-class passenger, just another middle-aged man thick with his liquor trying to carry his luggage despite the touch of bursitis. There was a chauffeur waiting for the man with the manicured nails. The chauffeur held an umbrella over the man's head, to protect him for the exposed few feet he had to travel between the terminal and the limousine.

Good thing, thought Jack, poor devil might drown. But as the limousine pulled away, splashing him with a cold spray of filthy water, Jack lost his tolerance: I should have told that schmuck that one of the engines fell off, he thought.

Jack boarded the shuttle bus to the long-term parking lot. One by one, the other passengers with their winter tans and tennis gear and designer luggage were dropped off, until, as he knew that he would be, Jack was the last one left. The bus deposited him deep in the long-term parking lot, alone. The wind whipping off the bay blew rain and hard pellets of sleet into Jack's face. He gritted his teeth and felt the grainy sand of a disintegrating filling.

He looked up, the way he would when feeling beset, and found a face full of hard rain. "I am going to try not to take this personally," he said out loud. "You're not making it easy."

Jack stood for a moment gathering strength, then hoisted his battered suitcase and began walking, bent into the wind and the sleet and all the other natural enemies in his path.

In the distance he heard a rumble that he took to be thunder. There were flashing lights near the main cargo terminal, but the old firehorse wasn't interested. Fuck it, he muttered. Fuck the wind and the rain and fuck my wet, spongy shoes. I do not brake for sirens anymore.

As he slogged along, wet and miserable, Jack harbored a simple dream: to once again hold a steady job. If only he had a steady job he could take tomorrow off—call in sick, maybe. Ah, to play hooky. To stay home and sleep. This would be a small slice of heaven.

But you couldn't call in sick if you didn't have a job anymore. No more civil service cushion upon which to rest his weary head. All he had was a self-proclaimed title and a growing family of unpaid bills.

As he splashed through the puddles and shivered in the rain, a terrible thought occurred to him: he couldn't afford to get sick. He had to be up and around in case a client showed up. He could not even afford a simple cold. He had to be out there.

Ah, fuck all the guys with manicured nails and six-figure incomes and chauffeured limousines!

He poked his head up like a periscope, squinting through the cold rain, looking for the big, gas-guzzling LeSabre. Just let it be there! Maybe it wasn't a stretch Lincoln, but it would do. Just let me get inside, he pleaded with whatever deity was listening to prayers in the long-term parking lot of La Guardia Airport on a cold, filthy night in November. Just let me get out of this shit and behind that nice, fat wheel. To feel the quick blast of hot air from that old reliable heater. Good old Buick. Just let me settle in on the ratty old seat and hear that engine spit hello. I'll be all tucked inside, cozy like a baby.

And when he saw the familiar hulk a few rows down, he smiled and relaxed. He nodded hello to the car, as dear to him then as a pair of open arms. Just a few more steps . . .

"Don't move," said a high, no-nonsense voice behind him. At that same unguarded instant, Jack felt what he was certain was a gun behind his ear.

He started to reach for the gun that wasn't there anymore, but he caught himself before he was murdered. "Aw, shit!" he groaned.

Mugged in a fucking rainstorm in the middle of nowhere, he thought miserably. Who else but me?

"Listen, pal, all's I got is about thirty bucks cash and some traveler's checks," he said. "You're welcome to the whole estate."

He was weary and disappointed at his own carelessness—not yet frightened.

"I don't give a fuck about your money. You're going to take me outta here, fella."

The voice behind his ear was like grinding gears. "Take it easy," said Jack, addressing himself as much as the man behind his ear.

Jack felt the man close in. An arm—a powerful arm—wrapped itself around his head and pulled him hard into the gun, which was now jammed inside Jack's ear. He could smell the man's sour breath, which seemed to give him substance, as well as something else that he could not quite identify. He wasn't sure why, but suddenly he was very frightened.

"Don't be tellin' me to take it easy, you piece of shit," said the man in a raspy, cruel whisper.

The man twisted the gun barrel viciously inside Jack's ear. The metal tore through the easy flesh. Jack felt the pain and then something wet spilling down his cheek. My God, he realized, it's blood!

The feel of his blood running down his cheek sent shivers through his body. It made him feel vulnerable and fragile. It made him put a different estimate on the situation. The softening influence of the wine was gone. He was cold sober.

"What did I say?" Jack tried to say, but his voice was

strangled and all he managed to communicate was his own terror.

The man behind him then relaxed his grip. He seemed to back off a bit, loosened up enough to pull back from some all-out outburst. "You don't want to fuck with me, fella. You really don't. Don't be tellin' me to take it easy."

The normal speaking voice of the man with the gun was somehow more sinister than the grinding gears. He's bouncing around like a loony, thought Jack. Anything can happen with this one.

"I just killed a man, y'see, and I'm a little crazy," said the man in a voice almost gleefully manic. "You want to be a little careful with me." Jack nodded against the restraining arm around his throat. "Now, where's your fucking car?"

"There," Jack managed to croak, jutting his chin to point at the LeSabre two rows down.

They marched carefully, like twin tightrope walkers, until they reached the car. The gunman put his mouth beside Jack's wounded ear—it felt like a reminder, a kind of punctuation mark—and he spoke: "Now be a good fella and open the trunk. I don't have time to convince you I'm a desperate man; you'll just hafta take my word for it."

Jack didn't need convincing. The other odor had come back to him. He'd smelled it first when the man behind him put the gun barrel in his ear. He couldn't quite place it, and, at the time, it was confused with the man's foul breath. But he knew that other smell, even if he couldn't make the quick connection. As he fumbled with the keys to the trunk of the car he remembered. It was gunpowder. He smelled cordite from a freshly fired weapon. And it came from the man's gun.

As soon as he made that connection, his heart sank. For hard upon that realization was another. The man had no choice. He had made his confession; he had worked himself into the state. The next step was inevitable. The next step always seemed inevitable. Jack thought, he's got to kill me.

Jack was in a panic. Wait a fucking minute, he wanted to shout. What the fuck is going on here! This is a mistake! He felt that wild, out-of-control helplessness of all the world's victims. He wanted to run. He wanted to beg. He wanted to turn this way and that way and start screaming, but he couldn't. He was standing on a land mine, and the slightest movement, the least little error, would be lethal.

In the end, the single thing that it came back to was this: the man had to kill him. He had killed once already. Jack smelled the proof. And he had confessed. The logic was infallible. You don't confess to strangers, you don't create witnesses, unless you intend to eliminate them. No, there was no doubt at all. Jack knew that he was the next victim.

I don't even know his face, thought Jack, as if that was an important omission. You should know the face of your executioner. He should look you in the eye.

"Let's get moving," said the man impatiently.

There was something else that gave away the man's intentions. It was in the voice. Jack heard a kind of wild, high-pitched excitement in the man's voice. He'd killed, all right. Now he wanted to kill again. The blood was up. One wasn't enough.

You are going to go down as one more Onion Field victim, Jack told himself. You're going to die like a sheep because you have a gift for bad timing and bad luck. They are going to find you between the cars or in some nameless lot, with the rain in your dumb, lifeless face and a bullet in your dumb, lifeless brain. Was it the champagne? Was that the fog that made him slow? He shook his head to clear it.

And as all this came to him, he felt the hard, sobering slap of real anger. It was as if he had pumped himself up, argued himself into a move. The one side insulting the other into action. And he became cold and deliberate and determined. He was in trouble—no doubt of that—but he was not going down without a fight.

Jack opened the trunk of his car, and as he did he improvised a plan. It was very simple: he would kill the gunman first.

All he would need for the plan to work would be a little luck. He was overdue for the luck. And he needed enough time to get at his own gun, which was hidden deep in a secret spot of his trunk.

The trunk of the car was a landfill of used tires, broken parts, wastepaper, empty cans, stained shirts, soiled paper bags and unidentifiable debris. The gunman took one look and turned away.

"Clear a space for my bag," he said with disdain. He didn't want the housekeeping chore.

Good, you asshole, thought Jack. Good, you lazy putz! That's one mistake. Just stay sloppy, please God!

Jack reached inside the trunk and began to systematically move his hand under the junk. He kept up a muttering, masking chatter about the terrible mess and how he always intended to clean it up but what with one thing and another, things kept getting in the way and he kept putting it off. And all the while his hand crept lower and lower toward the secret nest he had fashioned behind the spare tire.

The gunman sensed something, but he was distracted

by a fresh rush of sirens and flashing lights over at the main cargo terminal.

Just one more minute, prayed Jack. Just one more careless minute!

"It's the prime minister," he said to distract. "Coming to the UN. Cops run around like chickens for a week."

"Here we go!" said the gunman, and Jack felt a surge of fear. He's got me now. I'm a dead man! But then he saw that the gunman was referring to the activity at the terminal. He still hadn't tumbled to Jack's move.

Then Jack felt the cold, comforting barrel of his own gun hidden behind the spare tire. Oh, let it be loaded. I'm sure I left it loaded, except for the empty chamber on the barrel as a precaution. His hand was steady and quick. He slipped the gun out of the holster and took it off safety. By then his head was practically buried in the trunk. He grunted as he worked frantically.

"Hey!" cried the gunman, suddenly aware that something odd was taking place inside the trunk. "Hey!" he said at a loss, confused, unable to grasp what was about to happen, just as Jack pulled his arm out of the deep mess with the gun in his hand.

The gunman was about to say something else as Jack whirled and made his move. He dropped away evasively just as he had been taught and got off two quick shots. *Pock! Pock!* Straight at the gunman's heart. Two. Not one. That was the drill. You fired in groups of two and that multiplied the chances of a kill. Training.

As Jack was falling away to his left, keeping his right hand, his gun hand, free, he saw clearly that the first grouping had been lethal. One, maybe both, of his bullets had gone into the doomed gunman's heart. He was that clinical in his evaluation.

The gunman never spoke another word. From the

ground, Jack put two more bullets into the gunman's body. *Pock! Pock!* That's how it sounded—muffled in the rain. The gunman looked down at his crushed chest, amazed. His face registered wonder and surprise. He was dead before he had time to register fear.

Jack felt a flicker of pride. It was an instant of pure pleasure, an almost sensual thrill at his victory.

Jack was coiled in his own killing mood. He was up on one knee. His right hand was clenched around the gun; his left hand was rolled into a fist. His teeth were bared, and out of the tight spaces between them came a savage hiss.

He booted the loose gun away from the dead man's hand, then leaned over and felt for a pulse. His finger moved around the already clammy wrist, but there was nothing there to feel. He dropped the dead hand and it fell with a splash to the ground. Jack experienced a fierce satisfaction at the surface of the concrete. The rough texture of life. He brushed his fingers along the sandpaperlike surface. His fingers danced in the puddle from the rain. Every sensation was a triumph.

He looked around quickly, furtively, almost as if he was seeking a fresh target. Another threat. Something . . . anything with which to discharge this pent-up fury. Jack was in a murderous frenzy. It was lucky that there was no one around to kill.

He had seen this mood before. He knew it, although this was the first time he'd ever felt it himself. He remembered once asking a man who had slaughtered a whole houseful of people why he had done it. No reason. The man had had a quarrel with his wife, but after he killed her he'd murdered her parents and a grandparent, and even a strange boarder who happened to live under the same roof, all unconnected to the argument with the wife. How come? Jack wanted to know. None of the others had done a thing to him. They didn't interfere. They didn't try to stop him from escaping. Why kill innocent bystanders? Jack wanted to know.

The killer had shrugged. He had an explanation, but he didn't think Jack would understand.

Why? insisted Jack. Tell me.

They were there, said the killer. They fell within the killing range. They were simply caught in it. That simple.

Now, crouched and snarling in the airport parking lot, looking for fresh victims, Jack understood.

The mood passed. He realized that he had not yet seen the face of the man who would have been his killer. What would the face of death look like?

My God, he was young. And handsome.

"You see what happens?" he said out loud to the astonished face. "You see? Ah, schmuck!"

Always the moralizing cop. Even now, when he no longer carried a badge. Lecturing a corpse.

The rain suddenly felt good. Refreshing. It cooled the smoldering temper. He was surprised by it, too. Apparently, it had been raining hard all along. But he hadn't noticed. It was as if his scalp had held that storm in check while his own emotional storm ran its course.

Now he was back to reality, and he saw, between the rows, people heading to their own cars. It was funny. They were walking normally, steadily, without the jerky, quick, nervy movements of people who have just heard a string of shots. As if nothing at all had happened. Jack was amazed. The world had done a violent flip-flop, and as far as he could see, no one had noticed.

He took another look and saw that it had really happened; he had not had a psychotic episode in the rain. The man was lying in a puddle with his eyes open, unblinking in the rain. You don't get no deader than that, thought Jack.

He saw the bulky military travel bag that had been slung over the man's shoulder. It was caught under the body. It was for that bag that Jack had been supposedly clearing a space in the trunk. In a way, the bag had actually saved him.

Well, thought Jack, it's none of my business. I'll just turn the whole mess over to the Port Authority cops. Let them clean it up.

All that gunplay. At least two dead. Might have been me lying there like a dead fish instead of him. And all for that fucking bag.

Well, maybe I have earned a look inside. What harm could there be in taking a look? If someone came along, well, Jack was a completely innocent victim satisfying a small measure of curiosity. Nothing sinister in that.

It took, in fact, quite an effort. Jack had to roll the gunman onto his side to slip the strap off his shoulder. Then he rolled him onto the other side before he could pull the bag out from under him.

He took the bag under a nearby light stanchion. He was excited. A vague thrill of being close to something so dangerous it inspired murder. For whatever was in the bag was clearly in a tainted, forbidden realm. Drugs, he thought. Cocaine ready to be cut. Or pure heroin. He had seen the factories where they diluted it with lactose, where the fat women had to wear surgical masks and still developed vicious drug habits. Drugs, goddammit. Miserable, killer drugs.

He pulled the zipper on the canvas bag and the

money came spilling out. Like water. Big packets of bills, spilling out in the rain. Jack fell back, stunned, as if he had just pulled the top and out sprang a jack-in-the-box.

Jack was dizzy. He was afraid that he would pass out. He turned his face into the rain to revive himself.

He expected drugs. Where were the drugs? A load of drugs made sense at an airport, what with all the smuggling possibilities. And he had already made his peace with the idea that he had killed a drug dealer. In fact, he had already defended it. There was something noble about putting a drug supplier out of business. He had already calculated that he had saved so many kids from getting hooked, put so many junkies in clinics, driven so many street pushers out of business.

That would have been the payoff from nailing a guy with a bag full of dope.

But a bag full of cash?

A bag of cash made him a thief. Who would believe him now? A cop with money troubles, an unlicensed gun and a bag full of cash. They would see the money and roll their eyes and make assumptions like indictments.

There was a difference between dope and cash. A bag full of drugs offered no temptation to Jack. He would destroy it or turn it over to the authorities. There was no chance that he would convert it into the lavish street value money. He had seen many dirty things in his lifetime, but drug trafficking was the worst.

Money made it different. When it tumbled out of the bag, Jack had an incriminating thought: I could sleep tomorrow.

But he had no time for complicated self-examination. There were flashing lights and sirens in the distance.

Jack had two choices. He could yell cop; or he could run. They might or might not believe his version of events. In any event, he would fall under suspicion. Under the best of circumstances he would be nailed for carrying an unlicensed gun. He would do time—and all time for an ex-cop is hard time. He would be hounded forever. He could simply walk away, but they would find the body and they would track all the cars in the lot and sooner or later they would find him. They would match his gun with the bullets and that would be worse than the first choice. It was all inevitable. In his misery, he crawled over to the light stanchion and emptied his belly dry. All that champagne and beer pumped out in long, sour bursts.

His eyes were wet and he was exhausted, leaning against the post, when he realized that he had one other choice.

In that swarm of thoughts and decisions that raced through his mind, Jack knew that the first thing that he had to do was to get away from the airport. And in the same mental chaos, he knew that he would take the dead man with him. He couldn't leave the body behind. The police would find the body, begin an investigation, check on all the cars ticketed in the lot and sooner or later come around to him. Not that he had acted in anything but self-defense.

And the money would go along for the ride. He wouldn't keep it. He would never spend it. He would have to give it back. But it would be nice, even for a little while, to have a sack full of cash in his possession. Just to see what it felt like.

There wasn't much time. The thing hadn't crystallized. They were still in that shadow period of confusion and doubt. But it wouldn't last. Soon they would begin to seal off the airport. Already highway units and precinct cars would be heading for preassigned blocking positions. If his sense of timing was still working, he knew that he would have to get going.

Jack replaced the unlicensed pistol in the hidden nest behind the spare tire. He scooped up the dead man's gun, along with the loose bundles of cash, and stuffed it all back into the canvas bag. He jammed the bag deep into the recesses of the trunk, under the rear seat. Then he wrapped the dead gunman in his raincoat to prevent the blood from leaking all over the trunk. He saw a stain spreading through the arm of the raincoat. It would never come out. He realized that something indelible was spreading like the stain.

Before he lifted the dead man he thought, it's not too late. I'm innocent. All I have to do is call the cops. All I have to do is flag down a car and I can walk away clean.

But with the bile backing up in his throat, he knew that it was already too late. There were already too many pieces of tampered evidence. And as he lifted the dead man into the trunk he burned one more bridge.

2

Monday, November 2, 11:45 P.M., 130 Hours and Counting

Nora was working the bar when she spotted the little man worming his way toward her, motioning for her in that nervous, head-bobbing way that made her cringe. She nodded at Larry, the regular bartender, who looked up and saw Marty making faces and advancing in his own sweaty way. Larry saw the look on Nora's face and knew that Marty was in for trouble. He smiled and became a spectator at the silent struggle between Marty and Nora.

Well, what's Martin want now? thought Nora. Some more nonsense. Another excuse to lay his clammy hands on me; another opportunity to get in close and breathe his sorry whiskey breath in my face.

She let him wait while she finished the refills at the far end of the bar. She could see out of the corner of her eye that the man had no patience. He hopped up and down for a bit, like a man with a weak kidney, then started coming toward her. She finished up her work quickly and did a nice little pirouette and doubled back to where he had been standing in the first place.

Martin was caught midstream and looked around with an expression of panic and confusion. Nora watched with satisfaction as he stumbled and blushed, going one way and then the other, trying to recover, like a wobbly drunk attempting a straight line. He had his hands jammed inside his jacket pockets as if he could stiffen a soft backbone with enough push.

All nerves, she thought—a cold battlefield judgment. She could not imagine what use Michael found in him, apart from the money and the contacts and the convenience, which were important but not crucial. The important trait was character. And in a pinch, she concluded, this one would crack like an egg.

But Michael had his reasons. Besides, it was none of her affair. None at all.

She waited until Martin came back around and stood in front of her. She didn't speak—a family characteristic. Generations of proud, high-tempered Irish tenant farmers had learned to swallow their tongues rather than let loose a beheading rage. Let the other fellow explode; let someone else reveal something weak, something human, like emotion. That was the tight-lipped lesson that was passed along from generation to generation like the secret of fine stitching.

The nervous little man ignored her small revenge and stood in front of her and waited a beat, as if he hadn't been chasing her up and down the bar, as if he wasn't entitled as her employer to some show of respect. He gave up the little game entirely. "Mary won't be in tonight," he said with a smile worn out by too much leering.

Nora refused to take the hint, although the meaning of what he said was plain enough. She stared him down, forced him to his knees. "Her dad was in an accident," he went on, leaving an opening that she would not take. "He's in the hospital, but she doesn't know how bad. She has to stay with him. Y'see. I thought I'd give her the night. Poor thing."

She forced herself to let the little man suffer. He had earned it, made her suffer often enough. Then she saw something—a touch of resentment, a little flare of anger—when she wouldn't help him along. It came as a shock, something as noble as anger, from such a creature.

"Would you mind working the tables, Nora Kate?" he blurted out.

"I would," she fired back, leaving him, as she usually left him, tongue and jaw flapping in the wind. "Larry needs me at the bar."

Larry turned away. He had no appetite for involvement in a fight. He was a perfect bartender—a spectator.

Martin stammered. "Uh, ah, well."

"I'll tell you the truth, Martin," said Nora, turning away, forcing him to bend to her, letting the bristle of her tight red ponytail turn like a slap, "I don't like the tables."

"But, but, but . . ."

"It's no picnic working the bar, I give you that. I don't like getting pinched by all the young heroes who grow bold with ale." She let that sink in. "But, then, as a matter of fact, the tips are better at the bar. And the way you pay me, I can't be too proud, can I?"

"I'll make up the difference, Nora Kate. Whatever you lose in tips, I'll see that it's right."

She turned and faced him, showing him the full voltage of her contempt. He started to say something, but she stopped him by raising her eyebrows. Then she let him off the hook.

"I prefer the bar, Martin, but I'll do the tables," she said with an icy shrug.

Martin was baffled. He read it as one more instance of Nora's perverse impenetrability.

But it was more complicated than that. Nora was moved by an intricate sense of duty. Someone had to work the tables, and Nora Katherine Byrnes would not be the one to neglect the job. She would go, as all the women in her ancient line went, where she was needed.

Martin would have said something, made some remark to show his gratitude, but she was gone, whipping off the bar apron and replacing it with the one with pockets for the checks and the pencils.

There were only a few couples at the tables. Not much hope for tips—and Martin would soon forget his promise to make it right, she was sure of that. But the tables would be a blessed rest for her weary mind. The couples came to sit and lose themselves under the spell of the old wood in the dining room of the old house converted into a pub. They were enchanted by the shamrock napkins and the rusted blunderbusses mounted on the walls alongside the long, thin smoking pipes imported from the other side. You couldn't find pipes like that in America. Some effort had been made to fill the dining room with touches of Old World sentiment.

The bar, on the other hand, was a long, curved assembly line for hard drinkers—all business. Deeply stained wood and worn-down ruts around the stools where two generations and more of laborers had slumped into their whiskies after a long day on the docks or the high steel or running after crime in some far precinct or eating smoke in some doomed tenement.

Nora was the latest generation of barmaids who caught the restless fallout of the blue-collar customers. It was hard work. You had to stay awake just for the dodge and banter. The soft boys with beer bellies liked to touch and tickle. But more than that, they demanded a quick and nimble wit from their barmaids. You had to answer their crude jokes with something saucy. You had to play the dumb Molly to their sad wag.

"Now what's this?" she said, running into a thick arm laid down like a tree trunk, blocking her way out of the bar area. She was balancing a tray full of ale for the far table.

"Woncha sing, Nora, darlin'?" asked the fellow with the lumber arm, a brute named Callan who was waiting for his appointment to the fire department, who was making himself obnoxious with nightly farewell parties. The other men at the bar, thick with their whiskey, had been accompanying the jukebox to "Finnegan's Wake," or some liquid facsimile; now they stopped. They were waiting to see how she would handle the lunk. "Sing, Nora, dear. I could teach you one or two things about singing," crooned Callan, turning to see the effect of his salty innuendo on the others. "I could really make you sing."

The others—all of whom had at one time or another taken an unsuccessful run at Nora—leaned closer to witness the precise manner in which Nora would fend off Callan. They were not disappointed.

"Really?" she said, clipping his arm from underneath in one crisp, upward motion. Callan was leaning on the arm and the sudden absence of support sent him sprawling. Nora stepped over him, then stopped and looked down with pity. "And I could turn you into a tenor," she added brightly.

The others at the bar erupted in appreciation.

There was a lull in the dinner trade, and through the window of the Irish-style pub called the Shebeen, Nora could see the lights of the little boats nodding in Broad Channel, the little cove just off Jamaica Bay. She liked the look of small boats. She felt moved by them, so tiny and brave, riding gracefully in the chop of the sea. Like dancers, she thought whenever she caught sight of them through the window. Dancers bobbing on the cold stage of Jamaica Bay. She was, herself, a dancer, and knew the thankless sight of it.

She took the lessons and performed the endless exercises of a dancer. She disciplined herself and underwent denial and worked her muscles beyond the walls of pain. She never complained. Such was the price of being a dancer. It was not in her character to make a bargain with fate. She was a dancer and there was a price to it and that was that.

Not that she ever expected to appear in public as a dancer. She didn't even expect anyone else—apart from her teacher—to know her true identity.

She was a dancer, but not in this lifetime.

There had been a chance. Once. A teacher in Belfast had seen something in her and said, Be a dancer. You could do it. The teacher had offered to send her to a special school, to arrange for scholarships. But even at seven she knew that it was impossible. She understood from the moment she was capable of grasping any lasting idea that she was shackled by hereditary obligations, practical chains of responsibility. She had a father in the king's prison and a brother off God-knows-where and a mother dying of cancer.

She obeyed the daughter's duty and stayed home, and dancing was, not forgotten, but kept like a sigh in the dark chest of her lost hopes. And she was a soldier. She bit back the resentment and tried not to hate her dying mother. The disappointment only showed up as a crease in her face.

She learned to live with it. It was an old Catholic trick. If she couldn't be a dancer in this lifetime, she would be one in the next.

There was that spiritual dimension. She squeezed out the student fees and faithfully attended the lessons as if they were morning mass. She worked herself like a fanatic, keeping herself ready for the next life. Nora prepared and cleansed her body as she once prepared and cleansed her soul.

As she gazed out of the window of the Shebeen, as she paused to admire the elegant movement of the small boats in the cove, one of the monster jets came roaring out of nearby Kennedy Airport, crushing all thought, all conversation. Like everyone else, Nora Kate thought that she had learned to live with the jets, coming and going in their arrogant thunder. But she was roused to frustration by their overpowering presence. They were, in their own way, like the British army bullies with their long rifles who came marching through the Catholic neighborhoods of Northern Ireland, smothering talk and spirits under the click of their rough boots.

Nora turned away from the window. She busied herself at the tables, picking up empty pitchers, writing down orders, almost—but not quite, never completely—lost in the automatic tempo of work. This is good exercise, she told herself. Dancers repeat the same monotonous movements until they ache with the automatic repetition. Dancers learn to make even awkward steps look pretty.

She was a dancer on the dining room floor. No one carried a tray full of beer with quite the proud, high style as did Nora. She would overhear, sometimes, someone remark on it. That woman should be a dancer. She swallowed the smile, and the reply: I am, you know.

The pub was almost empty. She noticed. It was a habit. Like counting the house in the theater. Then a curious thought broke through her wandering mind: she wasn't needed at the tables; Martin could have gotten by without taking her off the bar. There was a reason. Intent. She could feel the conspiracy crawl up her spine.

Suddenly, standing at the alcove near the kitchen door, cold sober, was the would-be fireman, Callan.

"We need Michael," he said, and she shivered at the memory of urgency.

"What is it?" she asked dumbly. It was an instinct. It just slipped out. He gave her a twisted look. As if to say, you should know better than to ask such a question.

"Just get him," he said impatiently.

She nodded. A slip. Something weak slipped through my defenses. A human thing. Sorry. None of my business. Not anymore.

As she walked away, Callan staggered a bit, just for the benefit of the others, and sang over his shoulder: "Oh, you'll die a dry old maid, Nora Kate."

And for the benefit of the others, she called after him, chasing him with a quip: "I could think of worse fates." She paused. "And so could your wife."

* * *

She knew, as soon as she saw Callan standing sober in the alcove, that great sorrow was in the room. The foolish soldiers were rushing to arms, throwing themselves on grenades, killing and being killed—just from the straight-up sight of him. Oh, Callan, you silly bastard, I really don't like you this way. I like you better as a plain, witless drunk.

Callan took the wind out of her. She thought she had left them all behind in Belfast. Ireland was packed with sober boys drunk with foolish courage.

This was why she left. She wanted to save her unborn child from the doom and grinding hate of Ulster. She left because she came to see, at some ripe moment of clear-eyed maturity, that she didn't understand it at all. None of it. Not the least little bit. She saw the injustices and the implacability, she saw the cruel yoke, but she didn't see the point of suicide. The Troubles remained as much a mystery as the persistence of her religious faith. For, despite everything, she still found herself—at sad and troubled moments of her life—wandering helpless into a church, making choked and heartfelt confessions to dull, uncomprehending priests.

She told herself that she didn't believe—and that much she believed. Might as well talk to the blocks of stone left by the Druids. Might as well mumble dead prayers in a dead tongue to a dead God. She told herself as much. And yet her heart had its own convictions.

When, one day, to her amazement and delight, she discovered that she was pregnant and unable to bring herself to submit to a back alley abortionist, she ended up in a dark pew with her knees bent and her cheeks wet, praying to God.

She was whipped into submission by the terrible conflict. Finally, after all the other choices had run out, she went to her old maid aunts in Dublin in the South for sanctuary.

They took her in, as they took her in when her mother died, but there was a price. They gave her shelter and provided sustenance, in that strict, grudging family manner that left it an open question whether it came from emotion or obligation. Still, they took her in when it counted, and in the final analysis that was what mattered. Nora might not have understood the depth and complexity of her ties to her family—or to Ireland, for that matter—but she did grasp one overwhelming truth: she had to get away. She had to leave for the sake of the child, and for something she had always identified vaguely as her own mortal soul.

When she announced this to her aunts, the night she told them of her plans to come to America, she was in the last trimester of the scandalous pregnancy. All three women were seated around the thick, wooden dinner table eating cold cabbage soup and stale bread. They ate in the deep, oppressive silence that was the principal language of the house. Bridget, the older of the two aunts, sat pinched and stiff, the spoon moving from her plate to her lips like a machine. She took in Nora's news the same way she took in the cabbage soup—without any outward show of effect.

Deidre, on the other hand, clutched her hands together under her heart and made a sound like a whimper as she bit her lips. She stared at Bridget.

No one spoke for what seemed like a long time. Finally, Bridget put down her spoon.

"When is it you plan to go?" she asked, her voice neutral, yet already full of condemnation. She stared at the unfinished bowl of soup. Her hands were clasped as if in prayer.

"Soon," replied Nora quickly, feeling the exhilaration of having passed the worst, grateful that they were discussing tactical matters. "I want to get there before I have to pay for two seats." She held her hands on her high belly. "I'll smuggle him into America."

Bridget looked up. Her eyes were wide. The baby was not something that was discussed. Not openly. It was always some oblique, indirect matter: "When your time comes," "You need a larger dress; you are becoming apparent."

"You intend to go beforehand, then?" said Bridget.

"Why not? We have modern air-o-planes. Be there before you leave."

She sensed that the discussion was not done. Bridget had guns to fire. Nora picked up her spoon and took another mouthful of soup and a bite of bread. It stuck like cement in her mouth.

"And how will you get by in America?"

Nora shrugged. "I'll work. I'm not afraid of work."

"With a bastard in your belly?" shot Bridget coldly.

"With my baby. I'll work, Aunt Bridget."

Bridget shook her head. "You don't have the least idea," she said. "Go off to America without a plan, without means, without a friend in the world. You don't know what you're getting into, do you?"

"No," flung back Nora maliciously, "but I know what I'll be gettin' out of."

Her face flushed. She had not intended to be cruel. Bridget had taken her in. If she hadn't been kind, it was because kindness was not in her nature. But she had taken her in, and it was wrong to repay that with meanness.

"I'll be fine, Aunt Bridget. Really. They have doctors and hospitals and jobs in America."

Bridget sipped some water; lubricating herself for the fight, thought Nora. "It sounds to me as if you hadn't thought this through," said Bridget.

Nora was unprepared for an in-depth defense. She had expected disapproval and then sullen acceptance. She was used to that. When she first moved in with her aunts and did not grovel in shame and gratitude because she was unmarried and pregnant, Bridget smoldered silently. Her judgment was subtle: a moist sense of reproach, a head turned away quickly as a rebuke, the refusal to discuss directly the maternal fact. This was the limit. Bridget made her feelings known by mute, half-choked gestures and denial.

Not Deidre. Unlike the wire-thin older aunt, Deidre had some flesh on her bones; she had an endearing lack of willpower and a weakness for sweets and feelings that would not be denied. She spent long nights knitting baby things, grinning at Nora, signaling their great secret.

"Have you thought of the child?" said Bridget, softening, uttering the forbidden word. "Have you considered giving birth here?"

"No. Not here!" cried Nora, sounding to herself like a petulant child.

For that flicker of an instant, she could see how this must sound to Bridget, how it would play against her no-nonsense, grown-up ear. But Nora couldn't help herself; she sat back in the chair, thrusting up her belly like a holy shield. "The child will be born in America."

Bridget shook her head. "No," she said with uncanny

certainty, "you'll not be goin' to America with the baby in your belly."

Nora felt a flutter of panic, actual fear that her aunt possessed a secret power that could stop her. Then she got mad, more at her own obedient reflex than any real fear. "It's my baby. I'll go where I have a mind to go."

She lumbered up from the table, inching away from her aunt, putting some safe distance between them. Bridget sat there, hands folded, lips pinched, neck strained. "Sit down, Katherine," she said, nodding to the vacant chair. Nora remained standing, despite the fact that her knees felt unreliable. She didn't know why she was so afraid, but she was sweaty and sloppy with fear. She kept glancing around the room, as if she expected her aunt's demon allies to spring out from the shadows. Bridget waited, then spoke, staring down at her hands, her voice low.

"You'd better be clear about this, Katherine. I am not going to permit it." The words were driven home like nails, meant to hold. "I am not going to permit you to go to America in such a condition. If you want to endanger your own life"—she opened her hands—"that's your own business." Then she shook her head tightly. "The child is another matter."

Nora shuddered. Where did Bridget get such confidence? How could she be so certain of herself? She almost couldn't ask.

"How can you stop me?"

Bridget didn't answer right away. She was turning something over in her mind.

Deidre was frightened. "Oh, Mother of God," she cried into her knuckles.

"Be quiet, Dee Dee!" snapped Bridget. It drew another whimper.

"Aunt Bridget," said Nora, unable to keep the tremble out of her voice, "I am going and that's that. There's nothing you can do to stop me."

She intended to sound strong, but it came out feeble. It had the high-pitched sound of a plea. She started to clear away the dishes, but she stopped and turned back to her aunt. "Are you worried about the crime? Is that it? Are you afraid I'll get mugged and worse?"

Bridget didn't answer and Nora went on. "Because if that's it, if that's what concerns you, I can tell you it's worse here in Dublin. There's more danger on O'Connell Street than in Central Park. And up in the North, that's a fine place to bear a child, with the bombs and the rubber bullets! I'll take my chances in New York City, thanks."

"You know, Katherine, I used to think you were a patriot," said Bridget. "I thought you had that much gumption. I told myself that's why you did what you did. But you're not a patriot, are you? You're not a patriot, you're not a Catholic, you don't even believe in God. You don't believe in much, do you? You believe in running away when it gets a little fussy. What is it that you believe in?"

Nora was flabbergasted to be having this kind of conversation with Aunt Bridget. She had always assumed that her aunts were simply two more defeated victims of Irish civil strife. Sour, unhappy women blown by whatever ill wind came their way. It never occurred to Nora that they might be partisans, active veterans with hard opinions of their own. It stunned her that they might be passionate soldiers in the war.

"I believe in me," said Nora meekly. "And I still believe in possibilities."

"Oh!" said Bridget with a sharp, sarcastic voice. "You

believe in possibilities, do you? Well, that's good. Because here's something that's a little more than a possibility. I happen to know what you've been up to these past years. I know that you run with the IRA provos and I know all about your brother. I know names, details, occasions. Bombings. Shootings. I know enough to have you both hanged, let alone kept in the country."

"I do not believe this."

"Believe it."

"You are threatening me. You are going to turn informer."

"I am!"

"I don't believe it," said Nora, although she did believe it. "I'll do what I have to do to save the child." There it was, that old Catholic dogmatic reflex. Save the child. Kill the mother if you have to, but save the child.

It was a brutal standoff. And then Deidre spoke, startling both Bridget and Nora.

"You know, Katherine, dear, I think Bridget may have a good point." She nodded to her older sister, an old placating gesture, an appeal to be allowed to mediate now that the two sides had come smack against each other. She addressed Nora but faced Bridget. "We don't have any people in America. You'll be all alone. It will be hard at first, being a stranger, finding your way about." She kept nodding at Bridget, who, by her silence, permitted the mediation. "Why not have the baby here, then get settled in America? We could watch the baby, you see, while you get set up. Then you could send for the baby. It makes so much more sense this way, dear."

Deidre's plan did make more sense than her own, but that was not why Nora agreed. Nora saw the flint in

Bridget's eyes and knew that she was trapped. Bridget could burn down the house with the fire in her eyes.

Two months after Seamus was born, Nora went to America alone. She had no choice.

New York City came as a revelation. It was big and gaudy and filthy and dangerous, but it was also something wonderful, something she had never before experienced: it was free. She felt as if she could open her mouth and breathe. It was as if she had been living on one lung until this blaze of color and noise. Even the life of a downtrodden barmaid was grand compared to the gloomy ordeal of Dublin or the tightrope of Belfast.

And she felt certain that some undertow of fate had drawn her to America. She was bursting with it and wanted to show it to Seamus. She wanted his eyes opened before they were closed by IRA tunnel vision. She wanted her son to know the possibilities.

But one day Michael showed up at her door in America and told her her duty. She tried to refuse, to defy him, to tell him that he had no power over her here in America.

Michael listened without a word and let his silence erode her resolve. She had good arguments. She had a baby to consider. She was no good for a fight. She was tired. She'd resigned from the army. She was a dancer, not a soldier.

But in the end she could not resist his terrible, silent insistence. He wore her down simply sitting there in his battered trench coat, with all the old battles showing up like wounds on his exhausted face. He let the face speak for him, and in the end he prevailed. She took the job at the Shebeen.

When she considered it, she didn't understand why

she gave in. Partly, she knew, because she felt sorry for him, all alone in America, without proper support. Only his trench coat for protection.

She could not admit the ember of sympathy for the cause. But beyond all that, the real reason she agreed to help him was the stark fact that she was afraid of Michael.

And so she told him, okay, one more time. But it's the last. I'm out of it now. I have a child. He nodded in that weary, skeptical way that said over and over, we'll see, we'll see.

In life, she told herself later, you cannot pick and choose. You accept. You make do. It was a consolation she heard on her mother's dying knee. And so she sighed and performed her duty.

She slipped the winter coat on over the apron. Martin watched her go, sitting in a dark corner with the others. He made no move to stop her, but then why should he? This was why he asked her to work the tables, so she would be free to call Michael.

There was some sleet in the rain, and her feet were cold and wet. Sneakers were no good in the rain, she told herself, like some equipment manager for a dance troupe. Sneakers retain water, but you can't always pick and choose, and she leaped over puddles as she danced past Cross Bay Boulevard, deaf to the traffic, lost in her art.

She doubled back once and stopped in a luncheonette. She took her time and had a soft drink and saw that no one was following her or watching her. If nothing else, she was well trained. Then she stepped into the phone booth in the rear, a booth she had never used before because she never used the same booth twice. She kept the door open enough to keep the light off and dialed the number she had memorized. It rang twice and then she hung up. She waited another thirty seconds exactly and dialed again. Someone picked it up in the middle of the first ring and said nothing. She counted to eight, making certain that the silence was deliberate, then said, "You're wanted."

It was enough. She hung up and made her way back through the sleet and across the boulevard, a graceful dancer performing for an unseen audience.

3

Tuesday, November 3, 12:45 A.M., 129 Hours and Counting

Michael, as he called himself, lowered the telephone into its cradle like crystal. And then he simply sat there, very still.

It was not that he misunderstood the message. He knew that it was a danger signal. Something urgent. But he had something even more urgent to check out. His nerve. He was a man who had stood erect under fire, and before he could do anything else he had to know that his nerve was still unbroken. He had to know that the weapon was intact.

He sat with his back to the apartment door waiting to die. They could come any time. And they wouldn't knock. Not even here in America, with its dead bolts of civil rights. They would come crashing in without warning. They would explode through windows and doors and even walls, if they had to. And he wouldn't hear them until it was too late because they would be professionals. Like himself. And because they would be professionals, like himself, they would come in shooting. He would be dead by the time he knew that they had come.

Michael was not afraid of the professionals. He had grown accustomed to their long shadow. If he had any fear it was of his own side—his amateur allies.

Something had gone wrong. He didn't know what, but they wouldn't use the signal unless they were badly frightened. It was hard for him to assess the danger on foreign ground. It could be a real threat, or some weak-kneed dolt frightened by a noise. Damned Americans! A nation full of whiskey heroes. You didn't want that kind on a mission. You wanted solid men you could count on. Or nobody at all.

He thought this, but he didn't give in to temper. He kept that in check. He was only prepared to turn it loose at the right time on the right target.

He reminded himself that he was in a strange city and a strange country and at the mercy of an unreliable host. He hated being so dependent. There was a chance that they would all quit on him, now that something had gone wrong. That's what happened with the bold talkers. They had a tendency to duck when the guns went off. Look up in a firefight and you're all alone. Back home, on the other side, you could just winnow out that kind, send them on message runs or make them couriers. Find sturdy fellas for the real work. Here, he had to take what they gave him. And from the look of things, he was working with a lot of wet ammunition.

The Americans just didn't grasp the gravity of the business. They were unbelievably flabby when it came to security. They couldn't help it, he decided. Some innate urge to be celebrity freedom fighters. They all wanted recognition in their chosen field, no matter what field it was. And there was this strange quality of candor that he supposed came from too much freedom. No fear of cops or government assassins. They had lost the tic of educated paranoia.

The ignorance was apparent to Michael when they passed him around like a trophy. "I want you to meet Tim; he's very reliable." He couldn't seem to convince them that he preferred anonymity. He wasn't being coy. He was death. He lived in secret. All their "reliable" Micks and Seans and Dans were so many booby traps ready to blow up in his face.

And now they were exposing him again. He'd have to come out into the open and see if there was something more than panic involved. He had no choice. The mission had to be kept alive. That was the vital thing: the mission. Especially this mission. Everything else was tactical.

He was worried about time. There was only so much time for a job. You had to get in, get it done and get out. That was the secret of staying alive. Timing. Be quick and be ruthless.

He could hear the clock that had begun to tick from the moment he began the mission. The plane was a little more than five days off. Not much time to get the thing organized. Not much time to bring down an empire.

He sat there and it calmed him. It strengthened a brittle anger.

The first time he had consciously performed the exercise was when he was a boy in Belfast. He had walked calmly down the center of a street in the Bogside in the middle of a firefight. He was fourteen years old and, according to the adult gunmen of the Irish Republican Army, who shooed him away from their ranks on the grounds of his age, untested. Michael decided to make up his own test. There were the Brits on the one side of the street and IRA gunmen on the other, and Michael walked through the eye of the crossfire. Amazingly, when he came slowly down the center line, a sudden peace settled over the battleground. All the soldiers and all the gunmen fell into a dumbstruck truce at his display of raw courage.

But it wasn't so much a display of courage as it was a calculated thing. Michael guessed that the soldiers would be too confused to open fire. They would see him as a complete innocent; it would be sinful to molest such a witless creature. Even if they read it another way, even if they decided to bring him down, their aim would be thrown off by such a brazen target. They would be wild with opportunity.

Michael understood the fine points of human nature. He also had the rare capacity to calculate and reason in the windstorm of battle. The thing that set him apart from most, however, was the absolute lack of limits. The average person could tolerate a certain amount of risk, a certain level of pain. But there was a finite point beyond which that person could not go. Enough pressure, enough danger, enough pain, and the mass would break. Michael had no limits. None. You had to kill him to win.

Part of it was the fact that he was born poor and Irish Catholic under the Protestant boot; this provided a natural arsenal of resentment. But at bottom there was an inexplicable rage that even he did not completely understand. It was not connected to any injustice or any specific grievance or cause. It was something innate: flaming rage. It was the thing that made him dangerous.

Michael had learned to keep the volatility on a short leash. He had spent most of his life acting as his own drill sergeant. The training and testing began before he could remember.

When he was a boy—even younger than the reckless teenager who walked into a crossfire—he played a game with his friends. They would each buy an ice-cream cone and try not to be the first to take a lick. First one to taste the ice cream lost. It was a stupid game with no real point, except as a flexing of willpower. Usually, somebody gave up while there was still enough ice cream left to eat. But with Michael the game got out of control. One day he played with another boy of wild pride, and even after the other gave in and ate the melting ice cream, Michael held out. The game's over, the others cried, eat the ice cream! Not Michael. He was unwilling to stop. He waited until all the ice cream was gone, melted like a topping over his hand, then threw the cone away. The other boys didn't understand, except to recognize something freakish. No other child made war over ice cream.

Michael sighed and rose from his chair. He shut the lights and peeked out the window. As far as he could see, there were a few people out on the street; just normal traffic. The opposing windows were open and showing light, not black with watchers. There were no clean, inappropriate vans parked along the street. No laundry trucks or television repair vans in the night. He looked up and down and saw no ambush.

His car was parked two blocks away, in an open area

that gave him a clear field of vision. Always an open spot where he could see an attack developing. He walked past it once, careful not to look back, checking the dirt marks near the doors to see if anyone had been scuffling with the lock, working on getting in. He checked the windows with a glance for fresh smudges. His hand was clenched around the cocked automatic pistol deep in his raincoat pocket. Under the brim of his hat he scanned the streets like an early warning system. He noted the familiar signs, the undisturbed bushes. He marked out escape routes, always updating and improving his war plans.

The ambush wasn't there. Not this time. There would be a time when it would be, and there would come a time when he would probably miss it. A man eventually gets careless, drops his guard for an instant, grows tired or sloppy. Everyone. Even him. The enemy becomes creative or lucky. It would happen. There was nothing to do but keep going as long and as hard as you can. Change the routine, extend the odds—and wait for the professionals.

He noticed someone looking out of a ground-floor window of a two-family house. His hackles went up, but it was only a man taking a contented look out upon his world. Probably after a big meal and putting the kids to bed. Michael could see the sleepy, unguarded satisfaction in the face of the man in the window, snug and warm while the rain whipped outside. For a moment, Michael felt a jealous pang and wondered what it would be like to live on the other side of such a window. To have a house, a wife, children and a sleepy, unguarded view of the world. He wondered for one searing moment what it would be like to be not alone.

But then he shook the thought away. He was not a

civilian. He was a soldier. A soldier! There was a war to be fought and he had his duty. He pulled himself together and marched back to his car.

The second-floor meeting room of the Shebeen was where the Gaelic and Emerald Society cops and firemen held their monthly beer busts and parties. The walls were freckled with bits of Irish sentiment—long pipes and shamrocks and pictures of leprechauns out of Irish legends. On the plain pine walls were the modern travel posters advertising trips to Galway.

But the soul of the Irish rebel was represented by angry historical maps, with all the important battle sites marked and named. Here was where the rebels took the Dublin Post Office in the Easter Rising of '16. Here was where the cruel Black and Tans from Limerick were singled out and executed in the '20s. There were pictures of Collins and Pearse and Connolly, bathed and cleansed by time and distance. There was no sign of the modern Irish freedom fighter. The latest crop of rebels seemed tainted to the more conservative Irish-Americans. The latter-day IRA gunman carried the whiff of the terrorist. Considering the secret business conducted at the Shebeen, rebel sentiments seemed indiscreet, but it did thrill the tourists, and, in fact, the absence of the old heroes and epic poems in an Irish pub in the county of Queens would have been conspicuous. The dog had to bark, Martin declared when he hung them out in public.

Now Martin sat with his back to the epic walls, watching the staircase, counting out his chances the way he doped out horses at the track, and making quick work of the bottle of Irish that Nora had brought from the bar. He had moved to the empty upstairs room after

Nora had returned from making her call. His hand trembled as he poured the whiskey. Christ, he thought, finishing his calculations along with a huge swallow of liquor, he's going to murder me. Shoot me down like a dog in my own pub. I've given him more than enough cause. And he's that kind of a man.

"He did say he'd come?" he asked Nora when she returned with a pitcher of ale to wash down the whiskey.

"I don't know what you're talking about," she said in that thrifty voice, slamming down the pitcher like a gavel, hurrying away.

"He'll come," said Martin out loud. He had a fleeting hope that maybe he wouldn't come, after all. Maybe he'll vanish across the border into Canada. Or back to Ireland. You can't tell with such men. Well, this is what comes from playing out of your depth.

He drank the whiskey and the ale, and it had no effect. He was dead sober and worried sick.

Think, he told himself, but his mind was a blur. What would Michael do?

No telling. He knew from the moment he had laid eyes on him that he was one of those ice-cold killers who put bullets in people and never know a moment's regret. All that watchful patience. Like he was hoarding up his temper. Oh, Martin, you don't want to be around when the patience runs out.

Having met him, having stared into the eyes, you had to believe the stories. They weren't the sunny tales of doomed patriots who wrote poetry on their way to a British gallows. Michael's legend was one of powerful bombs and loveless courage. Operations meant to inspire fear, not poetry.

Of all the deeds attributed to Michael, the most chilling was the Mountbatten slaughter. There were other bombs and shootouts and daring escapes—enough to make a man famous—but nothing to match the cold-blooded outrage of that one. Michael had, or so the story went, swum out to Mountbatten's yacht, where the beloved seventy-nine-year-old earl and his fourteen-year-old grandson and a fifteen-year-old passenger were on vacation, and blown the boat to bits, along with everyone on it. The attack was technically brilliant, but it was also deemed heartless.

The other facet of Michael's myth was that he was impossible to capture. He had a phantom's ability to slip through traps and elude pursuers. He had been actually caught only once. The Canadian police grabbed him when he attempted to cross the border into the United States. But he got away. He disappeared in the Paris airport when they were trying to take him back to London for trial. Michael went into a men's room and did not come out again. There were no windows, no exits, no hidden doors. He simply vanished.

This, then, was the man for whom Martin O'Shea waited with bad news.

Concentrating on the staircase, Martin missed Michael's entrance. He had slipped up the back way and stood for a moment. Martin couldn't tell if the sudden chill was from the wind or from Michael.

He was a smaller man than Martin remembered. Smaller and less substantial. But then it was the legend and fear that fleshed out the character, thought Martin.

"Well, well," he said, scrambling to his feet, tipping over his chair. "Come in. Come in. It's a bitter night. Warm yourself. I've got a glass for you."

Michael closed the door and sat at Martin's table. He

kept his hat and coat on, and Martin shuddered at the hooded image. The man looked poised for a getaway.

The hands came out of the raincoat pocket and moved up to the table, and there was a flicker, a skipped heartbeat of apprehension, because Martin didn't know for certain what would be in those hands when they emerged from under the table.

But they were empty, and Michael folded them gently, one over the other. They looked soft, fluttering one on top of the other, and that made them more menacing.

"A drink, then?" pressed Martin, pouring a glass for Michael, trying to drum up some geniality. "Could use one myself."

Michael didn't bother to reject the offer. He just sat there waiting, pushing Martin with his silence.

Martin needed the courage; he couldn't help himself. "God bless," he said, emptying his glass in a single toss, his eyes wet from the quick fire of the whiskey. His voice was hoarse with worry. "No sense beating around the bush," he said, shaking his head, trying to smile, looking like he was already a corpse.

"You called," said Michael simply.

Martin looked at him. It might have been a joke. But he saw no humor. Or none that he was in on. "I called."

Michael nodded.

"I had no choice."

"Fine," said Michael. "You called. You had no choice. Why am I here?"

Michael reached over, and the soft hand was iron as he stopped Martin's shaky hand from going for the whiskey bottle again.

"Michael, we needed the money. You know that.

There's the thing. We needed the money. For the operation."

"I told you once, money is easy," said Michael, hard. Martin could see that he would not get much mercy here.

"I know. I know. Still, there's the fact. You can't fish without a pole, now can you? You need the pole to fish . . ."

Michael cut him off. He might have gone on like that forever. "What is it, man? Tell me."

"Oh, Michael, we did a foolish thing," said Martin, feeling the noose. "But I thought it was a piece of cake. The problem would be solved."

"Am I going to have to force it out of you?"

"You remember I mentioned a payroll? Do you remember that?"

"I remember that I told you not to commit useless felonies when there's important business on."

Martin shook his head and uttered a little cry of despair. "You did, I remember. Oh, stupid, stupid, stupid."

He reached for the whiskey bottle again, and Michael half tore his arm loose. Martin grew pale under Michael's grip. "Tell me, dammit."

"My arm!" whined Martin.

Michael released him. "Tell me," he repeated.

"I sent them in after the payroll," Martin said quickly. Michael closed his eyes.

"It looked such an easy thing. Beggin' for it. A golden opportunity. Oh, Michael, I thought I'd be helpin' out."

Trust fools, thought Michael. Well, what's done is done. It's too late to stop them and they could use the money. Wouldn't have to go askin' some other foolish patriot.

"How much did you get?"

Martin thought, Oh, Christ, now he'll kill me.

"How much?"

"I don't really know."

Michael's eyes glazed. "No more dancing, Martin. Tell me straight, what's happened?"

Martin swallowed. "There was a bit of trouble."

"What kind of trouble? I'm getting a little impatient with this."

"Some shooting. Somebody started shooting."

Michael's first impulse was to run. To go into deep hiding. This is where the discipline came to bear. He fought off the impulse. He forced himself to remain under fire so that he could learn the full extent of the damage. He spoke very slowly, very clearly.

"Who got shot?"

"Two of ours were killed."

"Two? How many did you send in?"

"Four."

"What happened to the other two?"

"We don't know."

Michael was very clinical—no sign of mourning for the dead—but detachment was necessary. Michael had made—in the smoke and confusion of the long war—the grim computations of his trade. He could measure lives against effectiveness. How much would it cost to throw a little fear into Britain's heart?

How much to clear them out of Northern Ireland altogether? For that was what he was trying to purchase with this single mission. Two dead? Not much when you put it in the macabre columns of history.

The other side would pay even more dearly. What

were a few Irish Republican Army soldiers against a prime minister? And what was a prime minister against a united Ireland?

A bargain. Worth it. Even if it meant, as it surely would, that he would be run down by the professionals and killed without mercy. Well worth it.

By that one act—the killing of the prime minister—the British Empire would know that they could never win. They would see then that there were men who would go on blowing them up forever. There were some, like Michael, who would never settle for a bad truce or a feeble compromise.

Then they would bend the proud knee. Then they would make peace. And not until then.

Michael ran his hand across his face. "The two who were killed, can they be traced?"

Martin shook his head. "Not for a while. They were imports."

"What about the other two?"

Martin took the opportunity to fill the glass again. "We're hoping that they got away. Hiding with the payroll."

"Hoping? You mean there's a chance that they took the profit?"

"No. None. Not these two. One's Matty O'Connor. Son of a cop. Good lad. The best. Would walk through fire."

"And what about the other?"

"Damian Boyle." His eyes were moist with guilt.

"Tim's boy?"

Martin nodded.

Michael remembered him. He was one of the lean and hungry types, brought over to meet him in a bar that they called safe. "You can trust him," Martin had said proudly at the time. Michael tried to explain: if this one knows, others will know; he couldn't count it an honor unless he boasted about meeting him. And then others and others and the secrecy was gone. They were so reckless and he couldn't make them see.

"Do the cops have them?" asked Michael.

"No. And even if they do, they'd never talk."

"God, you blind, stupid fool! In Belfast I'd have you up against a pitted wall, you silly ass!"

"I'd swear for them, Michael . . ."

"Don't swear, for Christ's sake. Save yourself for a mortal sin."

They sat for a moment. Martin lit a cigarette. "Well," said Michael eventually, "I'm not safe."

"That's why I called."

Martin felt a stirring of hope. Relief. "Do you want me to find you a new place to stay?"

Michael looked to see if he was serious. "No," he said. "You and I are done. The cops will find you. The only question is how long it takes them."

Martin nodded.

Michael's right hand left the table and went into his coat pocket. He leaned back, making himself some room. Some killing space, thought Martin in a panic. Oh, God, here it comes.

But it didn't. "I'll make my own arrangements," said Michael. "I may need some tactical support. But we won't meet again. I'll contact you when I need you. Don't try to reach me."

The head across the table bobbed: a great weight had been lifted from it.

"Find out what you can. From whatever cops you know. I'm sure you pal around with cops. But be careful. Don't let on about me. Not a word. Do you hear?"

"I was only tryin' to help, Michael. For you. I knew you needed some money to operate."

Michael turned his head. Just a bit. Enough to shut down that line of defense. This Martin was no different from the mob of them, he thought. Quick opinions. He's afraid of me. He thinks I'd kill him out of frustration or temper.

Michael thought, I could leave this silly country. Just get up from the table, get on a plane and vanish into one of the escape routes. It would be the sensible thing to do.

But he hadn't come to America to be prudent. He had an opportunity to unite Ireland. One stroke. Not many get that chance.

He turned to Martin and said matter of factly, "If they catch them, they'll talk."

Martin protested. "They won't. I wouldn't use such men." Michael stood, his hand in his gun pocket, wrapped around the automatic, gazing down at this sorry drunk with a mixture of anger and scorn. This Martin didn't understand a thing. He was dangerously sentimental. Finally, Michael asked, "Good lads, you say?"

"The best."

Michael nodded. "Well, Martin, they say that you need good luck most when your luck is running bad. Let's just hope that you got lucky tonight. Let's pray that all the fine lads you sent out to the airport tonight were killed."

In the cold blast of air that accompanied Michael's departure, Martin emptied the last of the whiskey. He didn't understand the high accounting of a professional.

4

Jack Mann hit the brakes and the old Buick skidded in the rain and came to a stop at a tipsy angle. The man in the parking lot booth was waving and calling him back.

I'm caught, Jack thought with terror.

What gave me away? A trail of blood. An arm dangling from the trunk. I thought I closed it. I'm sure of it. I tested it five times. Maybe when I went over that bump it flew open.

The picture was vivid, right there on that clear screen of his guilty conscience.

He rolled down the window and stuck his head out into the rain. He tried to show the man in the toll booth a smile, but it was closer to a grimace.

The attendant was trying to tell him something, but Jack couldn't make it out, what with the rain and the pumping of his own blood ringing in his ears. The attendant was pointing and yelling, and finally it began to come through.

"Windshield wiper!"

"Huh?"

"Windshield wipers! Your windshield wipers!" Jack turned around dumbly and looked at the windshield wipers. He could not comprehend. The man sounded like he was saying windshield wipers. They were right there, on the windshield where they were supposed to be. What is he trying to tell me?

The attendant—getting wet now in his frustration—had partly come out of the booth and was rocking back and forth, like a clock. Tick, tock; tick, tock.

"Your windshield wipers!" he screamed.

Jack had no doubt that he was screaming windshield wipers. The question was, Why? There was nothing attached to the wipers. They weren't about to fall off. They weren't even moving. . . .

The dawning was painful. A slow extraction of a monumentally stupid truth. Jack's windshield wipers weren't moving. In the middle of a rainstorm. He was driving blind. This is what the attendant was trying to tell him.

He groaned.

"Windshield wipers!" yelled the attendant.

"Right," replied Jack.

Not a great alibi, he thought. A little lame, but then the times called for something lame.

Well, at least he wasn't flat out caught. Not yet, at least. However, he had made himself conspicuous. He had planted himself prominently in the mind of the parking lot attendant as the asshole with the windshield wipers.

This is what happens when you cross that fine line

between guilt and innocence, he thought. You inherit the many-sided worry of criminal paranoia. Now all I will think about will be the parking lot attendant and the windshield wipers. It's the curse of the criminal class: small mistakes.

Tomorrow, when the teams of detectives come around picking through the garbage for clues, they'll stop to ask this attendant if he can remember anything unusual. Anything at all.

No, not really. Just some asshole tried to drive home, forgot to turn on the windshield wipers.

The detectives will exchange knowing looks and press the point because they are cops and cops understand that criminal lapses are just that stupid and just that ordinary. Criminals blunder over small details. It was an old cop's wisdom: when you see someone who's got the buttons wrong on his coat, chances are he's panicked, chances are he's paying attention to something else.

Jack knew. He had been trained to look for the incriminating lint, to spot the tricky errors in an otherwise routine picture. A police detective becomes, in time, like an urban tracker looking for small disturbances in the jungle routine. Windshield wipers not engaged in a rainstorm would be such a disturbance to a tracker.

At first they would ask their questions casually, patiently, maybe even fatherly, putting the attendant off guard, at ease. Inviting his help. Pretty soon, the parking lot guy thinks he's got a badge and a pension at stake and starts talking perps and running makes.

The clues would emerge and accumulate and, somewhere down the line, connect.

Jack saw this inevitability as clearly as he saw the

trunk flung open and the dead arm draped out of the car. He looked back at the toll collector squinting in the rain.

"Tired," he shouted, shrugging. "Had a bad day." He rolled up his window and drove off.

"Christ," he muttered critically to himself, "you sound like a fucking junkie burglar!"

Jack heard the approaching blocking force of tactical units and could not keep his foot off the accelerator. He knew better. Nothing attracts attention quicker than someone running away from a crime. Walk. Always walk. Or drive slowly. Do not move at an alarming rate, thus attracting undue attention. You see someone running, you stop him. A primer lesson he had been taught as a rookie cop.

A lot easier said than done. It may be smarter to go slow, but every adrenal instinct was to get away as quickly as possible. Fact is, Jack was running like a thief.

When he heard his tires squeal on a tight turn, Jack realized that he was being idiotically conspicuous and let the big Buick slow down.

The Grand Central Parkway glowed with traffic and lights. There were lights from the cars and the rain refractions. Lights from stanchions and from the airport. Jack felt as if he had been caught in a searchlight glare. For a moment, stunned by the flashing lights and quick traffic, Jack forgot his plan. But then as he made the turn heading east and slipped into the routine, impatient stream of late traffic, it came back to him. A simple solution to his problem: dump the body and the money as soon as possible. Leave no clues and get away from both as quickly as possible. Forget the nightmare ever happened.

Suddenly he saw the incoming police cruisers, cutting through heavy traffic like expert skiers. They were arriving from both directions, making artful, twisting loops to form roadblocks at the airport exits. Jack was struck by the performance of the police drivers, putting those clumsy cars into controlled skids. And then a pang, a remembered exhilaration at the easy, confident skill. He knew how it felt to be behind the wheel of a police cruiser on a hot run. There was a wild, breathless sense of raw power. But something else. Something that gave him an edge over the bad guys. He felt a divine immunity. He would chase down alleys and over closed roads with a kind of daredevil belief that he was protected from harm by the virtue of his cause. He was the good guy.

Not now. Not on this particular run. As he saw the cruisers closing in behind him, Jack was struck by the fact that he was driving in a cause that was not particularly virtuous.

He did not like this other side. It made him feel vulnerable. He knew that he had to get off the exposed highway. Suppose he had a breakdown or got a flat? He would be trapped with a dead body and a lot of unexplained cash in his trunk.

He left the Grand Central Parkway at the first exit. He drove into a side street and slowed the car and caught his breath. His heart was beating fast. He saw the ordinary houses and ordinary trees and was lost in the sudden silence. Getting off the main roads was like diving underwater—a slow, silent immersion in another dimension.

He knew the street, and yet he was lost. His normal

logical powers had been short-circuited by all the mental turmoil. How could a man think on the run?

He inched along—it didn't occur to him to look for a street sign—trying to get his bearings on a dark residential street in the heart of Flushing. He might as well have been in Asia. He could see the suspicious homeowners delicately peeling back shades and curtains, monitoring his slow progress.

He knew this street. Although he couldn't name it. But he knew it. This was where he had begun his police career twenty-three years earlier. He had been a rookie fresh out of training, and they had stuck him out in what was then considered the tame borough of Queens. He had patrolled this same block, answered the same calls from the same nervous homeowners. But it was as if he had landed upside down on the moon. He couldn't quite get the orientation. Was Northern Boulevard to the right or to the left? He put the Buick in gear and took a chance. He headed to his left and found Northern Boulevard, the main street. The merchants didn't stand sentry duty on Northern Boulevard. He was safer in a crowd of traffic.

He felt a little better, now that he knew where he was. He drove down Main Street and circled the police precinct on Union Street where he had once worked patrol. It was a risk. Cops knew him by sight. But he thought that he could make it to his destination without being recognized, for by now he had decided what to do with the dead boy in the trunk. He couldn't just roll him out onto the street. Someone might see. Note down his license plate. It was cold and it was brutal, but he would dispose of the body the way mob hitters got rid of their bodies—in one of the city dumpsters.

How did it come to this? Jack wondered. His mind

was a blaze of confusion. One step seemed to lead to another. How did it happen? Is this the landslide of crime? It all seemed so inevitable, so unavoidable.

He made a turn and left the station house behind him. Ahead, glistening in the rain, was the empty parking lot behind the shopping mall. It had the abandoned, bedraggled look of all midnight malls: a mouth without teeth.

Jack had the timing right. Too late for the four-to-midnight shift to be on their meal break. Too early for the burglary stakeouts to be on station. He had the parking lot to himself.

He cruised in and out of the shadows, checking for traps. Just for safety's sake, he drove through again. It was deserted. The rain had even driven the homeless into shelters. The shops in front were closed and locked, except for the fast-food chains further along. But he didn't want a dumpster behind a fast-food chain. The hungry scavengers would be picking through them for scraps. He wanted a dumpster loaded with plastic bags and broken bottles. The kind that discouraged visitors.

It nagged at him that he thought of such things. It stung his conscience that he thought so criminally clear. But he shook it off. He had to shake it off.

Jack killed the lights and backed the Buick into a slot in a far, badly lit corner of the lot. It was directly behind a pharmacy chain outlet. No one foraged in the waste from a discount drugstore. Might come up with some chemical contaminant.

Jack was careful to leave enough room behind the Buick. He needed about a foot between the car and the dumpster. He made certain that the car was at the right angle to block the view of anyone passing by.

Then he took a deep breath and plunged ahead. This was his moment of maximum risk.

It was slippery on the bumper, but Jack had to climb to the roof of the Buick and then pull himself up to the dumpster. He was careful, but there were few handles, and the muck made it ugly as well as slick. The top of the dumpster creaked and he looked around, but the sound was swallowed up in the rain. Good, the dumpster was almost full. He lowered himself again and slipped the last few feet, scraping his leg and tearing his slacks. It didn't hurt, but he knew that the excitement blocked the pain. Tomorrow it would be a purple mess. He checked the bleeding and saw that it was not out of control. Then he stripped off his jacket and his shirt. He had to be careful about being conspicuous afterward. He knew that after he had done what he had to do he would be covered with blood and gore.

His throat was dry and he ached for a solid belt of whiskey. Then he put the key in the lock of the trunk and opened it slowly. He knew what he would find, but there was always a small hope that maybe it wasn't true, maybe it was a dream or a wicked fantasy. Maybe he'd wake up still on the plane, still circling La Guardia Airport, sipping champagne.

But it was real, and when he looked, he staggered away, hitting his head on the dumpster. "Oh, Christ. Oh, good Christ!" he whimpered.

It wasn't death that frightened him. It was something far more shocking: the possibility of life. The man in the trunk had moved. He was still alive. He was trying to get out and had half turned around inside the trunk. But then Jack caught himself and realized that he was inventing things. The man was definitely dead. He had been dead in the airport. He had been dead all along. It was the rocking movements of the car that had rolled the body on its side.

He told himself, don't look. It's done. The man is gone. You have nothing to feel bad about. He was trying to kill you.

He got started. He bent his legs for leverage, then reached into the trunk and tried to lift the body. It was heavy and slimy with thickening blood and he had trouble getting a grip, but he kept at it, sliding his hands back underneath again and again. Finally he found some point of balance and managed to begin the lift.

Dead weight, he said to himself.

The body slid away again like a fish.

There was no choice. It had to come out of the trunk. He had to do it alone. There was no one to help, no one to call. He was on his own.

He reached down again and got under the shoulders. They were growing stiff. He pulled the dead man out. Hard to believe that this was the same agile youth bouncing up and down on the balls of his feet in the airport less than an hour ago. Now he was like slippery cement.

Jack tried to prop the corpse against the car, but there was no support in the joints. The body folded away. He lifted him again and held him steady with one hand while working for a better position.

He was breathing heavily. This is where I get the heart attack, he told himself. This is where the vise grips my chest and they find us both here dead and try to figure out this fucking mystery!

He rested then—grunting and wheezing, unable to tell his own sweat from the slime and blood—managed to get the body over his shoulder. His knees began to buckle, but he snarled and forced himself to stand up straight. Not now, you fucking knees! Not when I fucking need you!

The blood and rain were blinding him, and he worked by the sense of touch. He closed the trunk and there was a moment of panic when he thought maybe he'd locked the car keys in the trunk; he fumbled around in his pockets, balancing the dead man on his shoulders, while he checked it out. The relief when he found the keys almost made him drop the body.

Then he began the climb. Up onto the trunk. Slowly, so you don't drop the bastard. Carefully, so you don't slip. Make sure of the grip, like you're on the icy lip of some crevice of the Matterhorn. Ah, God, God! God!

He could feel the body sliding away again. The momentum was irresistible. He felt like crying when the body slithered off under the Buick. He could hear the head crack against the pavement. It made him cringe. It didn't matter that the man was dead. Or maybe it did. Maybe it was worse. There was something profane about injuring a dead man.

Fuck! Fuck! Fuck!

He thought of stopping. Just giving up. He was innocent of wrongdoing. He could just accept the incriminating accusations, admit the moment of temptation, and get it all out in the open.

But he couldn't surrender a lifelong habit of rectitude. He couldn't admit the foolish impulse that had brought him here in the first place. No. Despite the pain in his chest, Jack began again heaving and cursing and swearing in the cold rain. He summoned reserves of strength that he didn't know he had and began the maneuvering and lifting. First, up against the car.

Then, bending under the bulk like a fireman, letting his legs do the lifting.

He was learning. He made no mistakes, working carefully, systematically. He got himself and the body up to the rim of the dumpster, at last using his head, to bull it that final inch. As he sat there so near his goal, on that high perch with his burden in his arms, he looked up and found himself staring smack into the face of the dead man.

"I'll have nightmares from this," he told the dead man. "If it's any comfort, I'll probably never sleep peacefully again."

As he tried to catch his breath, he tried to imagine how the sight of him and his dead body would strike the cops in a passing sector car. A station house legend would be born.

"Then, then—you're not gonna believe this—it turns out to be an ex-fucking cop trying to lose a stiff!"

Jack Mann might become a locker room immortal.

Having recovered a little, Jack noticed that the lid of the dumpster was closed. Schmuck! Why didn't you leave it open? He turned to open it and twisted his back. I'll feel that later, too, he told himself.

Then he rolled the corpse into the hole. He could hear the plastic and paper popping and groaning as the body sank into its grave. "God forgive me," he mumbled. Then he reached over and piled debris over the dead man. He didn't want anyone peeking in and finding it.

Tomorrow, with any luck, the corpse would be gone forever, trucked out to some Rockaway landfill along with all the other nameless mob victims buried in that unmarked cemetery.

His work was finished, and he climbed down and

stood on the asphalt. He was winded and wheezing. His muscles were singing from the exertion. He stood for a moment, dazed by what he had done.

Then he fished out the car keys, opened the trunk and found a towel and wiped away the blood. He turned his face upward and blessed the rain.

As he struggled back into his shirt and jacket, he looked at the bag full of money. The plan had been to toss the money and the gun into the dumpster along with the body. One convenient burial. It would be as if the whole thing never happened.

But he hesitated. Maybe he should get rid of the money and the gun someplace else.

He needed time. He stuffed the bag full of cash deeper into the trunk, covered it with his own debris, climbed into the driver's seat and headed home.

He was too tired. And it wasn't only rain running down his cheeks. There were also tears.

5

Tuesday, November 3, 2:45 A.M., 127 Hours and Counting

She was cold and wet, although it wasn't the winter weather that made her shiver waiting for the bus on the little spit of land between the airport and the mainland of Queens. It was much worse on an inclement night in Belfast. What Nora felt through her coat was the raw wind of Michael back in her life.

This is America, she told herself. I don't have to be stuck with my old sad story.

When the bus finally pulled up to the shelter outside of the Shebeen on Cross Bay Boulevard, the faces of the other two passengers didn't help Nora's morale. The first was a middle-aged woman in a frayed coat clutching her purse in both hands like a rosary. She had the look of permanent fear stitched in her face and stared fiercely out of the window. A charwoman, thought Nora, from the look of her gnarled hands and wild hair and haggard face. You saw them like that in Ireland, Nora thought. Young hags, on their way to becoming old hags.

Halfway up the aisle was a man in rough work clothes. He bobbed like a puppet with the movement of the bus. There were specks of vomit on his beard. Nora could guess his story. Out drinking after a day's work and coming home surly and mean to his wife from high school and a batch of neglected kids.

Then she saw herself in the reflection of the bus window, her wet hair flat against her head. We look like outpatients from an asylum, Nora thought, glancing at the pale laborer and the huddled charwoman.

She listened to the hiss of the tires in the rain as the bus moved across Queens. The scenery made dramatic shifts. America, she thought gratefully—get on a bus and witness the changes.

The salt-sprayed houses of Broad Channel, with its pride of sagging docks, gave way to the haunted streets around the cemeteries of Richmond Hill. The crisp side streets were kept immaculate by the meticulous German immigrants who had settled there long ago, transforming the area, with their Octoberfests, into a kind of Bavarian outpost.

And then Elmhurst, with its cluster of department stores, patrolled in the night by an army of private security guards. On Queens Boulevard, the junkies clustered in the fast-food parlors, waiting out their long ordeal. There, a few innocent transients, like Nora, made bus transfers. They adopted a kind of conspiracy of blindness. Each side denied the existence of the other.

Late at night, the buses came in defensive bursts, arriving two or three at a time. It was as though even the buses were lonely and traveled together for company, thought Nora.

Most of the other girls who worked at the Shebeen lived in nearby Far Rockaway or Kew Garden Hills. They had boyfriends or husbands picking them up when they worked late. But Nora did not drive, and she had deliberately picked the far commute to Astoria. It gave her privacy. She could sit in her solitude and watch the world go by. She could grow glazed and blank for an hour on the bus ride all across the borough. From the Irish ghetto through the German and Hispanic and black ghettoes, to her own Greek island of Astoria. She had crossed all of Europe and landed in the Mediterranean on a bus.

In Astoria, unassimilated Armanians still bore an old grudge against the unassimilated Turks. In the Acropolis Diner, where she had breakfast, some of the waitresses spoke four dialects. You could almost believe the rumors that there were Magyar princes living in the rooming houses under the el.

In Europe, thought Nora, the hatred would burn holes in the night. In America, the princes and peasants became only one more quirky faction.

Nora Katherine Byrnes, from Ulster and Dublin, felt safe, tucked between the Cypriot Cleaners and five different styles of bakeries. She thought, I could raise my child here. I could live here and in time become a resident. Go to parent meetings at the school. Grow indignant about the garbage pickups. Support my local councilman.

It was a staggering thought for a woman who not five years ago was living under false names and hiding weapons for IRA gunmen.

* * *

Nora was deep in the reverie as she approached the private house where she rented a second-floor apartment. She was jolted alert by something strange. The absence of light from her window. She always left a light on. It was a small bulb and new, so it couldn't be burned out.

By the time she turned the key in the lock, she knew that Michael was waiting for her in the dark.

He was smoking. Sitting near the window, watching. She couldn't see him, but she could feel the weight of him. He had watched her coming along the street and, knowing him, probably read her innocent thoughts about schools and elections and the dull, ordinary ways of life. It made her angry that he could so easily brush aside all of her defenses, all the locks and remote hideouts, and force his way into her room. She wanted to remain angry, but Michael had uncanny ways of breaking through her closed moods.

"Do you remember Da?" he asked as she slammed her closet door shut. He was still looking out of the window, checking, no doubt, to see if she had been followed.

"Da?"

He nodded and didn't turn.

"No," she said briskly. "I never met the man. Listen, do you mind if I turn on a light? I'm not the nocturnal creature that you are."

"Wait just a bit," he said, not taking his eyes off the street. His voice was soft; it was the one he used to charm his way past all her outposts. Still, there was no mistaking the authority. She didn't turn on the light, but managed to feel her way to put on a kettle.

She thought, Well, he's not here for tea. Michael does not make social calls. He's after something again. But he'll get nothing from me. He's had my best as it is. Him, sitting in the corner like some cat with his coal-black eyes fixed like gunsights on the damned street. My street. The one I live on.

She closed her eyes and could see again the thing that drove her out, the havoc from the bombs. The cops and the smoke and the limbs scattered like bloody pieces of dolls. But they weren't broken dolls, they were dead babies. The mothers bent over in a pain beyond grief.

And here was Michael, still staring at her neighborhood. Damn your gunsight eyes, Michael. You can turn a common sidewalk into a battleground by just looking at it! You would escape, of course, in the bloody confusion.

Not that it was really her street that he was checking. She was a stranger here, too; tolerated. No more. Leave it to Michael to crack that secret, too, by bringing up her dead Da, reminding her that she had roots planted elsewhere. They both did.

"I remember Da," she said, striking the match and lighting the fire under the kettle.

"What do you remember?" he asked.

She was fussing with the teacups and the sugar. "I remember his face," she said. "I remember waking up once, and he was there."

Michael didn't move. But she knew that he was listening. She could tell by the depth of his silence how attentive he was. She was that tuned to him.

"I was six, I think. I hadn't seen him for a while. He'd been away on his jobs and in prison. Mother kept a picture hidden away and I'd look at it, so I'd know what he looked like. Then, one night, I woke up and there he was, smiling down at me like Christmas."

"He was a cheerful man," said Michael.

"He was a scarce man," replied Nora. She sighed. "Ah, little girls love their fathers. No matter how rare they are, we love our Da's. I will tell you something funny: from that night on I never woke up without looking for him."

Michael turned away from the window and stared at the black patch where his sister stood. He rose from the chair and closed the blinds, then walked over to the wall and turned on the light; Nora was struck by his competence, his ability to know where everything was.

On his way back to his chair, Michael touched his sister's shoulder. A light brush of his fingers, but Nora knew that it was a gesture of intimate understanding.

He kept his vigil by the window, pushing the blind open enough to see the street. "The thing I remember about Da was his laugh," he said. "The man had a great laugh."

"I remember the laugh," said Nora.

"My God, you could hear it a block away. Big, earth-shaking laugh. Surprised it didn't give him away on a job."

"Do you have a big laugh, Michael?" she asked, and he turned sharply and shot her a look. She knew that he didn't laugh much. Smiled only on occasion, and then only when he couldn't help himself.

"There's not much to laugh at these days," he said finally.

"Nor in his, I daresay," replied Nora.

He took the reproach, but he had something else on his mind. "He was not a careful man," he said.

"Well, in that regard, we might be grateful."

"I don't mean that, although judging from history, it seems that you take after him."

She laughed. He smiled.

"He used to wait up for me," said Michael. "When I'd be out with my friends, he'd wait up. I'd find him there at the window. Not Ma. She knew that I wasn't worth waiting for. But Da had to see me safe inside."

He shook his head.

"You know, he didn't want me to get mixed up in it. Not the troubles. Not the killin'." He shrugged. "He wanted me spared. Well, the man wasn't cut out for the harshness . . ."

"Who is?" said Nora.

"Some are better at it than others," he said. "Da saw that I was good at it. Too good. He told me as much. He said he thought I liked it. That was a dangerous thing."

"Well," she said, trying to push away the sentiment—she didn't need sentiment now. "A man wants his son in the family business. I've always heard that."

"I was just thinkin', sitting here at the window. It put me in mind of Da. The way he'd sit and wait for me."

The kettle spoke and she prepared the tea. "You've done fine, Kate. But then, I knew you would."

"You did?"

"I told Bridget you would."

"You told Aunt Bridget?"

"I was asked. Being the senior male member of the family."

She shook her head. "And just when did you pass this judgment on to Aunt Bridget?"

He waved the question away.

"You mean to say that you told Aunt Bridget I could

go to America? Is that it? You gave your permission?"

He smiled. "You really like a good fight," he said. "All I meant to say was that Bridget asked for my opinion and I gave it. That's that."

She slammed her cup down, breaking the saucer. "I want to be clear on this point, Michael. Was this opinion delivered before or after we had that little party at the house, the night I told Aunt Bridget that I was comin' to America?"

He allowed the room temperature to cool down. "Look, you came to me for money. You needed the money to come to America. I agreed to give you the money. I don't remember when I spoke to Bridget. But when I did speak to her, I told her that you would do fine and that she should support the idea."

He held his palms open, as if he had nothing to hide. But Nora knew that he had manipulated it all. He spoke to Bridget and prepared her for the outburst. He told her to hold the baby as a hostage—to see if she does well, would be the way he put it. He had given her money, he had smoothed things with Bridget, and now she had to repay the favor. The hidden chain of obligation was there.

Not that she could prove it. Not that she had any more evidence than the knowledge of Michael. But that was enough. She knew that every generous move was a calculated thing.

"I saw nothing wrong with saying a word on your behalf," he said.

She slumped in her chair, defeated, and drank her tea.

"I've seen Seamus," he said finally. "Fine boy."

Nora sat upright. "You saw him? When?"

"Week ago Sunday. Quick as a cat, he is. But he has a weakness for sweets, I think."

"That's Dee Dee," laughed Nora.

"Talks a blue streak. We know where that comes from."

"Oh, Lord," said Nora.

"And nice. A really good-hearted child. He offered me one of his own cookies. If you know him, that means quite a bit."

"I know," said Nora, although she didn't; she had only the secondhand reports.

"I told him he'd be comin' to see you soon."

Nora looked up. Her green eyes were moist. "Will he, Michael? Is that true?"

He sipped his tea. His face was like smoke, for all the solid truth you could find there. "I told Bridget, a child belongs with his mother."

"And what did she say?"

"She agreed. I'll help with the finances, of course," he said, peeking through the blinds again. "As soon as my work here is done. It won't be long. Less than a week."

So there it was. A bargain with the devil, but she was not prepared to argue. It had been more than three years, and she yearned to hold her child. She would do what he asked, if that meant she would get Seamus.

They sat and drank their tea quietly, like members of the royal family contemplating genealogy, duty and the ceremonies of tea. Nora was afraid to take too deep a breath—it might erupt.

After they were done, she offered to make up the couch for him, but Michael said he didn't need it. He was fine in the chair. He would be gone when she awoke. Too dangerous to stay the night.

"I need you to do some things for me," he said, and she nodded. She would not dare refuse now.

He spoke and she made mental notes. He knew that

she would not forget the instructions. She was reliable when it came to such things.

Michael kept a loaded pistol in his lap as he sat sentry at the window. He watched his sister prepare for bed and was moved strangely by the small, careful gestures of a woman of detail. The cups washed and dried and put away. The kettle emptied. The garbage covered. The teeth brushed. A hundred tiny habits that made her seem dear to Michael. The essence of attention.

When she left a blanket out for him in case he got cold, he felt a stab of unwanted emotion. A man like myself should be alone in the world, he thought. Nora Kate had no stomach for his work. Few did. Oh, she understood the small killings, the revenge murders, the little lessons.

But the large-scale political acts make her nervous. Michael had long since come to believe that the small killings were pointless. They might serve some local purpose, but as far as chasing the Brits out of Ireland, it couldn't work. Gun down some beardless English soldier outside of Falls Road and all you managed was a televised funeral with women weeping. It made the killers seem like monsters.

The thing was, you had to convince that it wasn't only the beardless kids who would die. No one was safe. Not Mountbatten. Not the prime minister. No one.

People like Nora were shocked by acts on such a scale. Geopolitics was too abstract for her to grasp.

But when you thought about it in a certain way, it was very creative. Michael had moments when he thought of himself as an artist. And artists were always misunderstood. James Joyce had been driven from his own land by weaklings. They were always after you to compromise. Tone down a harsh truth. But Joyce had changed the face of literature with a clear fact. Michael intended to change the map of Ireland.

Besides, he had no choice. The prime minister was about to act on her own. In four days she would be coming to the United Nations to hold secret meetings with the Americans; if it worked, she would deal a death blow to the IRA. The Sinn Fein intelligence network had learned that the British intended to make a deal to plug up once and for all American financing and gunrunning to the Irish Republican Army.

And it could be done. If they were determined, the Americans could stop it cold. It would be easy to trace the money from the St. Patrick's Day dinners and Northern Aid Committees. It would be easy to close up the ports of Boston and New York, where everyone knew that the Irish longshoremen turned a blind eye to the gunrunning. It wouldn't take much to impregnate the Gaelic fraternities with informers. All you had to do was to recruit a new breed of cop, unpolluted by the old folklore and romantic myths.

Without the Americans the IRA might as well close up shop. And the Americans would be given reason enough. In a world shifting away from the United States power policies, the British would support them in the Middle East. They would back them in Central America. England would be the loyal ally—in exchange for a crackdown.

A pretty good bargain from the American standpoint. Somebody had to stop it. When the leaders of Sinn Fein had come to Michael, they had had no plan. They thought that the Americans could be influenced by a dull noise. A few soldiers killed here or there. After all, they pulled out of Beirut when a few hundred marines were killed. Maybe they could be pressured by some bloody demonstration to see the error of closing down the IRA.

They left the means to Michael—the artist. And Michael intended to do it in one cruel stroke.

6

Tuesday, November 3, 3:00 A.M., 126 Hours 45 Minutes and Counting

Jack Mann carried around a picture of himself being stuffed into the back of a police car, handcuffed, twisting to avoid the cameras, humiliated. Not that such a picture actually existed, except in that steamy swamp of guilt that every cop carries in his conscience. But the image was so vivid that it might as well have been a tangible glossy print, mounted in his wallet, right next to the picture of Natalie.

Wait a minute, he told himself as he cruised into Rosedale on the far lip of Queens, I have not done anything wrong. I have not committed a crime. I am innocent. Whatever I did, I did in self-defense.

True, he had tampered with evidence and concealed a crime, which was, technically speaking, a criminal act, but there were mitigating circumstances. Any sensible district attorney, someone with a knowledge of how things work out on the street, would understand. The law could be merciful in the hands of humane people.

The tricky part would be explaining the persistent bag of money. If he had no larcenous intent, someone might well ask, "What is all that cash doing in your trunk?"

At this point, Jack declared his right to remain silent to his own overheated conscience.

He realized, during this frenzied passage of thoughts, that he was driving in circles mentally and physically. He had passed the camera shop and his dry cleaners, and it was the second time he had passed his own home.

Well, there was a perfectly good reason for the sense of dislocation. This was after the airport. Before the airport he could drive home while his brain remained on automatic pilot. But now was after the airport. The universe had changed.

He turned into the driveway of the home that he and Natalie had begun buying more than two decades and three mortgages ago. It was not much of a house, even in the present bloated housing market—the shingles were threaded together and cockeyed, the siding was ragged and needed replacing, and the driveway had rippled and cracked like old skin. But Natalie loved it, as only a child of the tenements can love a home of her own. She loved all the rooms where she could walk in and out, making a complete circle of the house. She loved the staircase and the smooth banister curving up to yet more rooms. She loved the cool sweat of the basement and she loved the dusty storage area in the attic. She loved the cramped, scratchy backyard.

But most of all she loved the deep draughts of her own breath in her own home. When they first bought it, when they knew that they actually owned it, she had walked through the rooms with her arms flung out, declaring her territorial happiness.

Jack was always surprised and pleased when he came home and found her chirping in the kitchen or sitting in the backyard, her face softened by a contentment that he could only witness, could only envy. To him the house was just a place. He had no sense of home or yearning for land. His home was Natalie. She was his shelter and contentment, not the fading wood and chipped cement.

As he drove along Elm Street, Jack had looked up and down the street to see if anyone was watching. There were always eyes on the street in Rosedale. This was the last stop in Queens, the last piece of land within the borders of the city proper. Thus, Rosedale became the grudging bedroom for cops and firemen who wanted to escape the urban terrors and yet were compelled by ordinance to live within the municipal borders. They preferred the far suburbs, but settled for this last-ditch compromise on the Nassau County border.

Suspicion and disappointment came with every mortgage. Not that it was unusual. Paranoia was an occupational disease among the uniformed services. No one worried more intensely, more creatively or more promiscuously than a cop or a fireman. Jack loved being a cop, but he was never completely happy living among all that suffering. It wasn't just the fretful backyard gossip about the encroachment of blacks that bothered Jack, although the bigotry was hard to swallow. What bothered him was a kind of sour gloom that poisoned the atmosphere.

One consequence of living in Rosedale was that every car that passed by at all hours of the day or night was watched by a series of unofficial volunteer block-watchers. As he had driven along, Jack could see the discreet ripple of curtains and blinds, as one after another of his neighbors checked, then recognized the old Buick as it made its way home.

The garage door rolled down like a freight train. Nights when he worked late, Jack took perverse pleasure in the virtuous racket of closing the garage. Slamming doors. Proclaiming himself in loud clumps of sound.

But this night he was caked with dried blood and there was an incriminating bundle in the trunk of his car.

He thought, I've never come home ashamed.

Fortunately, the basement had a private entrance. It also had a bed and a bathroom, complete with a shower. It had a desk and a personal computer and filing cabinets. It had an old black-and-white television set and a small refrigerator—both salvaged from the upstairs. Jack had turned the basement into a self-contained bunker during Natalie's long illness. He hadn't wanted to bother her with his late hours and homework. He had moved into the basement during her long dying. But another reason was that he could not bear to watch, and so he held out in the basement bunker against the enemy he could not defeat.

He stripped away his clothing, peeling away piece by piece the bloody shirt, the stiff trousers, the soggy shoes and sodden socks. They came off painfully, as if he were taking off a layer of skin, as if to remind him that he could not shed so easily what he had done. He worked in the dark because he was afraid to turn on a light, but the light from the street lamp outside was enough to make him cringe. One by one, he flung the articles of clothing into the furnace. He watched the fire for a moment and saw things in the flame. Then he shuddered and plunged into the shower. He scrubbed himself raw and thought of Lady Macbeth, a character he remembered from one of the plays to which Natalie had dragged him. He scraped under his fingernails and he soaked his hair and he scrubbed his back and even as he worked the soap over and over the same spot, he knew that he would never feel clean again.

The furnace was still bright when he came out of the shower. He put the killing and the disposal of the body out of his mind, into some mental future file, and he went to work on the car. His own flesh was pink as Jack took the debris out of the trunk and cleaned it or burned it. He kept rinsing the sink and washing the car, knowing that forensic units would still be able to find something to link him to the airport and the killing no matter what he did. A speck. A hair. A broken fingernail. He had been a cop long enough to know that there was no such thing as a completely sanitized crime scene. No matter how many times you went over it, no matter how careful you were, something remained.

The cleansing itself was enough to throw suspicion on him. But even though he knew this, even though he was aware of just how dogged and cunning cops could be when they sensed something, he continued cleaning, wearing nothing, growing slick with sweat.

What would Natalie say? he wondered. If she were still alive and came down here and found him in his birthday suit, working like a slave, what would she think, standing in that doorway by the stairs with that twisted grin of hers, that knowing look that invariably made him blurt out every secret?

"I only told you to wipe your feet before you come into the house," she would say in that high sarcasm that he knew so well and missed so much.

And she would know everything, because they operated on a plane of almost telepathic clarity.

It was strange, that they should know each other so completely, considering the fact that he was a blunt, Irish Catholic cop and she a subtle Jewish schoolteacher.

They had met on a blind date, and it was an awkward evening at first. He took her to a pub, him feeling bold and in his element, and she holding back, not saying a word, looking out from those deep, intelligent eyes. He began to boast to some friends about his work—for her benefit, of course—hinting that he had played some vital role in a crucial case. He was lapping up the admiration and attention, and when he looked over to collect Natalie's portion, there she was, beckoning with her little finger. Funny, he had just met her, but already, on that very first night, he knew that gesture so well. When he bent down she whispered, "Applause, applause!"

At first he was insulted. But then, when he got his sense back, he was bowled over by the purity of her insight. With one swift kick in his brag, Natalie let Jack know that she had taken his measure. He could fool the others, but not her. She was on to him.

Not that he was ignorant of the manipulation and uses of his own glib charm. He was aware of that easy guile and social sleight of hand that made him popular in the bars and station house. Now he had found someone who saw the plain vanity of his act and still whispered conspiratorially in his ear so that he wouldn't be embarrassed in front of his cronies, yet still know that she saw something better in him. Natalie had hope for him.

Later, when he took her home, they began to talk. It was strange, to let down the struts and guards and speak clearly. Even when they didn't agree, it was fine. Sometimes he saw her point. Sometimes she saw his. Even when they barely understood each other—him with his street-tough chip, her with her college-bred disdain of the rough; working-class style, they were still fond of each other, still enthralled by the music that they heard in each other's voice.

And when they decided to marry—an inevitability that became clear to them at roughly the same early stage of the relationship—both families were horrified and predicted disaster. But Jack and Natalie were amused. They knew a secret that nobody else in the family knew: they loved each other. They were compatible in ways that few other couples ever are. They hated the same things: cheap sentiment, phony patriotism, Helen Hayes. While their friends were taken in by the obvious conceit of a movie like *Rocky*, Jack and Natalie merely exchanged groans and silently agreed that they had discovered another public schmuck. Together they weathered the self-actualized, flabby human potential nonsense of the '70s and '80s. They had a warm contempt for Alan Alda and Phil Donahue, both of whom Natalie had described with laserlike accuracy as "repulsively sympathetic."

Not that they were a perfect couple. There were areas of their lives that remained closed to each other. She was baffled by the police work. From time to time she urged him to enter her uncle's furniture business. She argued that he had a talent for work and they would make more money and he would be out of danger.

He could not make her understand that he was a cop. One night, after they had been out to dinner and a movie, they were walking back to the car. A junkie put a knife to Jack's throat and demanded money. Jack acted on pure reflex. He grabbed the handle of the knife, ducked, whirled and kneed the junkie in the groin. The junkie dropped the knife and lay helpless on the ground. Jack stood over him and began to kick him in the ribs. It was very methodical. Very brutal. He aimed each kick to break a rib. The junkie pleaded, then wept and finally just groaned.

It was Natalie's scream that stopped him. "Look," he explained, taking her to the car, trying to stop her trembling, "this guy's a professional. If I take him to court, he'll be back out on the street before I finish the paperwork."

Natalie was sobbing, trying to understand. "He'll be sticking another knife in someone else's throat in time for the late show."

She still didn't comprehend.

"Maybe it'll be someone who can't protect himself. Maybe the next guy'll panic. You'd be surprised how many slit throats we clean up in the morning."

"But the man's sick," said Natalie.

"Exactly. He's sick. He's a junkie. He can't help himself. That means he has to do it. But my way, this way, what I do by breaking a few ribs is to put him out of business for a while. Put him in the hospital. Get him detoxed. Maybe give some helpless citizen a break."

"But, Jack . . . It's wrong."

He shook his head. "It's not wrong. It's true justice." He couldn't explain it any better. Still, Natalie did not understand, did not approve. It was a thing that lay unresolved between them.

Jack stood naked in the garage, looking at the empty doorway leading into his basement sanctuary. "I can't explain it any better," he said out loud.

He found himself, now and then, speaking to her. There were a lot of old habits he couldn't break. When he tried to sleep in their old bed, he stayed on his side. A year is not enough time. Not after twenty.

"What should I've done?" he said. "Ahhhh!"

He turned away and scrubbed down the car again, then showered once more and slipped on a pair of loose overalls. His legs ached and he felt his full forty-six years in every joint. Soon, he thought, I'll be thick in the gut. That's what happens when you get old. You thicken. Or shrivel.

Well, it has to happen. Jack had always been one of those youthful men—someone who could shave ten years from his true age and be believed. Not that he ever did. He got too much of a kick out of telling the truth and seeing the surprise. "Oh, no, you couldn't be that old."

But there comes a time when even boyish men grow old. The age settles into their faces from one day to the next, like a snow that falls overnight and marks the start of winter. Age comes often on the downward slope of forty. Suddenly, there are lines that run deep in the face.

He looked down at the overalls, no longer as loose as

they had been when he bought them, and thought, I'll never be thin again.

And he was hungry.

He began to watch an old Bogart movie on television and fell asleep before he could bring himself to go upstairs and make a sandwich.

7

Tuesday, November 3, 5:45 A.M., 124 Hours and Counting

Was it still possible?

Michael was up all night, staring into the dead eye of the empty street, and he still couldn't decide whether or not to go on with the mission.

The gun lay heavy in his lap. Nearby, his bag was packed and waiting. All the needed objects were within reach, ready, thoughtfully placed for a getaway. Such was his life—laid out for a quick getaway. In the next room lay his sister, Nora. She should be out of it, he thought. He had seen something in her eyes last night. A desperate hopelessness. A shallow breathing and wild swing of the eyes, like someone looking for an exit. He'd seen that expression before. It was the look of men just before they surrender. He shouldn't use her anymore, except that he had no choice. She was needed. But not quite reliable. Not the steady, fearless Nora he knew in Dublin or Belfast. Nora's turn was another factor to calculate. One more shaky factor in this dangerously sloppy country.

Was it still possible? How could he answer such a question, with so many slippery factors?

Michael could sense the first light in the sky. He couldn't see it yet, but it felt like a yawning stretch of the sky when he looked up. A gray November sky growing, not soft, but less dense. He could hear the traffic growing husky with the first delivery trucks of the day. And the scuffle of the early workers—crisp voices cutting open the day like a fresh apple.

It was early and he could see nothing in the street. Nothing, that is, that would raise an alarm, which was all that registered.

In her room, Nora heard the front door close. It was a gentle closing, not loud enough to detect, unless you had been lying awake all night like a held breath. Then she put her head down on the pillow and slept.

Michael fell in with the early workers heading for the subway. Blue-collar types. Construction men and low-level clerks and telephone repairmen this time of the morning. Later, the trains would be crowded with the secretaries, with their imitation high-fashion style, looking like pampered models. Unless you looked close and saw that they were just a bit too short to be models and their faces were not the striking faces of models but the faces of ordinary women made dramatic by makeup and flair and effort. There was no softness in the eyes, was what gave it away.

The men looked like lawyers and carried expensive cases, or cases that looked expensive. Always the look of things here deceived him. Everything was a knockoff. The clothing, the jewelry, the accessories, the people.

Strivers and jumpers. Made it hard on the cops, thought Michael. Couldn't tell if you were bashing some file clerk or a corporate lawyer. That's the trouble with this damned country: impossible to separate the real goods from the fake.

Michael felt more comfortable with the heavy lifting crowd, the prols, who had no pretenses, or only the hearty self-delusion of all Americans.

When he first arrived in New York City, Michael had taken some time to acquaint himself with the subways. It was a smart thing to do. He saw right away that the subways were the key to the terrain. They were what rivers and roads were to other towns. New Yorkers grew to understand them, appreciate their subtle effects. People lived off tributaries of the main lines—the IND or the IRT.

Each line carried its own distinct meaning and cachet. Individual stations were populated with implications. If you lived at the 125th Street stop on the Upper West Side, you were likely to be poor and black. If your stop was Fifty-ninth Street on the East Side, you were white and had money. Some stations were clean and safe and some were like waterfront dives.

And so Michael got the maps and rode the lines from one end to the other and studied the behavior and learned the basic protocol, which was that you traveled with an expression of massive indifference. Some riders even gave off an antibody of menace that kept them safe from the prowling hunters who stalked the underground.

After a while he thought he had the lay of the land. He had an idea of the subways and their intricacies. But, of course, he hadn't really penetrated the surface. Like some treacherous river with a calm surface and a demon undertow, the subway changed, shifted at unexpected moments and often had many meanings at the same time. Michael was no fool and understood such things, but the complexity and the sudden danger of this system were always a surprise.

The early-morning train from Astoria made its way toward Midtown, bodies whipping between the high handles and the footing like out-of-tune bowstrings, faces frozen in that permanent subway glare.

It wasn't too crowded now, and the beggars came through with their plastic cups. He listened to the steady whine of the beggars' appeal, "Please help out a homeless man!" "Just tryin' to get a meal!" "Spare some change, please, just some change!" which fell on the hard-hearted commuters like one more stammer in the long, lurching ride. Nothing broke the commuter mask of concentration. They had heard it all. Blind beggars who could see. Crippled beggars who could sprint. Women beggars pushing empty carriages. The commuters would get out of the way, but it was a rare coin that was tossed—like a basketball, for fear of contact—into the plastic cups.

Michael adopted the same commuter glaze and did not, at first, notice the fresh team of ex-addicts who entered the car. There were three of them and they were young and had the shaved, institutional heads of psychotics. Their plea was for funds for a drug rehabilitation clinic, and they didn't just ask and move on. They were wild with menace. They were like targeted missiles, aiming for specific passengers. They put themselves straight in someone's face and said pointedly that this was a good cause. There was no mistaking the hidden blade of extortion. They smiled wantonly and, since they had a superior force, one by one their targets submitted.

Michael blushed with shame and ignored them, turning like an old subway pro into his newspaper, adopting the usual mode of isolation. He could not endanger the mission by exposing himself, taking on a gang of bullies. Still, he was tempted. It was a bad sign that he felt such an itch to turn them inside out. Loss of control and discipline.

One youth with a shaved fuzz of red hair and a fuzz of red beard approached an old man in a corner seat. He took the top of the old man's paper and folded it down, and Michael made himself busy, searching his own paper for news of the airport robbery.

"Hey, mister," said the red fuzz in his stiletto voice, "doncha wanna see us stay off hard drugs? Doncha wanna see us stop muggin' and rapin' people?"

Michael saw that the red fuzz and his two friends had formed a semicircle around the old man. The other people on the train had spread out, giving them room to do their work. "Hey, old man, you don' seem to be gettin' the message. We are tryin' to do the right thing. Know what I mean? I could be out robbin' and things."

The old man looked around. He could expect no help. Not here. People on this train had all declared a separate peace. The old man's fate would tie them up, complicate the ordeal, involve them.

"What is it you want?" asked the old man. The three youths laughed. "Money," replied the red fuzz. "What else you got?"

The old man reached into his pocket and came up with a batch of singles. The red fuzz snatched it all away and it was more than the transit cop standing near the door could bear. He'd been watching it all from the corner of his eye with the haggard look of a man coming off duty, weighing duty against the bother. But the kids had gone too far, and the transit cop dropped his newspaper, revealing himself.

"Give him back his money," said the weary voice.

Red fuzz shook his head. "He gave it to me, didn't you, mister?" Red fuzz was glaring at the old man. The old man looked around for support. The two others were closing in, sealing off the cop from help. One was thin and had crazy eyes. But the real backup was the hefty youth, tall and powerful and itching for trouble, judging by his hungry look.

Michael was standing across the car and he knew that the moment when they would strike was close. "Oh, Christ," he muttered, then lurched, as if he had been thrown by the motion of the train. He planted a fist below the heart of the hefty youth. It wasn't a killing blow, but it knocked the wind out of the kid, who dropped cold to the floor of the car. The thin one made a motion—as if he had a knife in his hand, and Michael reacted quickly, clipping him on the jaw with his left hand. It sent the youth sprawling across two screaming secretaries.

Red fuzz began to run—or fight his way through the surf of a crowded subway car—toward the front. The transit cop was close behind, looking over his shoulder in awe at Michael, who retreated in the opposite direction, to the rear of the train.

"Mister!" called the old man. "Mister!"

Michael kept his head low, but he noticed a couple of construction workers, roused from their torpor, taking charge of the two youths.

I'm a fool, Michael muttered to himself. A complete

lack of discipline. I don't have the right to risk the mission. Not now. Not with four short days left and a busted plan. But this subway system is expensive. It costs a token and a piece of your soul. He couldn't just stand there and tolerate it.

The Double R line crossed into Manhattan from the Queensboro Bridge, and Michael huddled in the far rear, away from any commotion. There were little tears of rain on the window. Michael stared out of the grimy, smeared mess into the river. It was all a matter of timing. Could the train make it to the station in time for him to vanish into the Manhattan crowds? Could he put together another plan and carry it out in four days? Trust it to fate, he told himself. If the train makes it, fine. If it doesn't, there's nothing you can do. Not to worry. The water was choppy and cold. It would be hard work and tricky, if he ever actually got to perform the mission. The waters around the city were unpredictable. There were fierce currents as the rivers emptied into the ocean. His stomach hurt, waiting for the train to deposit him safely.

But, he thought, studying the wind whipping across the surface of the water, the mission was still possible. That is, if he could line up his support, keep his cover, minimize the damage from the idiots in Queens. If he didn't get nailed as a Good Samaritan. Still possible. Maybe. He didn't know.

Suddenly the train hit the platform, he was in Manhattan and the tempo of life changed. The passengers poured out of the trains at Times Square like a flood. The daily melting of the borough ice caps fed the industrial thirst. Michael moved with the crowd.

He emerged from the subway on Forty-first Street

and Broadway. The rain had stopped, but a strong wind was blowing. He could smell the sea in the air. It was too early for the call he had to make, and so he walked south until he found a coffee shop on the fringe of the garment district. From the outside it looked like a closet. A narrow storefront with a counter and just enough room to squeeze by. But the restaurant blossomed out in the back and became a big dining room with waitresses and booths. The garment center hotshots were already deep into their day, smoking thick cigars and making fat deals with buyers. Egg-stained plates marked the battlefields where manufacturers and buyers fought for their lives.

In one booth, bent over a couple of fruit cup specials, were a pair of ready-to-wear models, miserable and exhausted in the midst of their lifelong diet. They were not attractive, thought Michael, but then they were not on duty. At full attention, they might be different. Some people could do that with their faces through sheer effort. Will themselves to stature. But now the mannequins were tired and ached over their grapefruit and orange slices.

Michael sat behind them and a gum-chewing waitress seemed annoyed when he said that he needed a menu. He read it then, while she stood there, tapping her foot. Finally, refusing to be rushed, he said that he would have a bagel and tea. He didn't much care for American coffee, nor for the tea, for that matter. But the bagels were a treat.

"You want cheap knockoffs, go to Jeune Fille," said the man at a table across the aisle. "You want quality, come to Max Gross. Max Gross knows something about quality. Still. After thirty-eight years. In 1988."

He was not an old man, but there was something ancient in Max Gross's pitch. He sat back in his chair, having declared his high standards, having proclaimed his merchant creed, and blew cigar rings at the ceiling, as if that was where he lived—up there, without earthly worries. The buyer across the table looked worried.

The two models behind Michael spoke in rough borough accents.

"I told him. I said, you gotta move out."

"So? Did he go?"

"Are you crazy?"

They went back to their sullen fruit cups.

They all spoke as if they could not be overheard. New Yorkers lived their lives at full volume. There was a recklessness to them and their public declarations. Maybe that explained the airport. Maybe it was just another indiscretion.

There was a phone in the back of the restaurant, and Michael waited until he had it to himself. Then he dialed an emergency number he kept in his head. The phone rang once and he hung up. He waited two minutes exactly, then redialed. He let it ring twice, then hung up again. He checked his watch. He had fifteen minutes until the next call. At 9:02, he'd have to call again.

He motioned for the waitress and ordered a soft-boiled egg and another cup of tea. "That means I gotta make out another check," she said in that slow, sullen tone of reproach.

"Pretend I'm a brand-new customer," he replied, smiling. Meanwhile, Max Gross and his smoke rings had come down from the ceiling. The buyer wasn't buying. He had thrown himself across the table and was taking an entirely different tack with his buyer.

"Sam, listen, Sam. I can't meet that price. You can't ask such a thing. It's cutting my own throat. It's not realistic."

Sam nodded. The tide of battle had turned, and he didn't look worried anymore. "I'm sorry, Max. But, the way things are, I'm gonna hafta look for a better price. I really feel bad."

The buyer started to get up, but Max reached over and held his sleeve. Sam looked down at the grip. "What's the big rush?" pleaded Max. "Listen, we're not doing business since yesterday. I've been doing business with you for twenty years. All of a sudden, you're just gonna get up and walk out."

"Don't play games with me, Max. It's a bad season for games." Max let go of Sam's sleeve.

"Who's playing games? You think it's a game? I gotta make a living, not play games."

"It's very simple," explained Sam. "I can't use twenty-dollar tops."

"Who says I don't have fifteen-dollar tops?"

Sam sat down.

The models dabbed at their undisturbed lips. They pulled out makeup kits and went to work reestablishing lines that seemed perfect to the untrained eye.

"You could move in with me," said the second model, "but, frankly, things aren't so hot between me and Pablo right now."

"Are you nuts? You think I'm gonna move out and let that closet fag have my apartment? He'd just move his boyfriend in. Do you know what my apartment is worth?"

They were counting out the money for the check in small denominations of silver.

"Maybe you'll work it out," said the second model.

"Maybe he'll drop dead," said the first. They left quarter tips and smiled their grudging smiles at the waitress and walked their professional model walk into the street.

At 9:02 exactly, Michael dialed the number of the safe phone. He hung up after the first ring and redialed. He let it ring twice, then hung up again. He waited ninety seconds, dialed again, and when someone picked up the phone and did not speak for twenty seconds, Michael said, "I have a need."

He could hear the intake of air on the other end. He could always hear the catch of fear when the promises were called in.

"What can I do?" asked Thomas Flanagan, who was, publicly, the head of the longshoremen's union in the United States. In that public role, Flanagan was the tough-talking leader of a powerful group of rough men. But he had a private, more dangerous role. He provided logistical support for the soldiers of the Irish Republican Army. He had been informed, through a cautious intermediary, that he might be called upon to provide more than the usual free pass for the crates of guns on their way to Belfast. He had been informed that he might have to do something to assist a man on a desperate mission. Whatever this man needs, he had been told, you provide. Do not ask questions. Do not hesitate. This is Michael, the lion of the cause.

It was one thing to believe in a cause and proclaim your support, but it was quite another to receive a telephone call from a dangerous assassin.

Michael, aware of his effect, tried to calm the man down. He spoke slowly, reassuringly.

"Are you there?"

"I'm here."

"Is there a problem?"

"No. No problem."

Michael told the man what he needed and how fast he needed it. He could hear the suction on the other end. He had always counted on sheer boldness to quiet the qualms.

"Do you think you can handle it?"

"Yes. Of course. It's a tall order. But, yes, it'll be done."

"Tom, listen to me. This is important."

"Yes?"

"Right away. You hear? Not tomorrow."

"Do you mean today?"

"I do."

"My God, man . . ."

"I know that it's asking a lot, but there's a lot at stake. Now there's a good man."

"Today," agreed the union leader, who was accustomed to making impossible demands, who spent his life negotiating them down, but who understood that with this one, what was on the table was what he wanted.

Just then a man came up to the phone on the wall and stood next to Michael. He wanted to use the phone and he was using his presence as a pressure to force Michael off it. He would eavesdrop until this little jerk hung up. It was an old public phone tactic.

"Just a moment," said Michael to Flanagan. Then, to the man waiting to use the phone, "I'll just be a minute."

The fellow just nodded. He didn't take the hint and move out of earshot.

"This is a bit private," said Michael, smiling at the

man. The man folded his arms defiantly across his chest and stood his ground. One more minute, he thought, and I'll just pick up this little runt and move him away. Just take over the phone myself.

The man was big and brawny, and Michael instinctively began to take his measure. Too much flab in the gut to be any good in a fight. But he couldn't afford a fight. Not now.

Michael bent over the receiver. "We have to meet," he told Flanagan.

Flanagan gave him the name of a restaurant on East Broadway in Chinatown. Be there at three o'clock, he told Michael. Eat something, then ask for the owner. Tell him you're waiting for the man in the back room.

"Fine," said Michael, hanging up. The big man waiting by his side grinned triumphantly. Michael smiled back meekly.

As the big man came abreast, brushing past to get to the phone, he pushed Michael against the wall. Michael suppressed the impulse to respond, and withdrew, his tail between his legs. He was beginning to get excited again. This thing was not going away.

Michael just kept going, dropping his check and five dollars at the cashier. He made his way east, ducking in and out of buildings, making certain that he wasn't being followed. And he chastised himself.

"Good," he muttered under his breath. The strain was showing. That could have been a big mess on the subway. If he had been stopped, if he had been seen. If there had been cops on the platform. But he'd gotten away with it. And it felt good to put that big one on his ass.

New Yorkers were a lot like the Irish. Get pushed

around enough and you push back. Or develop an edge. A nasty temper.

He kept on walking east, and as he walked the debate went on. Was it still possible?

He walked fast. That was one nice thing about Manhattan. You could walk fast without attracting attention. Everyone was on a mission. He passed the loading docks where the blacks and Puerto Ricans were leaning against their hand carts, taking deep draughts of the drugs that kept them enslaved.

He passed the lumps of rags and some of them moved. The homeless men and women, hiding under their blankets of rags.

He needed cover. He couldn't be running around punching up bullies. New York was a perfect city for his plan. All you needed was money. A secret man with secret means could do anything at all in New York City without attracting attention. There were so many rich desperados on the loose already. Only the poor outlaws stood out.

The advantages to the city were dazzling. The subways, for one. They were dirty and dangerous, but they went everywhere. Better than renting a car and leaving traces.

At Fortieth Street off Avenue of the Americas, just outside of the park behind the great public library, Michael jumped into a cab. He couldn't see the driver, who was blocked by the No Smoking signs plastered over the bulletproof partition. All he could see was the smoke from the driver's cigarette.

He shouted into the spread of ventilating holes, "Plaza Hotel." Then he settled back and rested. He had decided. It was possible. The mission was on.

8

Tuesday, November 3, 9:45 A.M., 120 Hours and Counting

He awoke with a cold jolt of fear. It was that nervous quiver of feeling barefoot in a world full of broken glass. Not that vulnerability, or fear—or even broken glass—were unknown to Jack Mann.

You couldn't be a cop for very long and not face some mortal moment of truth somewhere along the line. During a small, neighborhood riot, bullets had flicked the pavement around him. He had been frightened, but he didn't lose his head. Some did. But he was relatively calm in the turmoil of a gun battle. Of course, it was one thing when he had the backup force around him. He had the security of brother officers. If he was hit, they would care for him. They would carry him to safety. They would protect him. But now he woke up all alone and in the basement of his own home, racked with the shiver of criminal guilt. He slipped on some underwear and his robe and tried to think, but his mind was a quick blur. He wanted to straighten the basement, but there was nothing to straighten up. He shut off the television and made up the couch. For a moment, he thought that he should be quiet—he shouldn't wake Natalie. But then he remembered that nothing could wake Natalie.

He went into the garage and checked the car, but he had cleaned it thoroughly. He would take it to a car wash, although he wasn't certain what good that would do. The thing he had to do was to clean out the trunk. That's where they would find all the clues. He opened the trunk, and there was the bag of money. Blood had settled into the mashed debris—the old papers and receipts and fast-food cartons—and he took out handfuls and carried them into the garage and dumped them into the incinerator. Something would remain. It wouldn't all burn. They have ways of detecting, Jack thought. Modern science could re-create the destroyed evidence. Somewhere in the back of his most paranoid mind, he was convinced that they could find a way to replay a videotape of the whole airport incident. One rational part of his brain knew that it was a crazy idea, but that other place, the crevice where he kept his lost faith, was crowded and cobwebbed with irrational guilt and terror.

Well, he thought, I've done what I've done and I have nothing to apologize for. If they could replay it, if they could see it, I would be deemed innocent. He was staring at the bag of money. The man was out to kill me and it was self-defense. He argued his case, alone between his garage and his incinerator, his arms filled with the bloody evidence, and he was his own worst prosecutor.

He had no more religious beliefs, hadn't had them for as long as he could remember, and yet he said out loud, "Forgive me, Father." Then he reached into the trunk of the car and took out the canvas bag of money. It was a bag. An inanimate object. He hadn't murdered the bag. But when he looked, he saw the dried blood and experienced another shudder of revulsion. He held the bag in his outstretched hands. As if he could keep from contaminating himself. It was heavy, and soon he began to think of why, exactly, it weighed so much.

Then, he had to admit, he wanted to count it. He had always wanted to count the money. Maybe that was why he didn't throw it away in the first place. Not to possess it. Not to steal it. But to evaluate his sin. To place it precisely. To count it. Then he would know just how bad to feel.

He lugged it up out of the garage and through his basement lair and up into the dining room, where the table was big enough to handle it all. There was something—a note—on the table. Without a second thought, he took the scrap of paper off the table, thinking that he knew what it was, and dumped the big pile of money out of the bag. He spread it out, smoothed it so that it made one pitcher's mound.

He still held the scrap in one hand. A note from Natalie. He went to the window to close the shades. She was always leaving notes. Little reminders of the complexity of two people living together. What would he like for dinner? Don't forget the cleaner's. How about this new movie that got such good reviews? Call me at work, it makes the other girls jealous. I love you.

As he was closing the shades, he suddenly remembered. He stopped in his tracks as the fingernails of memory raked goose bumps up his back. Natalie was dead. He was always forgetting. It had been a year and still he forgot, as if the lapse in memory could alter the fact. He still woke up in the morning and rolled over and started to talk to her and there was no one there to answer. He still started to dial his home number, and then sank back with the knowledge that there was no one there at the other end.

And now he held her note in his hand.

Only it couldn't be from Natalie.

He looked down and read it.

"Dear Uncle Jack: Large renovations and repairs to my hovel. Staying over for a couple of days. Hope you don't mind. Barry."

He spun around, wide awake and blinking with the glare of the note. There was a sheet and blanket on the unmade couch. He looked up startled and undone, and there, in the kitchen, like some back room interrogation lamp, was the kitchen light. And in the full glare of the light he could see his nephew, Barry, watching him beyond the pile of cash on the dining room table, waving a hero sandwich in one hand and a cold bottle of soda in the other. There was a huge grin on his face.

"Ham and cheese," said his nephew cheerfully, by way of explanation.

Barry liked to talk about his food, list his menus, as if the talking itself were one more tasty bite. And he had a big appetite. He routinely breakfasted on fat hero sandwiches and spent the rest of the morning nipping at packaged cakes. He sucked in soft drinks all day. And yet, amazingly, he wasn't fat. True, he had a soft flat tire permanently floating around his twenty-five-year-old belly, but, six feet tall, he remained at two hundred pounds—on the verge, but not quite pudgy. Not especially out of condition. The eating habits were, Jack was convinced, a reflection of Barry's essentially sweet, pleasant nature. Jack was grateful that it was food instead of drugs.

Barry was always in need of consolation. Anna, Natalie's sister, had died when her son, Barry, was still in high school. The father was a hopeless ne'er-do-well, seldom home. Jack and Natalie took Barry in, fed him, clothed him, but were never able to break through that high wall their nephew erected to keep out intruders. Barry had a jolly nature, but he also had a streak of mischief. He had been arrested more than a few times for car theft and petty drug deals before he was twenty. But even so, it always seemed so innocent, so devoid of true malice. Jack found in his nephew something rare: a good heart. Even in the midst of life as a small-time criminal, Barry managed to win his uncle's sympathy. Jack had no idea how Barry earned whatever money it took to rent a furnished room in Bayside, but he knew that it didn't involve heavy lifting or punching time cards. Barry was simply incapable of holding down a normal job. Whatever it was, he was also certainly involved in nothing sinister.

Nevertheless, Jack had inherited certain obligations concerning his nephew. As she lay dying in that cold, mechanical hospital bed, Natalie made him promise that he would look after Barry. Even if he didn't like Barry himself (and he did), he could deny her nothing under those circumstances. And so for the past year he had provided Barry with some cash, tolerated his eating binges whenever his nephew's refrigerator was bare, and made a few strategic phone calls to old colleagues to bail Barry out of jams. But in the end, it was one winning ingredient that enforced Natalie's last wish. Barry made Jack smile. Even when he had lived with Jack and

Natalie—when Natalie was still alive—Jack had always been cheered by his nephew's jolly nature.

"You're gonna get fat," he would say when Barry was chomping away at his second hamburger—and suffering the deep heartburn that frequently attended his own overeating. Jack would regret having said it, seeing his nephew bend over with pain, fearing that he had caused the chest pains.

Barry took his breakfast plate and moved to the dining room table, then pushed a channel through the cash. Jack seated himself across the canal.

"I slept fine," said Barry with a mischievous glimmer. Jack had no voice. He started to say something, but it got as far as his throat and stuck there.

"You know, Uncle Jack, if you ever want to confide in me, if there's ever anything about which you feel you want to unburden yourself; in other words, Uncle Jack, let me volunteer my shoulder. I can be an oak upon which you may rest your troubled conscience."

"Don't talk with food in your mouth."

Barry swallowed. Held up the sandwich. "Good ham. The cheese is a little old."

Jack ran his fingers through his hair. All the times he'd sat across the table from his young nephew and delivered sharp lectures about rectitude and accountability; all the mornings that ran into afternoons when he had explained with no hard proof of misbehavior other than Barry's unchallenged sloth the need for strict standards and discipline; it all came back to him now in his nephew's sweet smile of satisfaction.

"So, Barry, what's new?"

Barry held up his sandwich.

"Want one?"

"Don't be smart, Barry."

They sat for a moment, staring at each other across the artificial surface of cash.

"I suppose you expect some explanation," began Jack.

Barry waved away the suggestion. "Explanation? For what?" Jack turned away, looked at the window. "Listen, Uncle Jack, I was wondering, you happen to have a spare fifty? I'm having a little problem with liquidity."

"No," replied Jack, staring at the closed curtains. "I have no spare cash. None. I don't even know what liquidity is. It sounds wet."

"I was just asking."

Jack turned back and saw his nephew staring at the bulging piles of cash.

He pushed a wider channel between them. "Look, I am going to tell you about this, but I do not want it to go any further. Do you understand?"

Barry's eyes widened, as if to say, how could you doubt my reliability?

Jack thought better: "Oh, I'm not going to tell you shit. What am I, a moron? Telling you is nothing but trouble."

"Fine. You mind if I use the phone, Uncle Jack?"

"Listen to me, you big lump, I am going to tell you a story and if you are not silenced by it, if you do not immediately recognize my precarious position, my peril, I will have you arrested for bringing this boodle into my house." His arm swept over the table full of cash.

"I think, Uncle, you underestimate me," replied Barry in his News-of-the-World voice. "I have never seen a boodle in my entire life."

"Fine."

"Save this very substantial one on your table."

Jack proceeded to tell his nephew about the incident at the airport. Barry sat quietly, not even breaking for snacks, while his uncle re-created the past twelve hours. Even Jack was enthralled. As for Barry, he had no trouble believing every word. He knew that his uncle was incapable of lying. He did believe, however, that his uncle was perfectly capable of being naive.

"But why didn't you just leave the guy there?" asked Barry.

"If I left him there," explained Jack patiently, "the police would have routinely gone over the ground. They would have questioned the parking lot attendant, who might have remembered me. He would have a record of my license plate because this was a car left in a long-term lot for a period of time. If that didn't turn me up, they would eventually get around to checking the incoming flights. I arrived on an incoming flight in the time frame. I arrived at the approximate hour of the killing. They would have backtracked, found me and God knows what-all. No, I had to take him with me."

Jack shook his head, in part to control the involuntary shiver of his body.

"I had to take him with me. Removing him from the airport removed the connection. Now the police will not be looking for something that took place inside the parking lot. They will be looking for whoever this guy is."

Barry understood. He nodded. Then he asked a sensible question.

"Who do you think he is?"

Jack shrugged. "A stickup artist. A thief. A killer. I don't know. It's probably in the papers."

Barry nodded at the door.

"There's a newspaper on the lawn. Want me to get it?"

Jack hesitated.

"I don't even know if I want to know. Oh, I suppose so. Go get it."

The front page lead story was on the upcoming visit to the United Nations of the British prime minister. Speculations and hints about far-reaching, historic agreements. Straws in the wind. There were wrap-in accounts of the massive security precautions. The left-hand side of the front page, the off-lead, was about the airport heist. It was carried as a purely criminal act, and the newspaper account was lurid. A shootout during a stickup of a payroll being transported through the airport. An armored car stopped by four desperate men, a wild gun battle and four dead. Two bandits and two armed guards. Another armed guard was badly wounded. Two of the bandits escaped. They were the ones with the payroll.

"Listen to this," read Barry, unable to conceal his excitement. "'The thieves escaped with more than eight million dollars.'"

Barry ran his hand lovingly over the mounds of money. "Eight million dollars!"

"Not even close," said Jack. "That's newspaper bullshit. You know, like dope with a street value of eight million dollars. In real money, that could be anything."

"Why don't we count it, Uncle Jack?"

Jack looked at his nephew for a moment. When he spoke, it was with a weary, no-nonsense skepticism. "Putting all that money in your hands, Barry, would be like making you a hot dog vendor. Just too much naked temptation."

"Wrong, Uncle Jack."

Jack looked up, surprised at the new note of sober responsibility that had taken up residence in his nephew's voice. "You are mistaken. I understand completely, but you are wrong. We must take charge of this situation. Put it right. You have no business being in fear for your freedom. Not a man like you."

There was no irony in Barry's voice. He seemed sincere. He was being protective.

"All right," said Jack carefully. "We'll count it." They did it with methodical attention to detail. And Jack took a precaution: Barry worked the books while Jack lined up the bundles, stacked them, organized them into denominations and counted them. "It's not that I don't trust you to touch the money," he told Barry, although that was exactly why he was the one with his fingers on the money.

Barry nodded. He understood. He was content being this close. They worked quickly, as if there were a deadline. "That's another pile of two hundred hundreds," said Jack. "Right."

"How many's that?"

"Sixty-eight."

"So, how much is that?"

"That's one million three hundred and sixty thousand," replied the nephew, looking up from the paperwork, astonished. "And that's only the hundreds."

They began on the fifties. No use dwelling on the subtle meaning, the deeper possibilities of so much cash.

"One hundred twenty-one stacks of fifties," said Jack.

"That's one million two hundred and ten thousand dollars," said Barry.

"Eighty-nine stacks of twenties," said Jack, growing

grim, as if each increment were another nail in his coffin.

"That makes three hundred and fifty-six thousand in twenties," said a cheerful Barry. "For a grand total of two million nine hundred and twenty-six thousand dollars. Boy, do those newspapers lie."

They sat there as the morning dribbled away, staring at the big table, awed and silenced by the power of the raw piles of cash. So many thoughts raced through each. Barry looked at the table and saw vivid sports cars and buckets of champagne, naked women—and a long, expensive spree without those prickly stabs of worry about bills.

Jack saw something different. He saw a relentless pursuit. The money was a lost child and the parents would soon come looking.

"Well," said Jack with a sigh, "we really can't sit here all day."

"I could," said a smiling Barry.

Jack piled the money back into the bag—surprised that it almost all didn't fit into the three-foot-long container. Then he went down through the basement and into the garage, Barry close behind, and stuffed it back into the trunk of the car, under one of the spare tires, deep in the well.

"I am going out," said Jack.

"Where?" asked Barry.

"I am going to put my ear to the ground and my nose to the grindstone. I am going to try to find out what gives with this"—and he indicated the car trunk. "I am also going to figure out some way of getting rid of it."

"Uncle Jack!"

Jack held up his hand. "Please," he said staunchly. "I won't argue about it. The money is not mine. It is not yours. It is a houseguest who must be returned home. Nothing but trouble."

"Oh, but Uncle Jack, some trouble is worth it."

"No. I promise you, Barry, this is only grief."

They drove off after lunch in the beat-up old Buick with vague and troubled destinations. Jack wanted to dump the money and then go to a car wash, but Barry talked him out of it.

"You don't want the money to get wet. It might run," he said. "I'll wash the car," he promised.

They passed the Queens detective command, and Jack saw the activity and recognized a major investigation.

"God, they've got units from the Bronx, Manhattan, Staten Island, Brooklyn . . . everywhere," he said, noting the various precinct numbers on the cars.

He parked in an old municipal lot behind the precinct, where the cars were bent and smashed. "Uncle Jack!" whispered Barry. "You're not gonna leave it here!"

Jack looked around. "No place safer."

"Safe? Are you nuts? Look at the glass on the cement. They smash into everything."

Jack smiled. "Take a closer look," he said. "They don't hit cop cars. They never hit cop cars."

Barry looked and saw, among the rusted wrecks, the unmolested cars with the Police Benevolent Association stickers in the windshield—the same kind his uncle's car had—giving them immunity from the car thieves in the area.

They found the small diner on a side street. The windows were steamed and the traffic in and out was official—cops, detectives, insurance agents, City Hall hounds. Jack took a booth near the front.

"What's this?" asked Barry.

"It's called lunch."

A woman came over, stopped and leaned down and took Jack's face in her hands and kissed him. "How's it going, Maggie?" he said.

"It's too early to complain. Come back in an hour."

"This is my nephew . . ."

"Barry. I know all about you."

"This is Maggie."

"Charmed," said Barry, rising out of his seat, taking her hand and kissing it.

"The whole family," giggled Maggie.

"Couple of burgers, fries, Cokes, the works," said Jack. "Medium rare. Mo?"

"He's in the back."

Maggie came back trailing a big, bearded man with a huge belly. She was smiling as if she had personally cooked this dish.

"Tuna on rye, hold the mayo, little lettuce, right?"

Mo nodded.

As Mo moved into the booth like some oversized liner berthing in a tight pier, Jack introduced him.

"Tuna on rye, I'd like you to meet my nephew: burger, medium rare."

"Very tasty," said Barry.

"You're not bad yourself," said Mo.

Barry saw that this one was a cop, too. Uncanny how you could spot them. What was it? A certain subdued arrogance? No need to think it was the gun. That explosive power riding along the hip. But it was something else. Some indefinable psychic swagger that made it possible for them to intimidate—because that was what they did: intimidate. Some inner ear listening for trouble. Mo was a born cop. He lived on the top floor of an apartment house where he spent his nights listening for footsteps on the roof. While his wife slept beside him, Mo learned to tell the difference in the tread of a tenant and a burglar. A Jew, Mo married the daughter of a cop—a Catholic woman who counted Mo's policeman's nature as superior to their religious differences. She would wake up in the morning and look over at his puffy face and know that he'd been up all night standing sentry.

Jack and Mo ate their lunch, tossing around old stories while Barry listened.

"So she says, 'These two guys who grabbed my purse are young kids, Officer, how're you gonna catch them?'" said Mo.

"She said it to the wrong guy," interjected Jack.

"Well, they had a block on me and they're running easy. Like, 'Who is this cream puff on our tails?'"

Jack and Barry laughed, although Barry didn't know why. He merely sensed that there was an insider's secret.

"I go into hyperspeed," said Mo. "I am moving. I catch up to the first and he sees me and he almost faints. I cuff him, and I tell him to keep up because we have to catch his partner."

"Did he keep up?"

"For a while. But he got winded and collapsed. There was a precinct unit trailing us, and they picked him up. So, six blocks later, I catch up to the leader, who is huffing and puffing—really sucking it in. I figure I might even have a coronary here."

"This guy is fast," Jack said to Barry. "You would not believe it."

"He tosses the purse back at me and I scoop it up and keep going after him."

Maggie brought the coffee and there was a pause while they sugared and creamed it.

"So," asked Jack, when she had gone, "did you get him?"

Mo laughed. Lit another cigarette. "Not exactly. Some highway unit sees me running in the street with a lady's handbag and pulls me over, throws me up against the wall and tosses me. By the time they find my shield, this rabbit is gone."

Jack almost fell off his seat at that. Barry smiled and thought, Cops!

"Uh, listen, Barry, could you go check on the car?"

Barry was startled. "Sure, Uncle Jack."

When they were alone, Jack asked his old partner how it felt to be riding the passenger seat on a computer.

"I don't know, Jack. It ain't that bad. Listen, I'm not a kid anymore."

"You're not fifty."

They drank coffee.

"After I chased down those two guys? I was out of lungs. None. Was a time I could run all week. Fat as I am. Listen, you start to get old. Remember what Dorothy Parker said."

"Mo, they never let me join the Round Table."

"'After forty, it's patch, patch, patch.'"

Jack nodded. Then he felt an old comfort—the safe warmth of his onetime partner.

"Listen, pal, I'm trying to pick up something on this airport heist."

"Stay away," replied Mo, taking a last large mouthful

of sandwich, stuffing a piece of pickle in the side. "What, you got a client?"

"Maybe. I know there's a lot of heat and I know that there are markers getting called."

"This is an artichoke," replied Mo. "No telling what the next layer's gonna be."

"Give me a hint."

Mo looked around, bent across the table. "It's no big secret, but you know that this was a protected payroll."

If Mo had been paying more attention he would have seen his old partner grow pale. He would have detected the unsteady quiver in Jack's voice. But he was rolling along, giving up known gossip.

"Protected?" asked Jack.

Mo nodded. "The boys in Atlantic City were washing the hands of the boys in Las Vegas. You know how it works. Payrolls moving in cash under mob control."

Jack sat back and rubbed his neck.

"Whoever got this payroll is in for major grief."

"No shit," said Jack sarcastically. "But they're putting up a fifty-thousand-dollar reward."

"Yeah, that's Sally Bones. You remember him. One of their own posing as a lawyer. You don't need that kind of action. Hey! Ain't anybody getting a hot divorce? I'd think business would be good."

"No. AIDS makes everyone faithful. Tough times for keyhole peeping."

"Yeah, well, stay away from this one. This could be really tough times."

Jack and Barry drove home silently. A few words about staying inside. Not attracting attention.

"But I have to go out," said Jack.

Barry nodded obediently.

"I'm not leaving you any money. It'll keep you barefoot and pregnant."

"Where would I go?" asked Barry innocently.

Barry waited until his uncle was gone, then fished out the stacks of bills he had hidden under the cushions of the couch during the counting. He had four stacks of hundreds, six stacks of fifties and one stack of twenties—giving him a grand total of $144,000.

He was fingering the bills as he dialed the number of the chop shop.

He waited.

"Dino? It's Barry. Yeah, I know how much I owe you. I'll make it right. Trust me. Listen, you still got that Ferrari? I know, I know. Cash on the barrel head. I'll be down. Late this afternoon. I got healthy in a card game."

As he boarded a bus, he realized that he didn't have the exact fare. The driver kept the door open in order to throw him out. Finally, Barry gave up. "Keep the change," he said, tossing the flabbergasted driver a fifty.

9

Tuesday, November 3, 1:00 P.M., 116 Hours 45 Minutes and Counting

The floor manager in the men's department at Saks Fifth Avenue had been alerted to a disturbance by that inner-store telegraph of arched eyebrows, a tone of alarmed contempt, and the flustered attention of a swarm of sales personnel surrounding the suspect customer in the overpriced suit department.

"How may I help you, sir?" asked the floor manager, an unctuous, bottle-shaped fop who had adopted the retail stage name of Mr. Hilary.

Michael continued to examine the texture of a herringbone, then, without turning, said with stiletto confidence, "I will let you know."

Mr. Hilary—recognizing at once the sound of raw authority—scattered the overheated sales force: "Mr. Coleman, I believe that there is a problem in color matching in Ready-to-Wear. Mr. Marlowe, now is a good time to attend to the chaos in Outerwear."

No one replied. No one objected. They all bobbed and went off to their new assignments, understanding that the crisis was past. Or at least under control.

Michael enjoyed the stir, although it violated one of the rules of cover: not to call attention to oneself. He appreciated the confusion caused by his almost undetectable insistence. For though he was small in stature, and not impressive at a distance, Michael was commanding up close. He could shrivel a snotty clerk with the snap of his finger, which is how he handled Mr. Hilary.

"Yes, sir?" asked Mr. Hilary, moving in behind Michael, reacting to the snap of the finger.

"I'll want a tailor."

"Yes, sir."

"To take my measurements."

"Of course."

"I'll want several suits, a new topcoat, some other items. I'll want them altered and delivered to the Plaza today."

"Uh, alterations could take some time," said Mr. Hilary, bending down to pick up a lost petal from the carnation in his lapel.

Michael turned, handed him the herringbone, along with a plain brown suit, a deep blue suit, a sports jacket and several pairs of slacks.

"You'll see to it," he said, smiling frostily.

"Uh, weeelll . . ."

"My name is Michael Martin. I trust you'll take care of things for me, as I'm rather pressed."

Michael turned away. "Go fetch the tailor," he said. He always found it best to act like British aristocracy and take charge when they're flustered.

The tailor, summoned hurriedly, went grumbling over the surfaces of Michael's body as the floor manager attempted to calm him down, shushed him, smiling at Michael, who accepted the grudging attention without complaint or gratitude.

"How do you like the cuffs?" asked the tailor in a tone of pure complaint.

"I don't," said Michael. "The trousers will break at the shoe line. I would like some linen to show on the jacket. Not much. Just enough to display linen."

The tailor grumbled on, but now with some respect, for he liked a customer with definite opinions about cut and style. He hated the crude American rich men who had opinions without taste. This one knew what he wanted and made it plain, without the sniveling indecision that made him curse and stab his own fingers with anger and frustration.

Michael also ordered some luggage, shoes, underwear, socks, and settled the account with a charge card. Mr. Hilary put it through personally. Michael had checked in to the Plaza as Michael Martin—a name unknown to anyone except himself and a man in France who supplied a credit card without limit in that name. And, of course, the sales force at Saks.

"I will be out for the afternoon and there will be some things delivered from Saks," he told the nodding clerk at the front desk. "Send them to my room." He handed the clerk a fifty-dollar bill. "Have them hung up and put away."

It wasn't hard finding the restaurant on East Broadway. Michael was familiar with Chinatown. It was two-thirty when he arrived—he always arrived early so that he could see an ambush developing. The host seated him. Since he was hungry, Michael ordered soup and a dish of spicy chicken. The restaurant was empty except for a pair of lovers lingering over a late lunch. Could be, thought Michael, watching until he saw that they were too young and too soft and too besotted with each other to be a threat.

The men he expected arrived, looked around, focused on him carefully, blatantly, then dismissed Michael as one more obvious tourist and headed for an upstairs meeting room. They were very careless, thought Michael. They saw what they expected to see.

Not the owner of the restaurant. He sat by the cash register and never took his eyes off Michael. He knew the look of hunger that had nothing to do with food. Probably had to deal with rapacious warlords back in the old country, thought Michael.

Two bodyguards took up positions near the door. They had a strategic view of the staircase and of the street. Halfway through his meal, Michael summoned the manager.

"Mr. Flanagan is expecting me," he said.

"You are, name please?" asked the owner, playing his part, looking for the signal.

"I am a stranger," replied Michael.

He walked up the stairs slowly, to make them think, to give them time. He was like someone on the bridge of a ship at night, getting accustomed to the dark. By the time he reached the top of the stairs, Flanagan was standing up, waiting, smiling, holding out his hand like an idiot. Michael stood in the door, taking it in. There was Flanagan, stepping forward, the leader, flanked by a pair of rough goons. He's flexing some muscle, thought Michael. He wants to show me that he's not to be taken lightly.

"Could we talk alone."

It was not a question and Tom Flanagan was no cream puff. "Wait downstairs, boys," he said with the gruff certainty of a man who understood gesture.

Flanagan remained standing. He was taller, and the advantage was little enough. He shook hands and Michael was quiet, accepting the ritual, the small assertion, then sat at the table.

"Well, sir, I see that you found us."

"You gave good directions."

Flanagan leaned closer. "Terrible thing, last night. I'm glad to see you're all in one piece."

"I had nothing to do with it," said Michael, shrugging. Then he added, "However, something to be considered. A certain amount of pointless violence serves a purpose," he said with chilling aplomb. "It makes the other fellow less confident. You see, it throws off his calculations. He can't tell precisely where you'll draw the line."

Flanagan laughed and shook his head. "Yes, I can see that." Then, soberly, "But, Michael, this is different."

"How's this different, Mr. Flanagan?"

"This is Mafia. The payroll at the airport belonged to a crime family. They guard that with the same fierce protective eye as they guard their women's chastity."

Michael considered this. He turned the news around a few times, but didn't let it disturb the hard face of determination he had worn to the meeting.

"Well, all right, it's the Mafia; how does that make it different?"

Flanagan blew out some air. "How? My God, man,

we're talking about organized crime. That's like killing a cop. Worse. Cops are restrained from public revenge. The Mafia thrives on it. They welcome a chance to show off."

"Well," said Michael evenly, "they're going to have to eat this one."

"Michael, I don't think you appreciate our position. Those guys—the Mafia—they're like nations. They think that they can't afford to lose face. They go a little nuts when you make them look bad. And walking off with one of their payrolls makes them look very bad."

Michael thought about this. He lit a cigar. "I don't mean to be rude, Mr. Flanagan, but I think that they're in more trouble than I am. I mean, I don't care about their pride. I really don't."

Flanagan was wringing his hands.

"When they find out what happened—God forbid—they're going to come after you," he said. "They're going to try to make an example of you. Look, you're a big fish anyway. It would be a feather for them. Make them look strong. They'll pull out all stops."

"And what if I started pulling out the stops? How many do you think I could reach before I had to quit?"

Flanagan laughed nervously. As if Michael were joking, which they both knew that he was not.

"Let me make it clear," said Michael, leaning across the table. "I don't really give a fuck for the British Empire and I don't give a fuck for the Sicilian empire." Then he leaned back and puffed on his cigar. "It's not something we have to worry about now. They don't know me. There's no need for them to find out. And if they do . . ." He shrugged.

Flanagan looked confused. He thought, The man doesn't understand what's going on or else he's so far gone that he doesn't give a damn about living. Either way, it's crazy.

"Michael, I don't know what your mission is. I know that you're in a hurry. But I'm better off in the dark. I understand that. I know it's important or you wouldn't be here. I'm prepared to lend all support. All support. But let me just say something."

"If you're going to give me another scary lecture, save your breath. Tom, I'm here to do what I have to do. I'm here to die, if need be. Takin' a couple of nasty Italian fuckers with me won't bother me a bit. Not a bit. I won't die cheap." He shrugged. "If you're with me, that's fine. If not, good luck. But I'm going to do what I have come to do."

They took sips from the tea on the table. Michael sucked his fat cigar. He liked a cigar now and then. Gave a man something solid to hold on to. Ballast for an argument.

"Now what about the support?"

Flanagan always considered himself tough, having come up on the docks when fights took place with iron hooks and blood ran thick in the bars along the quay. But this one was some other breed. This one wouldn't flinch. This one was one of those wild, bared-breast-to-the-bullet death lovers—the kind that wouldn't lose a fight. The kind you had to kill to defeat. Flanagan was tough, but he had his limits and he was outclassed by Michael and he knew it. He'd seen that kind before, and they always frightened him with their suicidal courage.

Flanagan nodded. "Whatever you need, Michael."

"Fine," said Michael, giving him the instructions, accepting the envelope with credit cards and cash and a checkbook in the name of Vincent O'Dell.

"If you need more, there's more," said Flanagan.

"There's a safe-deposit box. The key is in the envelope. There's more cash in there. All in all, you have a quarter of a million dollars to operate with."

"And what about the logistics?" asked Michael, putting the items away in various pockets.

"Well, we can get what you asked for. It'll take a few days."

"I don't have much time."

Flanagan nodded vigorously.

"I understand. But it's not easy to get one of those launchers, let alone three."

"But you can do it."

"I can do it."

"And the two lads?"

"It's in the pipeline. They'll be here tomorrow."

"All right. I'll tell you where to have them meet me."

Afterward Michael rode an uptown bus through Manhattan. He preferred the buses. There was something peaceful and safe about the big, lumbering things, moving soothingly through rough traffic, comically bumbling up and down gently, with everyone loaded down with bundles, grateful for a seat. The subways were more jangling. They got you there quicker, but the price was rattled teeth and the stench of urine. The cabs were less risky, but they exposed you to a driver, and some of them were like airport X-ray machines, always studying the man in the back, trying to read him. The buses were better.

He walked across Fifty-seventh Street, stopping for a coffee, watching for a tail. That was the other advantage of the bus. Hard to plant a tail on a bus. After the coffee, he jumped into a cab and rode across the park and up to the Museum of Natural History.

He walked through the museum, doubled back out onto Amsterdam Avenue, where he bought a cap, then caught another bus downtown.

The habits of caution were ingrained and deep. He studied the faces he passed on the street without seeming to look. He looked in the store windows to see who was behind him. He paused in stores and surveyed the street. He ducked in and out of garages—looking like one more confused tourist—but all the while he was establishing a free zone where he was in control.

And yet, with all his stealth and caution, he had that feeling that he was being watched. That someone was on to his trail that he couldn't shake. It wasn't the first time that he had had such a feeling. Sometimes it was a true premonition. Sometimes it was the alarm set too tight. Nevertheless, it was something that he could not ignore.

He stood in the Plaza lobby for a moment, pretending to study the dinner menu, glancing over some guided tours, giving whatever was making his neck hairs stand time to catch up. Then he asked the bellman if his packages had come from Saks, and the bellman said that he had personally unpacked them. Michael took the elevator to a floor that was not his, and walked up three flights of stairs. He walked as softly as a whisper and listened for the inappropriate silences.

In his room, he stripped and soaked in a hot tub, making certain to set the mirrors so that he had a view of every door and window. Then he stuffed paper under the window lock and by the door so that anyone trying to slip in would make some noise. He lay down and took one of his naps, with his gun under the pillow and his ears still alert.

He dreamed the same old dream. They were coming

up behind him, and when he turned there was no one there. They were ahead of him, and when he rushed to catch up the street was empty. The city was empty. The world was empty. He was all alone in the world. It didn't take much psychological insight for him to understand the meaning of his dream. Ah, it's just a conscience, he told himself, as if that were a useless appendage like a tonsil that he should have had removed years ago.

He slept for an hour, then awoke with that cold sweat of dislocation. He looked at his watch and he looked out of the window. It was dark. He glanced around the room. The things he had inventoried were in place. Nothing disturbed. Then he showered and dressed and placed the little traps around the room to see if he would have visitors when he was gone—a thin dab of powder near the suitcase; a certain twist on the cap of the toothpaste.

Then he left. The brisk air cleared his head. Time to relax, he told himself, as if relaxation were one more inevitable body function that had to be attended to.

There was a bar uptown. Not the hottest spot in town—he could get in trouble at the hottest spot. But hot enough. A room filled with anxious clerks and junior executives. Hungry, upscale strivers who would judge any book by its cover.

"Name's Vincent," he told a young somebody at the bar after buying her a drink.

"Sarah," she said, looking him straight in the eyes.

"Cheers," said Michael, downing the dark beer.

"What?"

She couldn't hear in the din.

He put his lips next to her ear. "Cheers," he shouted.

"You English?" she asked, scrunching her nose at the

effect of the gin and tonic, looking at him for signs of aristocracy.

"How'd you guess?" he said, smiling with unfamiliar breadth, becoming, in fact, this fictional Vincent who was British. "Just here getting set for a trade show," he said during a lull in the music.

"Really?" she said, all interest now, having surrendered the other possibilities of the room. "An Englishman. Here for a trade show."

"Yes. I'm in menswear."

"Yes, you are. I could tell that the moment you walked in. I said to myself, There's a guy in menswear."

"Yes, well, lot of chaps here are in menswear," he said, going along with the joke. "Most, in fact."

"Except for the odd bum in women's panties."

"You think there are any of those in here?" he asked with mock horror.

"Well, I can tell you, being an old and steady customer, I wouldn't put it past some of these Wall Street heroes. I don't know what it is, but a lot of kinky behavior comes out of those stocks and bonds."

They spoke and bantered, and then there was a lull. Not a bad lull, just the sort of quiet spot you run into on a long highway.

"How about a walk?" she said finally.

"Capital," said Michael.

"Come on," she said, grabbing her coat. "You're not that British. Nobody's that British anymore."

"I suppose I'm not," he said, laughing.

She was hungry and so was Michael, and they agreed on a popular, overpriced Italian restaurant on Second Avenue off Sixty-eighth Street.

"You sure you can afford this?" said Michael, looking at the menu.

"Let's get this straight upfront, Limey," she said in a not altogether unfriendly manner. "I'm an underpaid menial in publishing. A junior editor. They pay us like they tip. You are, no doubt, an overpaid, underfed, up-and-coming hotshot over here on a lavish expense account. Whatever you've heard about American feminism, it does not extend to equal pay and sharing the price of dinner. So, young Cratchet, you are buying. If not, I'm going back to that Yuppie sinkhole and wangle a free meal from somebody else."

He laughed because he recognized the keen range of candor and truth that lay beneath Sarah's declaration.

"Now," she sighed, picking up the oversized, overpriced menu, "shall I order?"

"I'll have the northern Italian crow," he said happily. The food came quickly and in large portions. Salad. Veal. Pasta. She ate with an appetite, Michael noted. As they lingered over tea, they went through the usual revelations.

"Life on Long Island was dull, my schools were dull, my teachers were dull, even my parents were dull—although they are nice, decent, but dull people—and I was convinced that I was born in the wrong generation," she said amiably, in that happy glow of after-dinner contentment.

"How so?"

"Oh, I guess I wanted to be a hippie and a rebel and have my wild, overstated anger spilling onto the streets," she said glibly. "You know: Vietnam, drugs, civil rights." She shrugged. "All before my time."

He shook his head. "You Americans." And he laughed.

"Yeah? Well, we knocked your block off in the war. What's wrong with Americans?"

"Nothing. I like Americans. Just a little melodramatic."

"Oh, I see. Disproportionate in our emotions, is that it?"

"Something like that."

"Not constipated, like some members of a former world empire I could name."

"Tactless," he said, handing the waiter his credit card. Then he handed Sarah his business card, the one prepared to go along with the credit card: "Vincent O'Dell, Representative, Loch Knit Menswear, London, Ipswich, Aberdeen, Dublin."

She studied the card. "What exactly does a representative do, besides represent?"

He sighed, looked around. Nothing but diners in the restaurant. "Actually, a lot of espionage . . ."

"I thought you had a surreptitious air about you. Secret intentions. That sort of thing."

He laughed. "No. More in the garment line. Look to see what the next fellow is up to for spring. Actually, I'm trying to find out which way skirts are going."

"How does that affect menswear?"

"That shouldn't be too hard to figure out."

They were both smiling.

He was wondering how he was going to conceal his gun when he made his move.

10

Tuesday, November 3, 5:00 P.M., 112 Hours 45 Minutes and Counting

The small sign with black letters outside Apartment 3W said SALVATORE BONIFICE, COUNSELOR AT LAW. Underneath, in slightly larger gold letters, it said LONELY? MEET YOUNG PROFESSIONALS THROUGH OUR COMPUTER MATCHUPS.

Salvatore Bonifice—Sally Bones—conducted business out of one of those modern apartments with wafer-thin walls that had been converted into an office. The small bedrooms with the desks and cabinets never looked like anything but the improvised headquarters for a porn ring. All those formica-wood lamps and torn leather couches and artificial plants growing dusty on cheap coffee tables—it could have been a motel office, an airport, a 7-Eleven, a dental clinic—another interchangeable part in the assembly line of America. An anyplace, anything, anywhere.

Above and around and underneath lived the airline stewardesses and doubled-up secretaries who pooled together for the thousand-dollar-a-month rent. They all had small, hard, hunter eyes, looking for a male to snare. There were also tiny, one-bedroom apartments kept by the aging lawyers from Queens Boulevard on the pretext that there were nights when they worked late, but really for their sweaty, frustrating assignations.

The traffic into Apartment 3W ran a wide range of desperation and defiance. There were the thick-necked junior hoods with flattened noses and shiny sports jackets who were there to arrange for plead-outs on charges of possessing guns or drugs. Sometimes they were there bailing out a son, the next surly generation of grubby, small-time criminals.

And then there were the shy, painfully sad, lonely "young professionals"—mostly disappointed low-level white-collar clerks with no apparent social skills who had screwed up whatever courage it took to come there and now had to be posed and cajoled like babies in front of the video camera. Jack Mann waited while Sally Bones escorted one tight-lipped, hopelessly plain young woman to the door after the usual ordeal of forced smiles and maximized assets. The poor thing kept her head down as if she were coming out of a police lineup, heading for the six o'clock news.

Sally ushered her out, watched her go, kept smiling, shook his head. "Who'm I gonna find for a dog like that?"

"I don't know," replied Jack. "Maybe she ain't such a dog like you think she is."

Sally looked down at Jack, sitting on the torn-up couch. He motioned for Jack to follow him into what he liked to call his private office, which was located behind a door encrusted with undeserved civic awards from the Kiwanis and the War Veterans and Catholic Charities. Sally sat behind a desk that took up almost all of the room. It would have been the smaller bedroom in a two-bedroom on the A line, noted Jack. The master bedroom was where Sally conducted his interviews with the computer candidates. There, in front of the white screen and on a hard stool, the candidates squirmed and spilled whatever details Sally demanded. When Jack once happened to overhear one of the interviews, he blushed and moved out of range. They were conducted like police interrogations, and the subjects broke under Sally's harsh lights.

The guest chair in the small office was pushed in close, and Jack had the feeling that his shirt was too tight. Behind Sally was a view of the side street. Not even Queens Boulevard, Jack thought. Like all the other furnishings, it was false.

"Drink?" asked Sally.

"Scotch," said Jack, who had met Sally when he was a cop. He had had a low opinion of him even then, and it was hard to keep it out of his voice now, although he was scratching for help from this same demihood.

"Sorry. Out of scotch."

"That's okay. Whatever."

"Harvey's Bristol Cream."

"Fine."

Sally swiveled around in his chair, getting the glasses on one side and then twisting to get the liquor on the other. He poured stingy portions and then hit the intercom.

"Hey, I'm running outta liquor," he growled to his secretary.

"I'll pick some up tomorrow," said the sullen voice of

his secretary, a busty young woman with no obvious gifts beyond the obvious.

The door burst open and she stood there, chewing her gum.

"Yes, Gina?" said Sally, gritting his teeth.

"Gimme some dough."

Sally looked at her, looked at Jack, smiling.

"What is this, a stickup?"

"Ya want booze, I need something to give the man behind the counter. That's how they do it. You give them money, they give you booze."

"I'll give it to you later," said Sally, brushing her away. "As you can see, I'm busy."

She stood there. "I'm goin' home."

Sally looked at his watch.

"It's only five," he said.

"Yeah, well, my mother's sick and she needs me." Her nasal voice was thick with complaint.

"Okay, okay," said Sally, fumbling in his pocket. There was no room behind the desk and he was fat, and the whole exertion made him grunt and look ridiculous. He was fuming by the time he peeled off two twenties and handed them to the secretary.

"Get a bottle of Black Label scotch and one Red Label," he said.

"I'll be a little late. I gotta take my mother to the clinic."

"Okay. Fine. I hope she's better."

When she finally closed the door, Sally flung out a hand, as if to hurry her off.

"She types all day. Same letter. Gives it to me at the end of the day—five fuckin' mistakes."

"She looks competent," said Jack, glancing behind him at the door.

"Not a big letter," continued Sally, fuming. "Two fuckin' lines. No big words. Five mistakes. She misspells *hospital*. After looking it up. All fucking day long."

"I suppose she presses too hard."

Sally gave Jack a quick look.

"Some people do not behave well under pressure." Jack shrugged.

"She came in here and I thought she was here for the computer matchup, you know? God! So, I take her into the studio and I start to ask her to fill out the questionnaire and she just does it."

Sally shook his head, remembering.

"I should have known how dumb she was. But, my God, she had tits. Did you see the tits?"

Jack nodded to be polite.

"Then she says, 'Uh, Mr. Bonifice, is all this personal stuff necessary?' I still don't catch on, so I say, Yeah, sure. She just goes on filling it out. 'Do you really have to know what kind of fella I like?' Of course, I say. How'm I gonna find someone for you if I don't know what to look for? She looks at me. Not a brain in her head. Wide eyes lookin' at me. 'I already got a boyfriend,' she says. Boy! That opened my eyes. So then I tumble and I glom that she's here for a job."

"Me, too," said Jack.

"Well, the boyfriend doesn't last long. Who knows, maybe he had half a brain. Only a very dumb guy can take a broad like that. I mean, even tits get boring after a while. You gotta have something attached to them."

He sat there, looking at Jack, smiling, as if he had disclosed some great secret.

Jack smiled back.

Sally tried to stick his feet up on his desk, but they

wouldn't fit. Not without some very heavy pushing, which could propel him straight out of the window. This was something the man had to consider, thought Jack. Struggling back there, in that cramped space, if he wasn't careful he could shoot himself right out of his own window like a paper clip from a rubber band.

"What's your fucking story?" Sally snarled, still searching for some comfortable spot in that narrow alley behind the desk. "You do the job?"

Jack handed him the bill and receipts from Chicago. Sally studied them, as if Jack might have faked the signatures, faked the whole fucking trip for that matter. Like he was trying to steal the $250 fee, not to mention the expenses. Which came to $312.98.

"Phew!" whistled Sally. "I woulda done it for this. Whadja do, stay at the Drake?"

"I stayed at a men's shelter and I ate gruel. There was a bathroom down the hall, which I shared with the hookers. You couldna done it, Sally. Not with your touchy bowels."

Sally snorted and pulled out the top drawer, which pushed against the bulge of his belly, making it more prominent, like a push-up bra. He practically destroyed the desk-size checkbook, ripping it from the drawer, grumbling and making noises of protest all along. "Listen, why don't we make it an even five hundred bucks?"

Jack got mad. "Don't fuckin' nickel and dime me, Sally. I went cheap because I want to work for you again. I didn't sleep and I didn't eat, so don't fuckin' nickel and dime me."

"Okay. Okay."

Sally wrote out the check. He pressed the pen hard against the paper, squeezing out the last nickel. Five hundred sixty-two dollars and ninety-eight cents. Jack picked it up, read it over as if he was studying it, marking the spot for Sally so that he would know this was important on both ends. He folded it carefully and put it delicately into his wallet. Then he seemed to relax.

"I hear you got some of the airport action." It was a guess, but a good one, considering Sally's low-level connections.

"That's right. Where were you? I was handing out candy all morning. Playing with your dick?"

"I was getting some sleep after Chicago. Remember, I didn't sleep in the fleabag hotel?"

"You shoulda called me," said Sally. "You know something, Jack, you got no luck. You're never in the right place at the right time."

It had just occurred to Sally, but he was pleased by this insight. Sally liked to see people suffer bad fortune. He enjoyed a bad break befalling his fellowman. It made him feel lucky and he couldn't help smiling at his own good fortune.

Jack shrugged. He knew about luck and bad timing. "Now I got nothing," said Sally, holding up his hands, revealing how empty they were.

Jack nodded. He started to get up.

"Wait a minute," said Sally, waving Jack back into his seat. "You know, this is a pretty big deal . . ."

"I heard."

"Well, it doesn't matter what you heard. You take whatever you heard and multiply it."

"A lot of heat, huh?"

Sally raised his eyebrows; he was a man accustomed to speaking in guarded ambiguity against government wiretaps and bugs.

"Listen, listen," said Sally, trying to rise and lift himself to lean over the desk, managing to push a little closer, "this fuckin' thing is gonna rattle everybody's cage. The boys are after lungs."

Jack nodded.

"Major," whispered Sally, looking from side to side; Jack actually found himself glancing around to see if someone had slipped into the office. "Major, major!"

Sally reached into his drawer, cursing and muttering, and pulled out his thick calendar. He fumbled with a pair of glasses and began reading through it.

"Listen, I can't give you anything that's already out there, but hey, for an old cop. Whyncha check out some stuff? Go talk to some old pals. Ask a couple of questions."

He wanted Jack to use his connections. All the chains would be pulled to flush out an answer.

"I can give you, what? Hundred twenty-five a day, no expenses."

Jack hesitated.

"I'll take a hundred plus expenses."

He would have done it for nothing.

Sally peeled two hundred-dollar bills off of a thick roll and handed them to Jack. Before that morning, Jack would have been impressed by the roll.

"Here's two days," said Sally. "Call me tomorrow." He scribbled a phone number on a scrap of paper. "On this line."

11

Tuesday, November 3, 6:45 P.M., 111 Hours and Counting

The chop shop was buried deep in an industrial forest of rust and junk in Flushing. There were defensive perimeters of old cars, one piled on top of another, as if some playful monster had arranged it, stacked the cars like building blocks, to protect the inner workings of the shop from storm. There were mountains of worn-out tires, past all possible use, stored for no particular purpose, except the obvious—a barrier against intruders.

The local police knew what went on in the Western Motors Repair Yard. It was common knowledge that expensive stolen cars were torn apart and then put back together so that they couldn't be traced. But there was an understanding. The chop shop could remain in operation as long as it paid its fair share of bribes and as long as the business did not become a public nuisance. These terms Dino's father was always careful to meet. And his son was raised on these understandings, made to appreciate them as terms of honor.

Barry found his way through the labyrinth to the small office in the rear of that great worn-out heap. Dino was behind the desk, painfully smearing grease and ink over a maintenance form, scowling, as he always did when he had to perform the odious paperwork. The pen was stuck between his fingers like a thorn.

Young Dino didn't bother to look up when Barry came through the door. The sentries out front with walkie-talkies had already announced him.

"I'm glad you got the money," he said; he knew that if Barry didn't have the money he wouldn't be there.

"I got it."

"I always hate to hurt a friend," said Dino, looking up, smiling.

Funny thing was that he meant it. Barry was a likable guy. He had a sweetness that even a hard guy like Dino recognized and appreciated. Barry was just reckless and needed to be taught a lesson, thought Dino, whose notion of a lesson was the smashing of a major bone.

Barry took out stacks of twenties from his shopping bag. He counted $12,540, then put the rest back. At first Dino was agape, then he began to salivate. Large amounts of cash had that effect on him. But he hardly paid attention to the pile of payback cash. He figured that he already owned that. He was more interested in what Barry put back into the Bloomingdale's shopping bag with the old shirt pushed down on top as a stopper.

Two men who had been standing in the corner stiffened at the sight. Barry noticed them suddenly. He hadn't paid attention at first because there were always stray characters hanging out in the chop shop. It didn't matter. Everyone knew that Dino had a protected business. No one was going to commit a crime on this property. It was as safe as a police station.

But now Barry saw that the two strangers were dressed in Paul Stuart suits with custom-made shirts and quiet ties. Junior executives of crime.

"Lemme make a guess," said Dino, sitting down, smiling, putting the paperwork aside. "You knocked over a crack house."

Barry laughed, even as he noticed one of the two strangers moving between him and the door. "I told you," he said. "I got lucky in a card game."

"Right," said Dino. "I keep forgetting."

"Musta been some card game," said the younger, smaller hood. A long scar ran from his forehead across his eye and down to his cheek. Barry wondered how he wasn't blinded.

"It was a helluva card game," he said, and there was a quiver in his voice. He knew that he was in trouble. "Look, Dean, don't bother with a receipt . . ." Dino laughed. The others smiled. "But I really gotta go."

"Hey, what about the Ferrari? Didn't you wanna look at the Ferrari?"

"Yeah, I really do, but lemme come back another time."

"Hey, man, I kept that thing for you. I had another buyer, but I sent him away."

The small hood with the mean look spoke up. "Hey, you owe him a look. He sent a guy away. You wouldn't wanna insult him by not even lookin', would you?"

Everyone laughed except the man by the door. He just stood there, a sentry, knowing his duty without a word being spoken. It was as if a tree had fallen across Barry's escape route.

"Do I have a choice?" said Barry with a forced laugh.

"I don't think so," said the small hoodlum.

They walked into the back, through the noisy car shop bay where the mechanics and master cutters were splicing together the jigsaw of cars. They marched into a storage room, kicked out the two malingerers smoking a joint, and closed the soundproof door. They seated Barry down on the hard wooden chair, in the full glare of a bright light, and didn't even bother to try to take away the shopping bag, which he clutched in his lap.

"Tell me about the card game," said the short, smiling hood. Barry looked around and saw Dino with his arms folded across his chest.

"That's okay. That's Al. You can tell him almost anything." Al stood in front of Barry. On his right stood the other one, the tree.

"So, Barry, tell me about the card game," insisted Al.

Barry was sweating. "It was a card game. Classic poker. Five-card stud." He shrugged.

"Where was this fabulous card game?"

"A hotel. We took a room."

"Which hotel?"

"The Americana."

"Who played?"

"I don't understand."

Al laughed. The sinister Richard Widmark laugh. He looked over at Dino. "He don't understand the question."

Dino leaned over at Barry. "He wants to know who the other players were in this card game. He might wanna play with these guys himself, if they're such good losers."

It was damp and cold in this back room, but it felt as

if he had a mouth full of cotton. "Fellas," he pleaded, "what's goin' on here?"

Al opened his coat. Barry could see the gun. It was too big for such a little thug. Tucked nicely into the suit. Barry had a gun in the bottom of the shopping bag. By the time he got it out, he figured, he'd be dead. The gun was useless. He wasn't even sure if it was loaded. It was a gun he'd bought off some dealer on the street four years earlier. He didn't remember if it was loaded.

"Inform our dumb friend," said Al, nodding at Dino.

"Listen, Barry," began Dino, leaning in, trying to make it baby clear, "there's a fuckin' nuclear war goin' on." Barry looked confused. "Last night, didn't you hear about this?"

Barry shook his head.

Al took up the explanation. "Someone robbed a payroll at the airport. It was not a neutral act. This payroll belonged to people who do not get robbed. You know what I mean? It's like a doctor doesn't expect to get sick."

Barry held the bag tighter. As if it was threatened. This did not go unnoticed by Al or Dino or the thick hulk of a tree.

"I better make a call," said Dino, unlocking the door and leaving Barry with the two hoodlums.

"I think maybe that bag full of money does not belong to you," said the little thug when they were alone. "It's a guess. But I'm willing to bet your life that it's not your money in that bag."

"Hey!" said Barry, trying to fake indignation, "this is definitely my fuckin' money."

The small one leaned over and slapped him across the

face. It stung. "Watch how you talk to me, Barry. I don't like a punk with a big fuckin' mouth."

The big one cracked a smile.

"Now, tell me about the fuckin' money."

"I was in a card game—"

The little one slapped him again. Harder. Blood began trickling out of his mouth.

"No one loses that kind of money in a card game without some noise. We got people in the Americana. We got people everywhere. You think we wouldn't hear? Lemme clear you up on this. This is a very serious business. Don't fuckin' lie to me."

"I was in a card game at the America—"

The little one leaned over and slapped Barry so hard that he fell off the chair, spilling the contents of the bag over the floor. He rolled on top of it and could taste the blood in his mouth.

I'm not gonna get out of here alive, he thought. That mean little fuck is going to hurt me and then he's going to kill me.

Al turned away. He had hurt his hand on Barry's teeth. He didn't want to show it.

Barry felt the gun under his belly. His hand was wrapped around the grip. He rolled over and uncoiled and aimed and put a bullet in the belly of little Al, who looked down amazed at the spurt of blood and gore pouring out of his custom-made shirt all over his Paul Stuart suit and onto the floor of the room.

The tree leaped up in the air in sheer surprise. As if he could jump over the richochet. Barry could see his eyes open wide and the beginning of countermeasures. The tree wasted a split second, which was just enough time for Barry. He swiveled and fired twice into the face of the tree—obliterating it, mashing it into pulp. The tree fell as if struck by lightning.

"Ohhhh!" cried Al, who slumped to the floor. His legs were twitching. He was dying, if not already dead.

Barry was calm. He got up and stuffed a few of the stacks of bills into his pockets, leaving the bulk of the money scattered around the floor.

He thought, I have to run. I have to get away. The door was locked, and he fumbled with the knob. He had to just slide the bolt, but he got excited. Finally he managed to work the lock, and he slipped out of the room and into the bay. There was the buzz and hum of a factory. The high, metal whine of metal cutting metal. He saw Dino coming across the floor, looking confused at the sight of him walking unescorted.

A mechanic was working on the Ferrari a few feet away, listening to the purr of the engine, and Barry pushed him out of the way, closed the hood, and jumped behind the wheel. The mechanic seemed offended, ready to fight, unwilling to tolerate rude behavior. He didn't grasp what was taking place.

Dino was looking back and forth, undecided whether to run into the storage room and check on Al and the tree or to try to stop Barry.

Barry put the Ferrari in gear and released the brake and roared out of the Western Motors Repair Yard.

Sarah lay in bed trying not to shiver. It wasn't the aftermath of sex—although that was nothing to sneeze at. It was a sudden recognition of danger. She'd spotted the gun when she went to the bathroom. It was under his slacks, tucked away. Hidden. Almost. But unmistakable. Lethal metal look. A gun. No doubt. It didn't register at first. It did, but it didn't. A gun. So what?

Another jittery Bernie Goetz lying in wait in the subway. But then she saw him watching her when she came out of the bathroom. Not asleep. Alert in some kind of deadly animal fashion.

She climbed back into bed, her back to him, and clamped her eyes shut. Her head was buzzing with worry and fear, and she almost didn't hear him move. She felt the bed dip a little. That was all. And then his arm on hers. Her eyes fluttered and she moaned somewhere between fear and lust.

"Oh, God!" she cried as he turned her around, lifted her nightdress and took her again, this time in a harsher fashion.

Later, as they lay there spent, they spoke in that safe intimacy of the dark, each looking up at the ceiling as if they were talking on the telephone.

"Are you some kind of a cop?" she asked.

"Some kind," he replied, although he didn't know why he answered such a question. This was not his usual tactic of silence.

"I don't think you're a cop," she said after a while.

"Why not?" he asked.

She shrugged. He felt it. "I used to know some cops," she said. "The thing about cops is that they are very conventional fellows."

"Really?"

"They like to drink beer and talk tough, but actually they're very ordinary."

"Like uncles."

"More like aunts."

It was the first time she'd heard him laugh.

Then he remembered who he was. She could hear the air go out of his laugh. She could feel him tense.

She could feel the bed dip as he got up and went to the window and looked out onto the street.

He couldn't see anyone. But he thought he saw something move in the shadows across the street. Nothing definite. A quick movement and then it was gone.

"If you feel like talking," she began, then saw his face when he turned and looked at her. It was not quite scorn, but it was close and she felt as if he had slapped her face. She flushed and got angry.

"Don't let me keep you," she spit out.

"I have to go," he said.

He dressed like a whisper. Moving automatically, getting into his things, yet staying alert, aware of Sarah's position. She could actually see him listening. He made no attempt to conceal the gun. Checked it, put it back in the holster and tucked it behind his belt. Then he looked at her, as if to warn her that he knew she was watching, that he did this openly to emphasize it.

He kept looking through the curtain into the street. Something was out there. He was certain. He could feel the prickles of an enemy presence.

"I have to go," he said, standing at the door.

"Go," she replied bitterly.

Once the door closed behind him, it was as if he had never been there. He was a lost soldier deep in enemy territory. Only the ears and eyes were engaged. His mind was on a hair trigger.

The street seemed empty, but he stood for a long time in the doorway waiting to see something give itself away. When he saw an ordinary couple coming down the street he waited again, then fell in behind them, like a submarine slipping into a defended harbor behind another ship.

The couple speeded up, thinking that Michael might be a mugger, but he remained close enough to discourage whoever or whatever it was dogging him in the shadows. When he reached Second Avenue, he boarded a bus, then got off after one stop. He had his gun in his overcoat pocket now. He was spiked and ready to kill. A man coming alone down the street almost died. But then Michael recognized that he was just an innocent civilian out buying a newspaper. Suddenly he found himself in the heart of a cluster of Irish bars.

This city! he thought. You can't keep up with the damn thing. One minute you're in some posh Episcopalian section where all the women wear sable and all the men wear cashmere and the cops are doubled up on patrol. Then you turn a corner and you're in a working-class ghetto where the pubs are back-to-back and the drunks vomit every ten feet.

His hotel was to the west, he was sure. He'd lost his bearings for a moment, but then he saw the lights of the Empire State Building to the south and was guided by that star.

He ducked into an all-night restaurant and took a seat at the counter, where he could watch the street. If there was someone out there, he still couldn't nail him. Whoever it was was very good. He ordered tea and toast, and thought, giving himself a stray minute, that he liked that Sarah. He felt rested in her bed. But he shook the thought away; it was like sleep overtaking him on a highway. The thought of Sarah could kill him. He had sworn off women. He had taken an oath of celibacy.

He finished his tea and took a bite of his toast and paid his check and used another customer as a shield for his reentry to the street. It was getting late and there was no one waiting.

But at the hotel the message light was lit on his telephone. "A man who said you would know who he was," said the operator, reading from a slip. "He didn't leave a number."

Michael felt a chill run up his back. Maybe they were coming.

Wednesday, November 4, 12 Midnight, 105 Hours 45 Minutes and Counting

The phone kept ringing. Jack counted twenty rings. He stood in a phone booth off the Expressway, watching the Buick parked by the curb and trying to find Barry.

"C'mon, you little asshole," he muttered. Finally, on the twenty-first ring, someone picked it up.

"Barry? Is that you?"

"Uncle Jack?"

"Where the fuck have you been?"

"Here, Uncle Jack. Where could I go? I don't have a car."

"Why didn't you answer?"

"I thought you didn't want me to answer. I figured it was better to let it ring. You know, you really should get an answering machine."

"I hate those things."

"Yeah, but at times like this . . ."

"Is everything all right?"

"Yeah, sure. Why do you ask?"

"No reason, you little jerk."

"Oh, yeah. Everything's great. What about with you?"

"Fine. Fine. Did the phone ring a lot? I mean, were there a lot of calls?"

"Some. Hard to say."

"Hard to say? Why is it hard to say?"

A few teenagers were playing in the street. One of them sat on the fender of the Buick.

"Hey!" screamed Jack, leaning out of the phone booth. "Get off that car!"

The teenager blinked and ignored Jack.

"Listen, I gotta run," he told Barry.

"Uh, when are you gonna be home?" asked Barry, who had parked the Ferrari in the garage.

"I don't know. Maybe not until late. Why?"

"No special reason."

The teenagers had all climbed aboard Jack's Buick, which now looked like the jungle gym in *The Birds*. Stupid to challenge them, Jack thought.

"Watch out!" cried one of the teenagers in mock horror as Jack came out of the booth. "Here come the deee-tective."

"Gonna get us for sitting on a badass Buick," said another. "Thas a serious charge, ain't it, Parker?"

"A lot of time on that one," replied Parker.

Jack felt like an idiot. He hung his head and went around to the driver's side and opened the door and started it up. This is what comes of having guilt feelings, he told himself. You start acting like an asshole.

"Oh, please, mister deee-tective, don't shoot!" cried the first teenager.

"He be allowed to shoot first and ast questions afterward," said Parker. "Thas the law."

Jack started rolling with the teenagers all sitting on the fender. They fell off, one by one, and began screaming, as if they'd been hurt.

"Oh, I'm run over," was the last thing Jack heard as he picked up speed and pulled away, heading back into the airport.

The booth attendant at the long-term lot was still on duty. It was the same man Jack had seen the night before. He didn't recognize Jack, who left the Buick in a metered lot far away in case the car might be recognizable.

"The real cops were here all day," he said, looking at Jack's card with a miniature of the Private Investigator's laminated license on it. He handed the card back to Jack—a sign of disinterest. "I didn't have nothin' to tell the real cops, either."

"Well, I thought I'd get lucky," said Jack.

"Swept the joint clean. It was really something. They were crawling around on their hands and knees looking for clues."

"Did they find anything? Did you notice?"

"Nah! You kiddin'? These guys were pros. They weren't gonna leave clues lying around."

"No. I guess not."

Jack found himself in the airport bar, ordering a beer. He was feeling sorry for himself. Well, he thought, he would just dump the money and get clean. It was stupid to flirt with disaster like this. Then, absently, he began to clean his nails. He was using a book of matches. He looked down and blinked. He didn't smoke. He never carried matches. Where had they come from?

He tried to read the cover, but it was too dark in the bar. He took them over to a table and held them under a light. The cover said "The Shebeen, a touch of the old country on Cross Bay Boulevard in Queens."

12

Wednesday, November 4, 1:45 A.M., 104 Hours and Counting

They were belly up to the bar and spitting mad. "Okay, okay," said Tom Fiske, the writer, so-called, who worked behind the bar whenever Larry, the regular bartender, was too hung over or Martin too preoccupied to perform the pouring functions. "Are you ready?"

"C'mon, c'mon," said Frank, an impatient construction man who placed his clenched fists like loaded weapons on top of the bar. "Let's get something going, man."

Fiske, the so-called writer, slapped a fiver down on the wet bar; you could almost hear it splash. Then he filled up four mugs of ale from the spigot, all held in the grip of one hand, and set them down. One for Frank. One for Martin. One for himself. And one for this newcomer, Jack.

Jack—a little removed at the far end of the bar, but still close enough to be counted in the group—started to push a ten across the counter to pay for the drink, but Fiske held up his hand. "This one's goin' to be on our friend, here. Isn't it, Frank?"

"I'll be too old to enjoy it," said Frank, who did not like any kind of foreplay.

"The boys," said Nora in Jack's ear, throwing a thumb over her shoulder at the men at the bar. "They think they're expert at fine humor." Then she felt the swift burn of an embarrassing revelation—she had been caught with her emotions showing. There was no doubt that she had taken a sudden liking to this man, Jack, who had walked into the Shebeen out of the thin rain. He had a nice laugh and he also had a glint of something sturdy in his eyes. She wasn't sure which of the two traits was more attractive.

Fiske began his joke, and the usual happy hush that precedes a good joke fell across the bar.

"It's the olden days, see?" started Fiske.

"What are you talkin' about, olden days? What is this, a nursery rhyme or a man's joke? Let's hear a real story, for the love of Christ."

"You must be a pleasure on the job," said Martin. "What do you do, try puttin' up the roof before you have the foundation laid?"

"Never mind, never mind," shot back Frank, pounding the bar with his fists, a child demanding his satisfaction. "Have you got a joke or is this pissing in the wind?"

"It's the olden days," hissed Fiske, leaning across the bar, enjoying the sweat of the steelworker. "In France."

"Oh, in France, is it?" mocked Frank. He looked around. "In France," he said to Jack, nodding.

"Will you shut up, Frank, and let the man tell his

damned joke," shot Martin, who was in fact in a frenzy over something else entirely.

"Who's stopping him? Let's hear the fuckin' joke, if he's got one. Which I tend to doubt. I smell a long stall here."

"So this fellow Quasimodo is the bell ringer," continued Fiske, undaunted. "You know? The Hunchback of Notre Dame. Well, Quasimodo needs an assistant—"

"So do you, I think," laughed Frank, looking around, enjoying his own joke. Jack smiled at him, soothing, rather than as an accomplice.

"This young kid shows up from the provinces. Well built. Strong. But he has no arms."

"No arms?" asked Martin, as if the joke were a puzzle.

"Well, Quasimodo says, 'You can't be an assistant bell ringer. Not without arms.' The young man says, 'Just try me.' Okay. Okay. So he gives him a try, and the kid goes up to the bell tower and he smashes his head up against the bell. Nothing. A small, thin sound."

Jack and the others were smiling.

"One more time, begs the kid. Quasimodo is skeptical. But the kid begs and pleads and he takes a running start and he hits the bell and, again, nothing. A plink. Well, that's it, says Quasimodo. This is crazy. But the kid begs. Once more, once more. Please, please, please! So, okay, Quasimodo gives him one more chance, and the kid takes a long running start and smashes his face into the bell and it gives off a lovely sound. It rings out with a clarity and depth they had never heard before. Only the bell swings out and comes back and knocks the young lad out of the bell tower window. He falls a hundred and fifty feet and is killed on the stone slabs of the churchyard. Well, all the townspeople from Paris who have been drawn by the lovely sound come by and they stare at the dead boy. Finally, one of the citizens says to Quasimodo, 'Who was this lad?'"

In the intake of silence, Jack blurted out the punch line.

"I don't know his name, but his face rings a bell."

Everyone looked up, startled. It was quite a shock. Who was this strange upstart, comes in and steals a punch line? Only Nora laughed, but then she saw the wounded look on the others and she downgraded it into a smile.

"It's his five," she said, taking the wet bill and passing it over.

"It's not," said Fiske, smoldering.

"No," said Frank. "It's not. Why not?"

"Because that's not the punch line," answered Fiske.

"Oh, c'mon," said Nora. "The rules are that anyone can claim a punch line."

"That's not the punch line," insisted Fiske.

"Well, then, let's hear the real punch line," said Martin maliciously.

"Another kid comes in from the country," said Fiske, practically grinding his teeth. "Same identical face. And no arms. In fact, he's the twin brother to the first lad."

Fiske was addressing Jack, whose face was sunk into the mug of ale.

"Same deal," continued Fiske. "Let me ring the bell. Quasimodo finally agrees, and sure enough, on the third try, when he gets a beautiful note, the bell knocks him out into the courtyard and kills him. The citizens gather around and they ask Quasimodo again, 'Who was this young lad?'"

Fiske leaned farther across the bar and spoke straight to Jack. "Do you know the ending to this joke, too?"

Jack shrugged and said, “I don’t know his name either, but he’s a dead ringer for his brother.”

Fiske slammed the rag down on the bar. Frank came over and shook Jack’s hand. “That was lovely,” he said. “Truly lovely. For two years I’ve been waiting to see that man get his comeuppance.”

Fiske vanished and came back and slapped two twenty-dollar bills on the bar.

Frank moved closer to Jack. “I’m bettin’ on—what’s your name?”

“Jack.”

“I’m puttin’ twenty on Jack.”

“This is the story of St. Peter and Jesus at the Pearly Gate,” said Fiske.

“Give us some ale first,” said Nora, and Fiske did, never taking his eyes off Jack, as if he were a dangerous gunfighter who had to be watched.

“Jesus comes by and St. Peter says, ‘Listen, would you mind takin’ over for a bit, I just want to get a smoke.’”

Jack couldn’t help himself: “Is the punch line ‘Pinochio’?” They could tell from Fiske’s face that Jack was right. Fiske’s face just hung there, as if it had taken a sharp, painful, humiliating blow, which it had.

The seconds ticked by, and then Frank couldn’t stand it anymore. “What’s the joke?”

“You tell him,” said a disgusted Fiske, adding a shot of whiskey to his beer.

“Well, as I remember it, Jesus comes up to the Pearly Gates and St. Peter asks him to take over while he gets a smoke. ‘What do I do?’ asks Jesus. ‘Oh,’ says St. Peter, ‘just ask their names and what they do and if they’ve led a good life.’ So the first guy up is this little old man and Jesus asks his name. ‘Well,’ he says, ‘in your language, it would be Joseph.' 'Fine, Joseph, and what did you do in life?' 'I was a carpenter.' 'And were you a good man?' 'Oh, yes,' says Joseph. 'I took care of my wife and my only son.' Suddenly Jesus freezes. 'Your name is Joseph, you were a carpenter and you had an only son? Father!' The old guy looks over at Jesus and says, 'Pinocchio?'"

Everyone at the bar, including Fiske, laughed. Then Fiske got mad again and bent closer. "How can you tell an elephant is in your bed?"

"He wears a *E* on his pajamas," replied Jack.

"How can you tell an elephant's been in the refrigerator?"

"Because of the footprints in the jar of peanut butter."

Fiske looked at him carefully. "Are you some kind of professional?"

Jack laughed and shook his head.

He couldn't buy his own drinks after that. They were coming so fast that the bar was wet with spillage. He noticed Martin, however, stealing out of the back door, then coming back in and hovering by the telephone. Martin's eyes were all flickering lights, like some bad electrical connection.

There was traffic in the bar. Timmy Madden came off his night shift at Con Edison. He blew into his hands and put down three straight shots of whiskey before he was ready to settle for an ale.

"You better take it a little easy or the wife will have you homeless," warned Fiske.

"No problem," said Timmy, smiling like a thief. "Her mother's had a stroke and she's gone to Dublin to take care of her."

"God bless the mother," said Frank.

They all chuckled.

"This is Jack," said Frank, introducing his new friend.

"Glad to know you," said Madden, nodding down the bar.

"He's a professional; just beat Fiske at five punch lines," added Frank.

Madden's eyebrows went up in a kind of salute.

"Five, you say?"

"Maybe more. We lost count. The man was down in the dust bleeding, he was beaten so bad."

"Is this true, Fiske? Do we have a new champion?"

"It is," replied Nora. "Oh, it was grand."

"I was busy. I was tending the bar."

"You were beaten," said Frank.

"Fair and square," said Nora.

"Well, I had a bad night, but he's good—I'll admit to that. The man is fast."

Martin was outside again, taking the two young men who had come in out of the rain with him. They were hard-liners, Jack could tell. They had that unforgiving look. Baby killers, if it came down to that. Jack shivered and took another glass of ale.

They were in the shed down by the water. Martin had the only other key.

"Do you know how to operate all this?" he asked. The smaller man—the one named Kenny—shot the bolt on the Uzi, pointed it at Martin's heart and pulled the trigger. The click was loud, but not loud enough to drown out Martin's whimper of fear.

"God, man, don't do that!" he practically shouted.

"You've insulted our professionalism," said the thick one, who was examining the ground-to-air rockets.

All the equipment had been delivered during the afternoon. A truck came by and a silent man handed Martin a note. It said: "For the shed." He knew what that meant, but he didn't know it was coming or what it was until they started unloading. He could tell then that he was helping unload the spade that would dig his own grave. This is when he decided to try to make his own separate deal. He put in his telephone calls and connected to the right party. He didn't say much, just enough to establish his eagerness to cooperate.

Nora had gotten a call from Michael with instructions. He told her to tell Martin that two men would be down in the evening to look over the equipment. Martin was to let them in and stay out of their way. Michael told her where he was staying and said it was only for her to know and use only in dire emergency. Any other use of the information would put everyone in danger.

When Nora protested and said that she didn't want to act as a messenger, Michael hung up.

Martin didn't ask too many questions, but he was burning to know about the naval gear. Why the rubber boats and the inflatable pumps and the wet suits? He was too frightened to challenge Michael, but he had a terrible fear that his life as a pub owner was coming to an end. When Nora slipped and mentioned the Plaza Hotel, Martin made a mental note and asked no more questions.

"Give us a hand," said the young one—the one with the sadistic gleam in his eyes. Martin was quick and helped them move half the bundles into the flatbed of a pickup. They left behind crates of ammunition and high explosives stacked under canvas; it could blow the Shebeen to hell, thought Martin.

They drove off, leaving Martin wet and deep into his mourning.

Jack saw him come back in and slump into a chair in a dark portion of the restaurant. Something was going on out there. He hadn't heard much, but he'd seen lights and now the wiry old owner had come back alone.

"What's your funniest joke?" said Fiske. Jack turned his attention back to the company at the bar. The barmaid with the freckles was watching, and he sensed something there, too.

"Well, there's the one about the pig with the wooden leg."

"Pig with the wooden leg," repeated Fiske, trying to retrieve the joke, trying to remember. But he was blank.

"Tell us about the pig with the wooden leg," said Nora, putting a pot of shepherd's pie in front of Jack. She whispered, "You want to keep your wits with these fellows. Something hot inside helps."

"All right," said Jack out loud. "It's a traveling salesman joke." And there was a groan from the connoisseurs who flat didn't like traveling salesman jokes. They considered them crude, beneath their standards of sophisticated humor.

"Is that the best that a champion can do?" asked Madden. "A dirty joke?"

"Let's hear it," said Nora, angry at her shameless self.

"This traveling salesman sees this barnyard full of great-looking animals," began Jack. "And in the back, behind the donkey and the cow and the chickens, there's a pig with a wooden leg."

"If this isn't funny, you're gonna buy for the house," said Fiske.

"He sees the farmer and he says, 'You know, I've been admiring your animals; you have some fine animals here.' And the farmer says, 'Yep.'

"'You've got a nice cow and some chickens and a mule and some sheep. But, let me ask you something, does that pig have a wooden leg?' And the farmer looks over and says, 'Yup.' So the salesman cannot contain himself. He's nodding away and then he says, 'You know, I, myself, have never seen a pig with a wooden leg.'"

Some of them starting giggling, in spite of themselves, picturing a pig with a wooden leg.

"The farmer says, 'That's not an ordinary pig. That happens to be about the best pig in the whole world. See, about a year ago, the house caught fire. You can see the damage there where we haven't finished rebuilding. Well, sir, it was a real bad fire. The baby was trapped upstairs in the bedroom and no one could get to her. Firemen, everyone, were driven back by smoke. But that old pig, well, sir, he broke through the line of police and he climbed up the stairs and he low-crawled through the smoke and he rescued that baby. Carried her down through the smoke and flames. Never saw anything like it.' The salesman was astounded. 'Then, oh, 'bout six months ago, I was driving the pickup and I hit a pucker and she flipped on me. My leg was caught under the steering wheel. Couldn't get out. I was done for. I started calling for Jesus. Well, Jesus didn't answer, but that old pig come for me. Swam a creek to get to me. The flames was getting closer and closer to the fuel tank and he just put his snout under that steering wheel and lifted it straight up. Then he pulled me away from the truck and got me clear just before it all blowed up. Hadn't been for that there pig, I was history.'

"'That is truly amazing,' says the salesman. 'Unbelievable. I never heard such a story. But if you'll forgive my asking, how come the pig has a wooden leg?'

"'Mister, when you got a pig like that, you don't eat him all at once.'"

He was the champion after that. They were doubled over in pain from laughing. Madden knocked over a pint in his agony. Fiske just filled it up again and began groaning in his own pain of laughter.

Martin hadn't heard the joke, but he wished to God that he had. He could use something to distract himself. When he had Nora alone the kitchen, he asked her quietly, "Do you know what's going on?"

She felt pity for him, sweating like that, ready to burst with worry. "Listen, Martin, I don't know a thing. Michael uses me like a glass. I pass from lip to lip. I know as much as a glass."

"Do you know what they've got out there?"

"I don't. And I don't want to know. Listen, Martin, it's no use worrying about it. Michael will do what he wants and then he'll be gone, God willing. There's no point worrying about it."

She left him there, crouched over on a chair, like someone with a great intestinal eruption. It was late and the others were all gone. All except Jack.

"I thought I could give you a ride home."

"I take the bus," she said, afraid that he would not persist.

"I'd hate to deprive the Transit Authority of a fare," he said.

She wrapped herself in a coat and a kerchief.

"I wouldn't want to take you out of your way," she said. "Which way will you be heading?"

"I was going in your direction," he said, and that ended that.

They were silent in the car, except for her occasional instructions. "Turn left at the next light." That sort of thing. But as far as small talk or conversation, the act of sitting together in the front seat seemed to cover it.

Oddly enough, Jack felt as comfortable as if they were an old married couple. She looked bright-eyed and alert and without guile. A sound, solid woman with a wrist so small and fragile it might have belonged to a bird. When he glanced over and saw her there, in her tight little compact self, Jack wanted to take her in his arms, enfold her, radiate his own warmth into that frozen little package.

They stopped in front of her house and sat for a moment, both looking out of the front windshield as if they were staring at the passing scenery.

"I am forty-seven years old," he said finally.

"Congratulations," she replied. Then she softened. "I've no social skills. None. My basic tendency is to put an elbow out to ward the fellows off."

"I can understand that. Fellows can get pretty obnoxious."

She shook her head and snuck a peek at him. "You don't look forty-seven," she said.

"Fifty," he replied, and she laughed.

"You don't have many of the social skills yourself, now do you?"

"Out of practice," he said. "I was married for a long time and I'm not used to courtship."

She shook her head. "God, you American men! Shuck off wives like old boots."

"My wife died."

They were both shocked into silence.

Then: "Will you come up for coffee?"

"I thought you'd never ask."

13

Wednesday, November 4, 3:30 A.M., 102 Hours 15 Minutes and Counting

Martin sat alone in the dark booth near the front door, his soggy cap pulled low over his bleary eyes. He'd sent them all home, gone out to make certain that they'd gone, now drank the hard liquor in a hurry, storing it up. The knock on the door made him jump. It was the loud bang of a cop—just this side of breaking in. Arrogant bastards, thought Martin as he fumbled with the locks and bolts on the front door of the Shebeen.

They marched in like cops—clumping and careless and suspicious, looking everywhere, trying to catch you at something sinister. Martin stood there at the door, wanting to hurry them, afraid someone would see. The big one, the leader, sent his flunky to check out the place. He nodded his head and the young one ran off like a trained puppy to sniff for traps and ambushes. Then the big one walked behind the bar as if he owned the place, touching this and that, looking in the drawers, examining the papers. And Martin just stood by the door, shriveled up like his wet cap, feeling helpless, scowling and resentful, but knowing that it was all out of his hands now.

The big one pulled a bottle of Hennessey off the shelf, grabbed a few glasses and settled himself with a sigh in a booth. He motioned for Martin to join him across the table.

"You were right," he said finally, cracking the silence.

Martin wasn't sure what he meant. But now he had hope. "You found him, then."

"Oh, we found him, all right. That was no problem. No. We found him."

He threw back a drink and looked around to see that his men were still on duty. Two of them. One at the window checking the street. The other—the puppy—standing back watching them and the stairs, hands in his pockets, holding his cocked weapon, waiting for an ambush. The big one blushed and tossed down the rest of his drink. "Here's health to your enemies' enemies," he said.

The big one opened his coat and showed the bulge of his holster and the rack of his handcuffs. Sergeant Frank Palleo—known as Bobby to the men in his special antiterrorist task force—liked to establish up front that he was official. If you went against him, you were going against the law.

"You know," said Bobby, "he doesn't look like a big fish."

"Are you kidding? He's the biggest. I happen to know for a fact that he's done deeds that would take an army . . ."

The young one in front, Detective Sonny Federicci, leaned in and whispered something to Bobby. Bobby nodded and gestured for Sonny to move off and give them back their semblance of privacy. Bobby leaned across the table, pushed the bottle ahead of him. Martin poured himself a drink.

"Sonny reminds me that he didn't have the money."

Martin nodded, swallowed the rest of the liquor, and looked up at the ceiling with eyes filled with tears. "I knew that he didn't," he said. "I told you he wouldn't have the money. Didn't I tell you that? He's a big fish. Isn't he a big enough fish without the money?"

Bobby studied Martin for a moment. Blunt, brutal eyes. Could go either way, thought Martin. All depends on which way the wind is blowing.

"I did say that," whispered Martin hoarsely. "I did say that he didn't have the money."

"That's the whole trouble," said Bobby. "He doesn't have the money. See, if he had the money, we'd have something to work with. If you see what I mean. This way, we got nothing to work with."

Martin didn't know what he was expected to say. He just kept looking back and forth between Bobby and Sonny, who had cold, killer eyes. No pity in them anywhere. Martin felt the pressure of not being able to speak, of being dumb, of not knowing what tack to take.

Bobby didn't move. Sonny shifted his weight impatiently. He wanted action. He wanted to hurt Martin, who could sense the tense anticipation, the straining at the leash from the younger cop.

"You don't think I have the money?" said Martin, his eyes swiveling wildly back and forth. "You don't think that, do you?"

Bobby shook his head. "No, nah. You don't know dink about the money. If I thought that, I'd let Sonny give you a deep massage. You wouldn't be that dumb, to hold out like that. But let me ask you something, which is really bothering me: What's this Michael doing here? I mean, what the fuck is he doing here?"

"I swear, I haven't a clue. He wouldn't tell me. These people are tombs. They don't talk. They go to their graves silent. But I know it's big. I know that much."

"How do you know that?"

It was Sonny, and Martin was startled by the source of the question. Bobby looked reproachful.

"Well, I know it's big or he wouldn't be here. There's no way that a man like Michael would come out into the open if it weren't something major."

"What else do you know?" asked Bobby.

"I know it's soon. This weekend. He dropped enough hints about being out of here. He doesn't like America."

"No shit? What's it, something we said?"

Sonny laughed at Bobby's joke.

"It's soon. He couldn't wait. He's takin' a lot of chances because of the time pressure. He wouldn't do that unless he had to . . ."

Bobby smiled and leaned back in the booth. "Martin, how could you be so stupid? How could you think we could be so stupid? Did you really think you'd get away with it?"

"Get away with what? Please. Get away with what? I have no idea what you're talking about."

"I know you did the job. You think I have no friends on the street? You think I don't know what goes down in my own backyard? Don't insult me. You recruited the team. You knew about the job. You sent them out."

"I never knew about the mob payroll job. I got a few friends. I admit that. They were helpers. Michael asked for helpers so I got him helpers. But I would never do a stupid thing like putting them on a mob payroll stickup. That's crazy."

"Only a true asshole would do such a thing," said Bobby. "And if this guy is who you say he is, he's not a true asshole. Am I right?"

"He doesn't know the territory."

"You, on the other hand, are a true asshole."

"Christ, no one would put them on Iennello's payroll. No one sane."

"That's right, Martin. Don Iennello is not the sort of man who tolerates that sort of thing. It makes him look foolish. And he hates to look foolish. He puts ice picks in the eyes of people who try to make a fool out of him."

"Please, tell me what to do. I called you because I know that you can help people in trouble. I thought if I helped you stop this Michael from doing whatever terrible thing he is about to do you could help me. I don't know what to do."

"See, the trouble is, even if we catch the guy, he still doesn't have the money. We still have to find the money. In order to even talk to Mr. Iennello, I have to have the money. I can't go empty-handed. How would it look?"

"What should I do? Tell me."

Bobby emptied another glass of liquor, rubbed his mouth, then grabbed Martin's coat. "You find out about the money."

Then he and his friends clumped out. Loud. Like cops.

Wednesday, November 4, 8:00 A.M., 97 Hours 45 Minutes and Counting

Dino managed to clean up the slaughter that had taken place in the chop shop. The mechanics and laborers knew that something had gone on, but when you worked in a mob chop shop you looked away a lot.

Dino called in a reliable and muscular cousin, and he backed up a van and he loaded the dead bodies wrapped in cheap carpets (no use wasting an expensive rug) and he drove out to Far Rockaway, where he dumped the bodies into the city's waste.

It was a neater and safer thing to do than calling the authorities. For one thing, it would have been bad for business to report the killings. The police would have been forced to close him up, even if they were sympathetic and compromised by corruption. The press would have made it look bad if the police didn't close up an illegal chop shop after a double homicide.

There was another factor that went into Dino's calculations. Now he knew the solution to the mystery of the airport robbery. That information was worth more than the Ferrari Barry had stolen.

He was, however, astonished that a soft pillow like Barry had managed to pull off such a high-wire heist. But you never know about people. Imagine Barry killing two experienced gunmen and then brazenly driving out of the shop like that!

Dino made an appointment with the man who would appreciate the information. He had to be careful. This was a man who trusted no one, whose first thought was a suspicion. He had to go to him candid and innocent. He took his time and he took care getting ready, like getting ready for a date. And he wanted to see him fresh. Not tired and cranky. Morning would be fine.

After cleaning out the debris from under his fingernails, after combing his hair and putting on his best suit, he went to see Don Daniello Iennello, the crime boss who controlled business in his neighborhood. Iennello conducted business—such as it was—out of a small private club with blacked-out windows in the Howard Beach section of Queens. He ran small squads of numbers runners and cells of dope dealers and branches of loan sharks. Nothing big. Nothing on a citywide scale. Not like shaking down a whole union. But Iennello was the man to whom Dino and his father paid protection and he therefore represented the nearest high rung of Mafia authority.

Outside of the Howard Beach Fish and Game Club on 104th Street stood a man with a hand inside his coat. The man stood there all year long. In the stench and suffocating heat of summer and in the sting and bitter wind of winter, the man was a staunch sentry. He never took his hand off the grip of the automatic pistol loaded with twelve rounds of explosive ammunition that he kept in his pocket. One round would stop a bus, but the man at the door didn't expect to have to stop a bus; he was expecting a tank.

"He's waiting for me," said Dino, and the guard at the door blinked, which was all the permission he would ever grant.

Inside the club, two other men with granite faces stood on either side of the door. If one flagged or seemed to get distracted the other would snarl, snapping him back to attention.

"Defense in depth," was the way Iennello, a private soldier (who never saw combat but acted as if he had) in World War II, put it. "If they wanna come in here, they gotta expect to take some losses."

Who it was, exactly, he expected to try to break

through his outer and inner rings of defense wasn't clear. Certainly not the police. Cops were welcome. A lot of cops just walked in on their own. They had to pick up their bribes. They had to pick up their information, which Don Iennello gave out like Christmas envelopes. To stay in business, he traded off one thing against the other—recognizing that there were certain lines that could not be safely crossed. He could not inform on a brother member of the mob. But he could disrupt pirate operations. Cowboys who thought that it was safe to go out and peddle crack without a license from the local capo. Unconnected, unprotected criminals, without the whole life insurance of a mob friend. Such things were fair game. Probably Iennello feared the other mobs, or maybe some lone avenger. Someone getting even for some act of brutality he had committed in his wild youth when he spread violence like business cards, then forgot it. There was no telling. But Iennello felt better when he looked up from his endless game of solitaire and saw the guards on full alert.

Iennello was an old man, and his digestive system was sending out messages that he could no longer eat the hot sauces and spicy meals of his reckless days. The message was usually delivered in the form of gas, and sometimes the boys inside the clubhouse preferred to be on the outside. When the flatulence was bad they would roll their eyes, and Iennello would notice and get angry. He had to ignore them because to recognize the reaction would be to admit that he was farting. Instead, he simply got angry every time the aftermath of his long lunches escaped.

"It's Dino," said one of the guards.

"I can see that," said Iennello testily. "You think I can't see?"

He was on the phone, whispering. He was always whispering into the phone. As if the taps couldn't pick up a whisper. "All right, all right. I hear what you say and I appreciate the suggestion. Don't worry, I know how to reach you if I need you."

He dropped the phone and the guard picked it up and put it into the cradle.

"No, Boss, I was just tellin' . . ." he began.

"Don't tell so much and watch the fuckin' door. What am I payin' you for, you dumb shit asshole."

"I'm sorry, Boss."

"Watch the door!"

Dino stood there, smelling something funny, and sensing an ominous mood.

"You, sit down," said Iennello.

The table was situated in such a way that conversations were difficult to overhear.

"You want coffee?"

"No, thank you, Mr. Iennello."

"Scunnzato. Coffee. What's wrong with you?"

Dino waited for the coffee, watching Iennello's fiery looks at the two guards. Listening to his long, moist farts. Swamp gas, he thought. It smells like methane. We're all gonna die here in this fuckin' fake hunt and game club.

"How's your father, Dinatto?"

"Uh, he's fine. Fine."

"That's good. Good. I like your father. He's a good man. Raise a nice son. How's business? People buy cars?"

"Great. Great. Everybody wants a car. This is America."

One of the guards brought the coffee—thick, Italian

roast in small demitasse cups. The old man poured in some anisette and a twist of lemon.

"Now," he said, leaning back, ready to listen, "what is it that you had to see me? What's so important?"

Dino leaned across the table, messing up the solitaire arrangement, causing a look of annoyance on Iennello's face.

"Don Iennello, I think I know who pulled the airport stickup," he whispered.

The old man sat upright. He looked around. "Boys, wait outside," he said to the guards. When they were gone he turned back to Dino. "Fuckin' FBI probably has this place bugged anyway." He shrugged. "You gotta be careful, but you can't stop breathin'." Dino laughed, which is what he thought was expected.

"Tell me," said Don Iennello, folding his arms across his scrawny chest.

Then Dino told the old man about Barry and the windfall and the twin killings. The old man didn't seem to mind much about the death of his two underlings. He hardly noticed. He was only interested in the money—and Barry.

"A Jew?" asked the old man after hearing all the details, or as much as Dino knew.

Dino nodded.

"That's funny," murmured the old man. "You don't expect a Jew to act that stupid. Italians act stupid. I woulda sworn it was some Wild West gavonne, some cowboy from Brooklyn who thought he was gonna retire."

"This Barry used to deal some small marijuana for me," said Dino. "Not much. Nickel-and-dime shit."

"Why you use a Jew?"

"His uncle's a cop. Was a cop. He's retired."

"Nothing worse than a Jew cop. They gotta be good."

"The uncle's not a Jew. Just the nephew."

"And he takes care of his nephew."

"He kept him out of jail a few times."

"Sure."

"They were pretty close. This Barry, he lived with his uncle sometimes."

"Lived with him. Ah, ha."

"He had his own place, but when he got in trouble, which was a lot, he stayed with his uncle."

"This uncle, is he a thief?"

"Nah. Straight as an arrow. A real Boy Scout. Kept trying to straighten Barry out."

"So you don't think the uncle stole the payroll."

Dino laughed.

"You gotta know this guy. The uncle. Jack? He wouldn't steal second base. The man's pure as . . . as . . . as anything."

The old man smiled. "Sure. Sure," he said. The old man thought for a minute. He finished off his coffee and lit one of his thin, twisted cigars, which smelled almost as bad as his refried lunch.

"I want you to work with me," he said finally. "You know, this is a DellaCorte family matter. One of the five major crime families. I'm not in that league. I work for Don DellaCorte. If we solve this case, if we bring him the money and the head of the villain who stole it, this would be a very nice thing for me. It would put him in my debt. And I would take care that you were not forgotten."

"How can I help?"

The old man leaned across the table and put his hand on Dino's arm. The fingers—all bent and stained—

looked to Dino like the cigars that the old man smoked. "You will be my good right arm in this matter. I have some friends. Cops. We need a cop to help us in this."

Dino shrugged.

"He's gonna help us. He calls me and he offers to help. You can't do this alone. My friend will help."

Dino felt a shiver, a premonition. This smelly old fart was cunning and calculating, and he could almost hear the gears at work, he could almost feel the talons sinking into his flesh. This could be bad. This could be very bad.

Wednesday, November 4, 8:00 P.M., 85 Hours 45 Minutes and Counting

Barry was at the window in the front of the house when he thought he heard something out in the backyard. He tiptoed across the house and peered out of the back window. Nothing there but shadows. He then made his way to the front. Did something move behind that tree? Someone walked a dog. "I can't stay here," he said out loud.

But where would he go? He couldn't just leave. Not now. That would put his uncle in a trap. He went into the kitchen and made himself a thick sandwich; he didn't even remember eating it later. He stood by the window, eating his sandwich, staring into the street, sipping on a beer.

When he thought about the lives he had taken in the back room of the chop shop he began to tremble. Then he began to cry. He pulled a chair up to the window and wept and fell asleep.

Suddenly he awoke, pulling apart the drapes. Barry squinted out into the street and his heart dipped. For there, across the road, was the unmistakable car bearing trouble. One of those plain sedans with two men in drab suits in the front seat. It could have been a police car. It could have been a mob cruiser. The one thing that it could not have been was a normal, routine piece of traffic. Not even American Express sent goons like that to collect debts on their card.

Barry did the only thing that he could think of. He cleaned the house. He washed the floors and scrubbed the sink and dusted the living room, taking a break every now and then to look out front and confirm that the men in the drab suits were still waiting.

Why were they waiting? For reinforcements? Of course, they couldn't storm the house with two guys. No. They didn't know that Barry was inside. There was no car out front. The Ferrari was tucked away in the garage. They were waiting for someone to come home.

Which is what jolted Barry out of his chores. "Uncle Jack!" he cried. He would be coming home sooner or later. He would walk into the ambush. Barry couldn't allow that.

Nora was sitting in the bathroom, looking into the mirror. She shook her head. Not like her to tumble into bed with a stranger. To spend a day puttering in the kitchen and falling back into bed. To feel the arms of a man around her. To nuzzle in, to burrow down and feel that deep, deep comfort of a heart beating not your own. Not like her at all. And yet she was lulled by this man.

Jack, with that plain, uncomplicated face—she thought of him and smiled. She thought of him even though he was in the bathroom. She could hear the water running, and she smiled again. Whatever he was, whoever he was, he was no stranger. This was a warm, compassionate man, with the smell and vulnerabilities and strengths of a man.

She giggled. A thing she seldom did. At the crucial moment he had gone limp. It was an endearing thing. Almost like a reassurance that he wasn't dangerous. They lay together, cuddling like children, for an hour. There were no carnal moments. Except later, in the middle of the night, when she had awakened and saw him there, so innocent, so peaceful. And she had felt a great female stirring—a primal sob of desire and sympathy—and she folded him in her arms.

In the morning there was a honking and commotion in the street. Her first thought: Michael. Nora looked carefully out of the bathroom window and saw the landlord pacing back and forth in a rage. He was unable to get his car out of the garage. The reason was the rusty bucket of bolts—Jack's Buick. It was parked in the driveway, eating up half the sidewalk.

Nora tiptoed into the bedroom and lifted the car keys out of Jack's pocket. She put a coat over her nightdress, then went downstairs.

"I told you about the driveway," the landlord had shouted. He was a mean-tempered Greek named Plato who had tried on more than one occasion to test Nora's availability, despite the fact that they all lived together under the same roof—him with his wife and five children and Nora. Now Plato was indignant, marching up and down the street, ranting against the real wound of Nora's rejection. "I miss work. I lose money. What car is this?"

"This is my friend's car," she said, climbing behind the wheel, adjusting the seat.

"What friend?" said Plato, turning to look up at Nora's window. "You got a friend up there?"

Nora rolled up the window as Plato ran after the car. "I told you, no friends. No boyfriends. No sleepovers. This is my home!"

Jack had heard the shouting and then the familiar sound of his engine. He got to the window in time to see the car pulling away. He watched it heading down the street, around the corner, out of sight. He got a big lump in his throat. It was partially a fleeting thought that he had trusted someone who had betrayed him. He felt like a sailor who had been rolled on a drunk. But then he thought, it's not that bad. She couldn't know about the three million dollars in the trunk. At the worst she was stealing his car.

He found a kettle and put some water on the stove. He made sure there was enough in it for two, thinking that would drive away the bad thoughts. Then he heard a knock on the door. She forgot her key, he thought.

"Mister, pack up and move out!" shouted the intruder, barging past him, standing in the middle of the room, looking around for evidence of depravity. Jack, who was fully dressed by then, grabbed the man by the arm.

"Who are you?" he asked, pulling the man back toward the door.

"Me, I am the owner. The landlord. Never mind that. Who are you? I don't allow this in my house. Mister, pack up. Now. You hear me?"

"In about one minute, unless you're out of here, I'm gonna tear your arm out of your shoulder," said Jack calmly. "This is a private home and as such it is protected by the second, third, fourth and fourteenth amendments to the Constitution. You heard about that?"

The landlord looked as if the wind had been knocked out of him.

"No unreasonable searches," said Jack. "No forced entry and no denial of due process."

As he pulled the landlord toward the door he saw Nora standing there in the hallway, smiling.

"I tell my lawyer," said the landlord, hurrying down the stairs. "I go to call him now."

Nora came in and closed and bolted the door. "I'm afraid I've caused you some trouble," said Jack.

She tossed him the car keys and smiled. "I liked the way you handled him," she said. "He'll not cause me any trouble. In any case, we haven't given him any cause, have we."

Jack blushed. "A technicality," he said. "Easily fixed." She came into his arms. He held her face and kissed her noisily on the mouth. She felt him rouse and then she groaned. They stumbled into the bedroom and became naked and kissed each other in long, tender relief. Nothing was rushed. Nothing frenzied. Just a slow slide into each other—almost like a confirmation of their first impression.

Later they dressed and then sat drinking tea, silent, each wrapped tight with private thoughts.

"Do you work tonight?" he asked.

"I do," she said.

"Why so far away?"

She shrugged. “It’s something to do with privacy,” she said, a little more harshly than she intended.

He nodded. “I understand privacy,” he said. “Not that it means much to me. But it means a lot to some people, and I can respect that.”

“That’s rare. Not many can.”

He gathered his things and looked around. Collecting memories, she guessed. He thinks he won’t see it again.

“I’m old,” she said when he stood by the door, ready to leave. He looked puzzled. She shook her head. “Not chronologically. But old. Older than you, I think. Crotchety, too. I like my mornings quiet and I like to read in the evenings by myself.”

“Are you driving me away, Nora?”

She smiled. “No, Jack Mann. I’m laying down a road map. So you won’t fall into a ditch.”

He pulled her to him and kissed her. She held a hand against his face. It was a small gesture, huge with significance.

And so they had spent the rest of the day.

14

Wednesday, November 4, 9:45 P.M., 84 Hours and Counting

They were waiting where they had been told to wait, on the northwest side of the street, facing Park Avenue and Sixtieth Street. Two good Irish Republican Army soldiers.

"I believe that you're expecting me," said Michael, keeping them both in killing range just in case he'd made a mistake, just in case that back-of-the-neck premonition he couldn't shake was right and he'd been followed.

"I don't know," said the young one, the bright Mick with eyes like lit coals. "We're strangers."

"We're all strangers," replied Michael, and he was surprised to hear a croak in his own voice. It had the sound of defeat, or at least resignation. They knew the signal, and he was relieved. It wasn't a trap. Or at least not one that he had fallen into carelessly.

It was still early enough, and he took the two soldiers

for a walk through Manhattan, pointing out the sights possessively, like a loving tour guide. "New York is getting ready for Christmas," he said, showing them the lights and trees and merry windows of Fifty-seventh Street.

"Good Christ, it even makes Dublin look small," commented the thick one, the one called Dan. "Dublin's a little village compared to this."

"Dublin is small at Christmas," said the quick one. "That's because it's Cat'lic. Small and sad. But Belfast t'rows a nice Christmas party."

"I'll call you Mick," Michael told the younger one.

"The name's Kevin."

"Never mind. You're Mick to me."

They stopped in an Irish pub and had a beer. "Like piss," said Dan.

"So's this pub," said Mick.

"Now, now," said Michael. "A little thin, maybe. But this is America."

"In Dublin you can bite the ale, it's so t'ick," said Dan. "This tastes like pisswater."

"The difference is that in America people can afford to buy the damn ale," replied Michael. "There's the real difference."

The two exchanged looks. Michael could have felt the looks go back and forth even if he hadn't been staring in their direction. As if to say, The old man has gone soft; the old man has forgotten what it is like to hate.

"Never mind," said Michael, smiling. "Listen, Dan, go across the street. There's a phone booth there. Call this number. Tell the woman who answers that Aunt Dee is fine."

Dan nodded and knew enough not to ask what it

meant. He understood that it had meaning and that was enough.

"And, listen, Dan, while you're at it, see if you notice a watcher."

Mick picked up his ears. "Is there someone on our ass?"

"Can't be too careful," said Michael.

A waitress came down from the dining room and asked if the "boys" would like anything from the kitchen, because they were about to run out of the house special.

"And what would that be?" asked the bright-eyed Mick.

"A trencherman's plate," she said.

"Is that with hairy bacon?" asked Mick. "Because I like my bacon hairy. Reminds me of the old country."

"We won't be dining," said Michael, subduing young Mick with a glance.

"If you don't mind me askin', how much time do we have?" said Mick when the waitress left.

"Enough," said Michael, looking at him coldly.

For the first time Mick could see a long drop in Michael's eyes. "I didn't mean to be nosy," he said quickly.

Michael changed the subject. He wanted to know some details. They were staying in Queens, said Mick. Someone's house. He shrugged. It was the way it worked on the other side. You moved into someone's house—a stranger. They asked no questions. You offered no explanations. You came and went and then one day you were gone. How the thing was arranged was someone else's business. His job was mechanical. He planted bombs. He sprayed streets with automatic fire. He laid low.

"How old are you?" asked Michael.

"Twenty," shot back Mick. "I don't expect to get much older."

"None of us will live to collect a pension," said Michael bitterly.

Then Dan was back. The woman had answered the phone and he had delivered the message and she had rung off.

"Did you see anyone?" asked Michael.

"Just a lot of Americans," said Dan. "No watchers."

"Good," said Michael.

"Oh, she said one other t'ing," said Dan. "She said, 'Luck.'"

It was the warning that they were being watched. That it wasn't entirely safe. It wasn't the alarm to call it off. Just the yellow caution light. Nora could be trusted. If she sensed something wrong, there was good cause for concern. Michael thought about it, but he had come too far to turn back now. The plane was already on the tarmac on the other side. It was under guard now, being searched and searched again for bombs. They had no idea that the danger came from an entirely different quarter.

"Tomorrow night we make the practice run," said Michael, and the other two exchanged excited looks.

Barry waited until it was dark. Then he tried to slip out the back door. His plan was to wait for his uncle on the usual approach road, flag down the Buick and warn him off.

He had the gun inside his coat and the money stuffed into his pockets, along with a ham sandwich for emergencies. Outside, as he turned to make certain the door was locked, each of his arms was grabbed in a viselike clamp.

"Barry? How the hell are you?" said one of the men behind the grip. Before he knew what was happening, they had stripped him of his gun and his money and even his ham sandwich. Then, as easily as if they had a key, they opened the locked door of his uncle's house and took him inside. Seven men came in trailing. Serious-looking men with deep frowns. Standing back out of the way was Dino, looking a little out of his depth.

"Dino?" pleaded Barry.

"Can't help you, pal. These guys are judgment day." He tossed a look over at the frosty men.

"Sit down, Barry," said the obvious leader, a rough man with a battered face and a body as hard as stone. You could see it scrape against the fabric of the suit and shirt. The leader spoke gently, but it only made the force of his command more urgent.

"Put the cuffs on him," he told one of the henchmen. When the henchman opened his coat and took out the cuffs and Barry saw the belt and the holster, he knew that they were all cops.

The henchman handcuffed Barry behind his back. There was a gentle knock on the door. Barry half hoped it was his uncle, although he didn't believe that anything could save him now. It was just the two men who had been parked out front.

"One of youse guys stays in the car," said the leader.

"Right, Bobby."

"I want you should stay awake, too."

"Right."

The house was swarming with men picking apart the furniture. They were cutting up the cushions and pulling apart cabinets.

Bobby pulled over a chair and turned it around and sat across from Barry, facing him, resting his hands on his chin on the back of the chair.

"Listen, I know what you're thinkin'," said Bobby. Barry couldn't speak.

"You're thinkin' that you're a dead man. Am I right? Tell me the truth, am I right?"

Barry smiled. He felt some relief. The man spoke as if to reassure him. And if he was right and they were cops, he was safe. Cops would only arrest him. They wouldn't execute him. And then he thought, what's Dino doing with a squad of cops? And as the thought struck him, so did Bobby's fist. Straight in the face. It knocked out two front teeth and started a flow of blood from his broken nose.

"You know, you could be right," said Bobby, rubbing his fist, which had a slight scratch from the broken teeth. "You could be a dead man."

Barry was conscious for a few seconds, and then he passed out. Not for long. When he awoke he was still handcuffed and the two guards were propping him up. He tried to speak, but choked on a mouthful of blood.

"See, Barry, you and I both know where that money came from," said Bobby, bending in, sounding reasonable. "I mean, you had it in your possession and possession is supposed to be nine-tenths of the earth's surface, but you and I know it ain't your money."

Barry managed to speak. "Could I call a lawyer?"

Bobby rolled his eyes. "Did you hear that? Hey, Sonny, you catch that? He wants a lawyer!" Bobby shot out a left that snapped Barry's head, closing an eye and restarting the flow of blood in and out of his head. The pain got really bad and he passed out again.

They were holding him up, doubled over, because he

was spilling blood and bile all over the carpet. Barry worried that his uncle could be very upset. Then he thought that was stupid.

"I'm your lawyer," said Bobby, smiling maliciously. "You can tell me anything. I promise."

Barry heaved again.

The teams came back from the other parts of the house. "Nothing," they reported, and one of the henchmen searched each member as they reported in.

Barry was alarmed; they trusted no one.

"Get the car out of here," he told Dino. "We don't want it traced."

Dino took the keys and went out to the garage. Barry felt a curious abandonment. As if his last friend had left him.

Bobby came back from the kitchen sucking on a can of beer. He nodded to one of the men, and they lifted Barry to his feet. Bobby turned and back-kicked Barry in the belly, emptying out the last dregs of his stomach.

One of the goons was washing Barry's face with a wet cloth and whispering in his ear. "It's only gonna get worse. He's gonna pound it outta ya. One way or another, you gotta tell us what you did with the money."

"Was your uncle in on this?" asked Bobby almost gently.

There was something in his arm. He didn't know what it was. Funny, he hadn't eaten anything but his stomach bubbled with gas. His head was light. It wasn't the beating. He knew that it wasn't the beating. Then the pain in his arm rolled up and into his chest. Like a vise grip. He'd never felt it before, but he knew what it was. And then Barry smiled. He didn't know why. He just did. And then he felt a terrible, clear pain all across his chest. And then he felt nothing.

Bobby was stunned. He saw the kid's face turn pale and then purple. He knew what it was, too. The punk had gone and died on the carpet of his uncle's house. Lying in his own blood and vomit. No doubt. A coronary. He'd seen enough of them. But a kid like this . . . ?

"Take the cuffs off," he said.

"Do we torch the house, Sarge?" asked plainclothes detective Sonny Federicci, no longer careful about names and titles.

"No, you asshole. The dough might still be here," said Sergeant Frank Palleo—Bobby.

"But we searched it good," said Federicci.

"We could have missed it," said Sergeant Palleo. "No. We wait. Let the uncle come home. Maybe he'll show us where it is."

Jack saw the cars parked out front. Then he saw the lights flickering upstairs and downstairs and he just kept going past the house. The lookouts across the street never even noticed him slow down, pick up speed and then go by.

Jack turned two corners, then hid the big Buick behind the all-night grocery store four blocks from his house. He backtracked on foot, making certain that he aroused no attention. He settled into a blind across a lawn from his house, shielded by bushes and a tree. He sat there and watched. And he checked his gun.

Whoever they were, they were very careless. They parked where you couldn't miss them. They ran lights like it was Christmas. Was it the mob out to reclaim their money? He doubted it. The mob was more discreet when it came to setting up an ambush. More likely they were cops. All those nonchalant men behind the wheels of their showy cars, all that insouciant display of power; he knew the signs. Had to be cops.

"Fucking Barry," he whispered out loud.

Maybe they had even been listening when he called. Barry had sounded nervous. Still, you couldn't blame him. You couldn't hate him. Barry was not good under pressure. Barry was foolish. But he was not someone you could blame or hate.

Jack watched them leave his home in teams and pairs. He counted five. Finally there was only the car across the street with the two plainclothesmen drinking coffee. He didn't see Barry leave. Maybe they had brought him out earlier.

When the house was dark and he hadn't seen any movement or light for half an hour, Jack made his way to the basement window. He broke the glass with his scarf wrapped around his hand. He pulled the latch, then crawled in. He felt funny, breaking into his own home, but then maybe this wasn't his home anymore. He could sense the strange presence. He could feel a difference. He thought that he wouldn't need a light, that he would know his way around by memory, but he kept stumbling and bumping into things. When he turned on his pencil flashlight, he saw what had been done to the interior. The living room was a riot of broken and ripped furniture. They had been searching for the money, no doubt. The stuffing had been torn from every couch and chair.

Then he saw the body. It was Barry. No doubt about that. He was lying in a puddle of his own spent life in the middle of the living room. No doubt that he was dead. The battered face and the open eyes and the stench of raw vomit and the excrement left no question about it.

"Barry!" he said, as much an apology as anything else. "Damn!"

Suddenly he sensed something else. He made his way to the closet, but all the blankets were shredded, as if they'd suspected that he'd sewn the money into the linings. Moving slowly, he managed to get near the door leading down to the basement. Then he lunged and stumbled down and up through the window he had used to get in and was out in the yard.

By the time the police hiding in the house were able to get out of their own nests, Jack was gone.

"Tell Ryan to stay on him," ordered Bobby, who had been watching from behind the refrigerator door.

"Orange Two, this is Base, stay on the subject leaving the house," said Detective Federicci into the radio.

The radio crackled, but there was no answer.

"Orange Two, Orange Two, this is Orange Base, do you copy?"

"Orange Base, this is Orange Two; you're breaking up," said Plainclothes Officer Tommy Ryan, stationed one hundred feet away in the unmarked car.

"Orange Two, Orange Two, stay on the subject fleeing the goddamned house!" shouted Sonny Federicci. "Do you fuckin' copy?"

"Yeah, I copy, but what subject are we talking about?" said Ryan. He was standing in the front door of the house, having given up on the radio.

"Christ, he just ran outta here," said Bobby Palleo. "Didn't you assholes see him?"

"We didn't see no one, Sarge."

"Should we seal off the neighborhood?" asked Federicci.

"Are you nuts?" shot back Bobby. "You want Borough Command to start getting curious?"

"Sorry, Sarge."

"Where the fuck is your brain?"

They ran out, looking to see which way Jack had run, looking for fresh tracks. But all they saw was a few blinds going up and then down. Bobby told Sonny to torch the house. Discreetly. Jack was hiding behind a tree near the garage when he saw the detective go into his home. He heard a crack, and in a moment he saw the smoke and flames. Poor Barry, he thought. One more insult.

There were things inside the house that he would have saved—pictures of Natalie, old letters. Then he thought, Fuck it. This was a rough game and he'd better start acting like a player.

15

Thursday, November 5, 12 Midnight, 81 Hours 45 Minutes and Counting

The apartment building was old, built in the twenties when they put in long, lavish lobbies without calculating the square-foot cost, back at a time when doormen wore wing collars and looked like Russian aristocrats. It was located in downtown Brooklyn, on the fringe of the expensive area, the part known as the Heights. The tenants still called it Brooklyn Heights, but that was a conceit. The building was in downtown Brooklyn.

The landlord, a skinflint, liked to point out to prospective tenants that it was a "classy" building; it even had a doorman. But the doorman was a lush who had been glued together strictly for the sake of appearances. Minimum wage and minimum effort. The doorman could barely manage to stay awake, much less climb into a uniform. He usually showed up for work—when he did show up for work—in a plaid shirt sour with the stink of liquor. Still, the landlord could say with some technical justification that he had a doorman, and boost the rent as if he were still employing a Romanov.

Jack waited across the street until someone went in, then trailed behind like a pilot fish. The doorman was suffering either in anticipation of a drunk or the aftermath of one—either way, he didn't pay much attention when Jack marched through his checkpoint. And the tenants didn't care because Jack was white and looked reasonably respectable.

Mo was married to a woman named Christine, a Catholic who was convinced that she was going to hell for marrying a Jew. Jack's wife had been Jewish and, Jack himself being a lapsed Catholic, the tangle of religion became a running joke among the four of them. It seemed to ease the embarrassment of the mixed grouping. Always, Christine regarded the sight of Jack (a fellow apostate) as some kind of absolution—a forgiving and comforting presence.

She came to the door in her dressing gown, peered through the peephole and let Jack in.

"Mo didn't tell me you were coming over!"

"Is he home?"

"Just gone down to the store. He'll be back in a minute. Just enough time to get him jealous."

"I need a drink," said Jack, collapsing into a sofa. She looked at him and went straight for the liquor cabinet.

Jack sipped the whiskey and waited silently for Mo. Finally, they heard the key in the lock.

"There he is," Christine said with obvious relief.

She rushed to the door. "Jack's here," she told her husband.

"Is he dressed?" quipped Mo. "Or it's just you running around naked?"

Christine pouted and left them alone in the den with an open bottle and a couple of glasses. Jack waited until she was well away. "I'm in big trouble," he said.

Mo lit a cheap cigar, nodded and asked, "What kind of trouble?"

"It's complicated. I'm not sure. I think there may be a warrant out for me."

"Why? What for? You didn't pay your parking tickets, or what?"

Jack looked over at his old friend. "It's serious," he said.

"I can see," said Mo. "What can I do?"

Jack took some more liquor and drank with a long sigh. He looked around. A nice room. Warm. A cozy little den with wood paneling, something that he could never manage to put together. He was always leaking papers, leaving half-read books scattered over surfaces, forgetting cups of coffee, spilling crumbs. Of course, Mo had a talent for neatness and order. It was what made him a good cop. He kept his desk neat and he kept his files up-to-date and everyone under his control behaving nicely.

The glass was empty again and Jack filled it up. Mo's face showed a frown of concern. "Don't be my mother," said Jack.

"You don't usually drink like you're trying to drown," said Mo.

"You Jews! You think that liquor is some kind of toxic waste!"

"It is."

"Not always. Sometimes it's medicinal."

"So is radiation. Doesn't mean you should go out of your way."

Jack leaned forward in his chair and put his hand on his old friend's knee. "Mo, listen, I'm in trouble."

"You wanna tell me about it or you wanna sit here and get shitfaced?"

"Both, I guess."

"Tell me, Jack."

Jack sighed and his shoulders sagged and he clutched back a sob. "Barry's dead," he said.

Mo fell back in his chair, and his face drained of color. The half tolerant, half provoking smile vanished. Then he recovered, became the solid policeman, the sturdy partner, the reliable shoulder for his friend.

"What happened?" he asked.

Jack shook his head. He swallowed some tears. "I really don't know," he said. "I came home, he was dead."

"Was he dealing?"

"No. I'm sure he wasn't dealing."

Mo stood up and walked around the room. "Listen," he said, "remember 1967?"

Jack remembered.

During the Arab-Israeli War of 1967, New York City Patrolman Moses Berger joined the Israeli Defense Force. He took a plane and told the authorities in Tel Aviv his background, and they signed him up. Mo had been a tank commander in the American army in Vietnam, and his services were welcome. The problem was that such services were against American law, and Mo would lose his job and his pension if it came out.

So Jack covered up for him. When Mo was wounded on the Golan Heights, Jack made certain he got home without attracting attention. He checked him into NYU Medical Center, where they treated his burns and his shrapnel wounds—recorded as treatment following a car accident. They would joke later that it was the only known case of shrapnel injuries resulting from a car accident. "Vehicle," said Jack. "Technically, vehicle was correct." Jack got a friend with diplomatic connections to create false documents, and Mo's job and pension were saved. It was not a small favor, since Jack had put his own job and pension at risk. When Mo had tried to express his gratitude, Jack waved him off. "That's what partners do," he had said, ending the discussion.

"Yeah," said Jack now, "I remember 1967. I bought a new Buick. So what?"

Mo smiled. "Tell me what you can tell me."

Jack shook his head. "I can't tell you much. I came home and I saw cops all over my house. I hid in the bushes and I waited until I thought they were gone and then I went inside. That's when I found Barry."

"Oh, boy!"

"Somebody did a real job on him. The kid's face was all punched in."

"What did you do?"

"I snuck out. They were waiting for me."

"They were waiting for you?"

"I saw them burn down the house. Some plainclothes fuck set off a thermit charge and burned it down with Barry still inside."

"Cops?"

Jack nodded. "I know a couple. Citywide anticrime. Cops."

"You're not telling me everything."

"I can't. I really can't."

Mo was quiet, sucking on his cheap cigar. "You want me to go down and check out the computer? You want I should find out what's cooking inside the Atex?"

"If it's not too much trouble."

Mo nodded. "Okay. Did you eat? Are you hungry?"

"I'm not hungry."

Mo put on his jacket. "I'll tell Chris not to bother you." Then he stopped at the door. "Listen, Jack, if you need me, I'm still good on the street."

"I know."

"You need backup, someone to watch your ass, someone to run an errand. You need something."

"I know."

The lieutenant on duty at Borough Command in Queens was surprised to see Mo. "Isn't this your night off?"

"I forgot something; left my wife's anniversary gift here," said Mo.

"I thought your anniversary was in September."

"I'm a little late."

The lieutenant was a man without any sense of humor. He looked puzzled, but he was too busy prowling the aisles, annoyed at the idle chatter of the night crew on the computers, to dwell on Mo's presence. To Lieutenant Kevin McElvy the men were like lazy cattle, grazing in tall grass, not earning their paychecks. Not that there was anything to do. But the lieutenant wanted to see the men busy. IDLE HANDS ARE THE DEVIL'S WORKSHOP, said the plaque on his desk.

"Hey, Loo, we're sending out for pizza; you want in?"

That was just like them, he thought furiously, eating pizza and drinking beer when they should be working!

"No!" he snarled.

"Okay, but it's Joey Maleno Pizza. Last chance," said the baby-faced rookie. He seemed to like to annoy Lieutenant McElvy. "Hey, Mo, you want a couple of slices?"

"Nah, thanks anyway; I gotta get home," said Mo. "It's my anniversary."

"Yeah, no shit? I didn't think Jews celebrated anniversaries," said the young cop.

"We do," replied Mo. "We have the traditional feast in which we cook the firstborn son of a young Christian colleague."

The baby-faced cop—whose wife had just given birth to a son—blinked in shock. "Hey! That ain't funny!"

"How would you know, asshole?" said Richard Deitz, another old cop farmed out to work night computers.

"Okay, okay," broke in Lieutenant McElvy, who saw in the nasty exchange the living proof, actual evidence, to support the wisdom written on his plaque. "Let's get some work done. Berger, if you came in here to get something, get it. Don't be disrupting my crew."

Mo ignored him, sat down at the computer terminal, opened a few drawers, then logged into the mainframe computer. He punched up the warrants outstanding file and was relieved when Jack's name wasn't there. He punched up fire department runs and read the details of the fire. Then he punched up the material about the airport robbery.

Jack and Chris were playing gin rummy when Mo returned. Mo looked haggard and motioned Chris out of the room, then took a reviving slug of whiskey.

"That was some fire they started at your house," he said. "Still going."

Jack blinked. He didn't know what to say.

"They found the body."

Jack nodded. He noticed the dust floating in the light, suspended in the air, like his own life.

"So far no identification."

"It's Barry," pronounced Jack. He felt a steep slide of emotion as he uttered his dead nephew's name. Not fear. Confusion. It was not the first time he'd felt it. How did Barry die? Did cops actually beat him to death? He found that hard to believe.

"There's no warrant out on you," said Mo.

Jack sat up straight. How could that be? He'd seen them. They were cops. He was positive. Not a doubt. He'd recognized at least two of them. Anticrime cops. Routine procedure was to put out a warrant when you were after someone. And they had to be after him. And if they were hunting for Jack, where was the warrant? Unless . . .

"You wanna tell me about it?" asked Mo.

Jack didn't hear him. He was too busy turning over the gears of this new information. Cops. Cops for certain. Cops who burned down his house. Cops who probably murdered his nephew. At first he thought that they'd stumbled onto the dead body and that the arson was harmless. But not now. Now he thought they were part of some scheme. Under orders to maintain secrecy. One thing was certain: somehow, although he didn't know how, this was connected to the robbery at the airport.

"What did you find out?" he asked. "About the other business—the airport?"

Mo reached into his pocket as if he were pulling out a fifty-pound weight. "I told you to stay away from this," he said. "This is a can of worms."

"I remember," said Jack. "Objection noted."

Mo sighed and put on his glasses and looked at the piece of paper. "Irish," he said.

"Irish?"

"Like, from Ireland. The two dead stickupmen at the airport were soldiers in the Provisional Wing of the Irish Republican Army. Here on a job, according to Intelligence."

"Why would they pull a common stickup? I mean, if they're IRA soldiers, why would they stoop to that?"

"Isn't that how they get their money? I thought that was how they operated. Pull a job, finance an operation, keep going. Isn't that how it works?"

"Not an ideal method. If they were here on an operation, they should have laid low. Get their money in some regular way so they don't put themselves at risk. Save the risks for the operation. Now they're exposed."

"Well, we do have some other parties interested."

"Like who?"

"Like the State Department; the FBI; CIA; Interpol; Royal Ulster Constabulary, Special Branch," ticked off Mo. "Like I said, a real can of worms."

Jack nodded. "I'm grateful for the help."

"I owe you."

Jack began to get up. "Mo, where do these people operate? I mean, where is their territory? You know, like the German-American Bund had nests in Yorkville during World War Two. Where would the IRA soldiers find sanctuary?"

Mo looked around as if he'd find someone under his couch. "All over," he said. "There are rough pockets up in Inwood. Where they play soccer. All over."

"Queens, too?"

"Oh, sure, Queens. Very big in Queens. Far Rockaway. Lots of pubs along the boulevard."

Thursday, November 5, 3:45 A.M., 78 Hours and Counting

By now Jack was beginning to wonder about Nora. After that first night, when he slept over, he had found her whispering on the phone when he came out of the toilet. She had had that brittle smile—a child caught in the act—when he gave her a quizzical look. He had thought nothing of it then. Just something you came across when you broke into someone's life. She could have been juggling boyfriends. Gossiping about him with a friend. Or was it something darker?

He sat in the car across from the bus stop and waited for Nora to come home from the bar, turning over possibilities. After what had happened to Barry, everything took a sinister turn, everything seemed shaded and heavy with implications.

He looked around and saw no one else waiting in the shadows. Maybe he was being paranoid. Maybe. But the longer he sat there, waiting for her to come home from the Shebeen, the more certain he was that her appearance in his life and her connection with the bar was not a coincidence. She was guarded, silent, withholding details about herself. Of course, Irish girls were like that. But this one was past that natural reticence. The soft affection she had showed him in the night was a slip, atypical, not the iron core.

"Nora!" he called when she stepped off the bus.

She froze and twisted and seemed to bend into a

crouch, ready to strike out. Then she saw him standing under the street lamp, recognized him, and she stood up straight. It took her a moment to smile. As if she had to weigh it.

"You frightened me out of my growth," she said coldly.

"I'm in trouble."

She looked around.

"Let's not stand here then," she said, pulling him along to her apartment. He felt something protective about her.

They moved silently and quickly through the streets. There was no breath wasted in talk. Past the locks and into the apartment; she put the kettle on, then sat across from him.

"My nephew Barry's been killed," he said.

"Oh, Mother of God!" she said.

He watched her, looking for something to betray her, but she seemed genuinely shocked. She took him into her arms and comforted him, and he allowed himself to rest for a while.

"There's a spot, you know, in the west of Ireland," she cooed in her lullaby voice, as he lay half asleep and half awake. "It's outside of Galway on the coast—the place Yeats described as having a terrible beauty—where there is a separate peace. There's no war and no rebellion and the Troubles are held at bay. You can sit in a pub and look across at the island of Aran and not get blown up and not get shot. I've thought about making a home there, near the colleges and the coast, lapping up the sanctuary."

Jack was by now asleep and thought that he dreamed it all.

16

Thursday, November 5, 4:00 P.M., 65 Hours 45 Minutes and Counting

He awoke to the sound of the kettle. Nora was wrapped in a towel, fresh from the shower, and singing softly under her breath, plucking fresh underwear out of her drawer.

"I guess we overslept," he said, smiling.

She turned to face him, and he was shocked by the transformation. She was radiant. She closed the drawer and came over to the bed and bent down and kissed him.

"I wanted to let you sleep," she said.

He yawned and she slipped into his outstretched arms.

They lay like that for a while, not speaking, hardly breathing, feeling a strange and alien contentment. Then she moved—a tiny shift of position, like a cat nuzzling closer—but he felt her breasts flicker against him and he was stirred. "Nora," he said, and she looked up from the nest of his arms and he bent to kiss her. "Oh, Lord," she moaned and pressed in and reached up and pulled him closer.

"Nora," he repeated in that deep-throated voice of passion, and his hands unfolded the towel and she shifted to make it easier. She pulled away his blanket and they both stared at each other. They were white and trembling, as if the long abstinence was a shadow that kept them pale and nervous.

Later, when they were drowsy and content, the phone rang and she wrapped herself in her towel and in her secrets to answer it. She listened, her back turned to Jack, and made single sounds in response to the party on the other end.

"Yes. Fine. I understand."

Then she took her underwear and her clothing into the bathroom and dressed. The phone call had enveloped her in modesty and stealth.

"Will you be at the bar tonight?" he asked.

"I will," she said.

He dressed quickly and burned his tongue on the hot tea. She was in a hurry. He could tell. But he didn't feel jealous. Whatever errand she had to run was no emotional threat. It was something far more dangerous.

Thursday, November 5, 8:45 P.M., 61 Hours and Counting

They took the subway out to Queens and bought cold cuts and bread and soda in a delicatessen and retrieved the pickup truck from the locked garage in Flushing. Then they drove out to Long Island, eating along the way. Michael read the map and picked out the landmarks. Twice they got lost, and twice he found the way back. Soon they were glimpsing signs and smelling the ocean.

"The water's choppy," noted Dan as they rode along the shore out past Amagansett.

"It won't be so bad out in the bay," said Michael. They found the house marked for them on the map.

"Rich bastards," muttered Mick.

"Without the rich bastards we'd be using a slingshot," replied Michael.

He didn't know why he was so cantankerous with these two. They were soldiers doing their duty. Maybe it was just the fact that he didn't like working in a group.

He looked around the house. It had huge glass windows and sun decks and a counter that ran like the deck of an aircraft carrier along the wall of the kitchen. There was a barbecue out back. It must be nice during the summer, he thought. To sit on the sun deck and get fat . . . Then he pushed away the thoughts of pleasure.

There was a changing room and steps leading down to the beach. You couldn't tell if it was raining or if the wind was whipping up the surf. They were in their wet suits and heavily laden. They carried weapons and ammunition and a deflated rubber boat. Michael also had an air compressor.

"Real ammunition," instructed Michael. "In case we have to fight our way out."

They swam out deep, lugging the equipment behind with a rope. At a signal they dove and made the last few hundred yards underwater. It was a struggle with the air compressor. Finally, Michael hooked it up and turned it on, and the compressed air made the rubber boat unmanageable. It leaped up out of their hands, shot up out of the water like a submarine blowing its tanks.

On the surface, Michael pulled the boat to him. "We'll try it again," he shouted, and the other two nodded. They were experienced divers. It took a while to deflate the boat, but they finally got enough air out to make it sink again. It was difficult work, and Michael was breathing hard as he struggled to attach the air valve again. The other two were also breathing hard, he noted with satisfaction. Dan held the boat steady and used his weight to keep it down, but it was a fight. Mick had to come in and wrestle with the leaping rubber boat as well.

Finally, at a signal from Michael, they turned it loose and it shot to the surface. Michael was quick, right behind it, lugging the rest of the equipment in a waterproof sack. It took two heaves to get it into the boat, and then he climbed in afterward. Mick was on the other side of the boat, tearing away the waterproofing from the weapons. He had the rifle out, and Michael had the rocket half undone.

"You stay in the water and steady the boat," shouted Michael, and Dan nodded. Good lad. They were both good lads in a fight, he could tell.

Mick was down in the boat, the rifle cradled in his arms, ready for action. Less than three minutes since the boat hit the surface. Michael was attaching the wires and loops and steadying the rocket on his shoulder. He checked the sky to make certain it was clear. He checked the shore to see that it was far enough away so that the rocket wouldn't be noticed. Then he sighted on a cloud and launched the heat-seeking missile. The boat rocked unsteadily, but the thing worked!

The rocket went out over the Atlantic and finally ran out of fuel before it found anything hot enough to home in on. It fell harmlessly into the ocean. If anyone saw it, they would wish on it, thinking it a shooting star.

Michael stood there for a moment, rocking with the motion of the boat, enjoying the triumph. The plan would work. He would have to fine-tune it a little. He'd thought of some changes already. But he was burning with the knowledge that it was possible. It would work!

He nodded to Mick, who let off a few rounds to see how the boat would handle the kick of the automatic rifle. Then they wrapped the weapons back in the waterproof bags and eased back into the water.

Michael pulled out his knife and tore apart the rubber boat. The rubber boat was expendable. The practice run had been worth it. He cried out, "Christ Almighty!"

The other two smiled. They were witnessing the joy of Michael, the legend.

"It's Jack!" bellowed Tom Fiske, who was back to being a writer. Liam was behind the bar. Then, turning to the bar, Fiske cried, "Liam, give my friend here whatever will lubricate his throat—this man's a great high tenor when it comes to wit."

Nora had a slight shock when Jack pushed his way into the Shebeen. It was something that she saw in his face. Something hard. A certain set look of utter determination, an expression not unknown to her. And then she realized that she didn't know much about the man. Not much more than his name, if that was his name. For all she knew, he could be working with Michael. A whisper of caution crept into her greeting.

"How are you tonight?" she said crisply.

"I'm fine," he replied, and she picked up a thin crust of frost in the voice. He didn't seem like the same man that had charmed her into bed and kept her there half a day. But then he softened. "And how are you, Nora?"

"I've been better," she said, turning away.

Callan, the fire department candidate, who had a soft spot for Nora, saw the exchange, understood at once the intense meaning underneath. He followed Nora to the kitchen.

"Who is he?" he asked, indicating the space over his shoulder where were located the bar and Jack.

"Who?"

"Don't be coy, Nora Kate. Who's the suitor?"

She shrugged. "He's two pints of stout and then gone," she said. "He's none of your business."

You could only press Nora so far. Callan pinched his lips. "Michael will be here in an hour," he said. Then he looked at his watch. "Less than an hour."

"Oh?"

"Well, we don't want him to walk into anything dangerous, do we?"

"Michael can take care of himself," she said briskly. "Now come on, let me get on with my work."

She brushed past him, annoyed more with herself than Callan. Jack sat at the bar, his head low, and took in the traffic. He saw young Callan grab Nora at the kitchen door and he saw Martin skulking around near the back, his eyes busy out the rear window every few minutes.

Jack gritted his teeth and thought of Barry. He'd have felt at home here. Tossing around jokes and lapping up ale. Barry had been the joke teller, not Jack. He had been expert at punch lines. Whatever Jack knew, he'd picked up from Barry. And realizing that, he welled up with sadness and rage. He couldn't put the battered face out of his mind. The pack of matches that had come from the Shebeen. It had been in the bag. Mo said that the job was connected to the Irish and here was a nest of Irish patriots if ever he saw one. Nora was up to something, although what and how deep he had no idea. But there was a connection.

He had no choice but to work quickly and find it. It had to be here. He had felt it deep in that gut instinct that had served him so well as a cop.

And then he had seen Nora and his instincts had fallen apart. Now he smiled at her, and she smiled back. A simple thing, but it melted the ice that had built up between them.

"Well, now," she said, stopping at his spot at the bar, "I can put up some food, if you're hungry."

"I won't say no to a hamburger," he said in that oblique, self-protective fashion of the Irish.

"And would you say no to some cheese and some French fries?"

"I might, but I wouldn't mean it."

She laughed, picking up on the fact that he was mimicking her.

No point in being too cautious, she told herself. This was a fine man who'd probably had a bad day. She was not a cold IRA soldier anymore. She wasn't operating in enemy territory, suspicious of every shift in the wind, looking for hidden meanings behind every wisp of mood. She had come to America to escape just that fear and hesitation. Her aim was to bring her child to live in such open air. Michael was an extortionist, forcing her to take calls, arrange meetings, operate as a cutout. Technically, she knew that she was an accessory to some great criminal act. But Jack wasn't that sort.

There was that wide, unguarded grin of his to attest to his character.

Jack moved to a table with his cheeseburger and French fries and glass of ale. Nora stood behind the bar like a clucking mother smiling at Jack's appetite.

"What is it you do for a living?" she asked afterward, taking a seat across the table. "Do you mind my asking?"

"No. Not at all. I work for the telephone company."

He didn't know why he lied, but he was in the middle of a case and this was a location in the heart of the investigation. Nora was closed-mouthed and discreet—he'd stake his life on that—but habits are hard to break, and he was in the middle of the cover before he could back out.

"The telephone company," she repeated. "Now there's a firm that won't go out of business."

He laughed. "They might. If I keep getting stuck with overtime."

"Is it a good job? In what capacity?"

"Administration."

"Administration! Sounds grand. And what is it that you administer?"

"Accounts and records. Mostly delinquent accounts and records. I'm the fella orders them to shut off your phone if you don't pay your bill."

"I wouldn't say that too loud," she said, looking around. "There's a couple of them in here as had their service stopped on more than one occasion."

"There's a couple everywhere. You should hear the stories that they tell."

"Well, if they lay you off, you could do a book."

"I could."

They both laughed. She felt bad about being suspicious. Then she angled her head and looked at him. "The telephone company! I would have guessed something else," she said.

"Really? What would that be?"

"A politician, maybe."

His eyebrows rose.

"Not a politician himself," she quickly added. "Not a councilman or a senator. More likely the man behind the man. The one with the good eyes who knows how everything works and tells the politician that he's a fool."

"I'm no politician," he said modestly, laughing, turning his head away. "I don't have the duplicity."

"Oh, it's not duplicitous," she said indignantly. "Maybe in some parts of New York City, with your crooked mayor and corrupt borough councilmen—"

"Borough presidents," he corrected.

"Borough presidents, then. All the same, where I come from, if a man doesn't talk plain, or at least have some wit or a plain man of common sense behind him, they'll send him back to the field, picking potatoes."

"That's Ireland. Here we advertise ourselves. We brag about being witless."

"We're not above that, too, you know. It's the TV. Makes liars out of saints and fools out of sages."

He put his hand across the table, and she blushed and flinched as if she had been touched with something on fire. She looked around to see if anyone else noticed.

"Will I see you later, Nora?"

"Jack," she said softly, smiling, "this is a little fast for me."

He pulled back.

"I don't mean that I'm a tease or a schoolgirl," she

said. "I don't do this very often, you see. I just have to catch my breath."

They drove back carefully, keeping under the speed limit. Dan took the wheel in case Michael had to make a break for it.

"We're only a day or two away," said Michael, refusing to divulge the exact time even to people he trusted. The other two exchanged looks.

"We will go or not go soon—this week," continued Michael. "Today's Thursday. By Sunday night we'll be home or in hell."

They nodded. They understood. Mission safety depended on a certain amount of doubt. Michael knew the time and place of the strike, but if he told them they would pace themselves accordingly. They would lower their high level of excitement. This way they'd both stay sharp. On the edge.

"I'll be glad to get back to Dublin," said Mick, unable to mask the high excitement of the impending mission.

"Not me," said Dan. "I'd like to stay around here for a bit."

"Don't even think such a thing," warned Michael quickly. "The escape is just as important as the mission."

"I didn't mean it," said Dan. "I was only joking."

"We'll all get drunk on O'Connell Street when it's done," said Mick.

"If we're lucky, we'll never see each other again," said Michael. "That's the truth. There's no drinks around the bar for the likes of us. There's no family or home, for that matter. That's for the others, the softer ones. That's not what keeps us going."

They were on the expressway, and the traffic was light. The houses on the fringe of the highway had their windows framed with lights. The vast shopping malls glowed in the November night. Soon the Christmas lights would go up.

"You both have to lie low now," said Michael. "If one of us gets caught or tumbles, we're all done for."

He went over the plan with them again. They knew what they had to do. They might be flaky when it came to other matters, but as far as their work was concerned, Michael could find no fault at all.

"We'll try the two rubber boats," he said. "That way we'll have a backup. If the primary boat is having trouble, Dan will abandon the backup and assist. Do you get that, Dan?"

"Yes, Michael."

"The diversion might be unnecessary, but it's always better to have a fallback. Good to have both of them down there just in case."

He was talking now out of nerves. Even Michael had attacks of nerves. It gave the other two heart.

Michael drove by once. It looked all right. Then he dropped Mick off at the corner and handed him a slip of paper. "Here's a number," he said. "You ask how's business. If the coast is clear, she'll say 'It's the regular crowd.' If there's trouble, she'll say 'Oh, you know, off and on.'"

Jack was on his second cup of coffee. "What's he so nervous about?" he asked Nora, indicating Martin, the owner.

"Oh," she said, flustered, "he's the owner. He thinks there are burglars comin' in by boat to steal his business."

It registered. A lie. At least an evasion. Jack counted that and took a long step back from Nora. "He sweats like the informers in H-Block," he said.

She looked surprised. "What do you know of H-Block?"

He shrugged. "Only what I read."

A disturbance hung in the air. A small, thin texture of something not quite right. Enough to frighten a rabbit in the forest, but qualified and dismissed by Nora in the pub as a misunderstanding. Something had thrown her off her usual alert status. The thing that lowered her guard was Jack. She simply couldn't believe that he was a threat to her safety. She could believe anything of Michael. He was capable of betrayal and heartless cruelty. But Jack was soft and tender and sensitive. At least those hours they spent together were convincing.

When the phone rang Nora answered and told the inquiring caller that the pub was filled with regular customers. It was the "go" signal for Michael.

"The water looks cold," said Dan, indicating the chop in the bay.

"It'll keep us awake," Michael replied, looking around, checking the area.

They'd met Martin down by the shed. The pub owner kept flinching at every passing car. "What is it, man?" demanded Dan. "Are we followed?"

"He's just nervous," said Mick. "Isn't that right, Martin? You're just a nervous little mouse?"

Martin fumbled with the lock until Michael took the key out of his hand and unlocked the shed. The bottle was still behind the door, a few inches off the jamb, and the dust was piled where he had left it, so he knew that no one had been there; the shed had been undisturbed.

Michael examined the crates carefully all the same. People who set booby traps were sometimes clever, and you couldn't be too careful. Then he removed his thick pistol. "Hide this in your pocket," he told Martin after showing him the mechanism and the safety device. "If we're discovered, or if we shouldn't come back for any reason, hold it up at the sky and fire at an angle out over the bay. It'll warn us off. Will you do that?"

Martin couldn't speak. He was sweating and shaking like a man in the last stages of pneumonia. "Will you do that?" persisted Michael.

Martin nodded. It was as much as he could manage. Then he turned and headed back to the warmth and safety of the pub.

"He won't," said Mick with scorn.

"No, he won't," agreed Michael. "But it will make him think that he's in on it. You want them to feel implicated."

Inside the shed, they struggled into their wet suits; one man remaining on guard with an automatic weapon while the others changed. Then they encased the weapons in waterproof bags, took the gear and slogged into the filthy bay, the mud sucking at their feet as they went. In high water, they put on their flippers and the going was easier.

The three were attached to a line, like mountain climbers on an ascent. They moved deeper into the water, studying the shoreline and the boats, moving by inches, braced for an assault. This was the most vulnerable moment—in relatively shallow water, moving slowly with no means of escape, loaded down with weapons, ammunition, a bunch of explosive charges.

Finally the water was deep enough, and they dived into the dark bay, foul with oil and debris. They swam through human waste and dead fish, staying close to Michael, who was in the lead. Dan was on his left and Nick on the right. Each of the trailing men navigated by the back of Michael's flippers. Finally Michael stopped, turned and showed them a tight fist. It was the signal to remain in place.

The two men remained down while Michael let out the line by loosening the knot, and rose slowly to the surface. He was careful not to break water too quickly; he didn't want to attract attention. He took a moment on the surface, looking first at the sky, then turned and found the fixed points of light on the land: the pub and the nearby diner. He triangulated the two points with the runway lights and thus had a pretty good idea of his position.

Not bad, he thought. He could navigate in the bay. He was a few points off, but now that he knew the waters, he could manage. He waited on the surface, removing the face mask, listening. He wanted to see a plane land. He studied the horizon and stared hard. He saw the lights first. Little pinpoints in the sky. Hanging there, suspended. Almost without movement. A child's toy held by some monster hand. And then he heard it. A low growl like some approaching tiger. As it got closer, it grew into something inconceivable, the roar. A great thundering sound. Pushing down on him, trying to drown him, throwing the water into turmoil.

Suddenly his heart leaped, as if into the sky. He wasn't being pushed down. He was being sucked up by the plane. Oh, dear God, he thought, it is so close! He could reach up and touch a wing. He could see it all, oh, dear God!

For a moment he lost his head completely and

screamed up at the passing jet. "I owe you, you British bitch!"

And then the plane had passed and the silence was even thicker. He looked around to see if anyone had noticed.

There was work to do. He had to be methodical. He was a few hundred yards off the point where he had decided to plant himself. Work to do.

He replaced the face mask and let himself sink quietly. The other two were treading water, and he signaled for them to follow. They fell back into the same formation and continued the swim. Michael glanced at his underwater watch. Only half an hour since he started. Two hours left in the air tank. It seemed longer than half an hour, but he trusted his equipment. He'd checked it out minutely. That was one thing they taught you in commando training. Half an hour factored into the plan.

Once again he held up his clenched fist and the others stopped. Michael rose and checked his bearings. Another plane went over, and it was an inspiring thing.

No one has ever thought of this, he told himself. It's so easy and so obvious, how come no one has ever thought of this?

Methodically, Michael lined up the shore lights and the runway lights. Slightly off. Not much. Not enough to make any difference. And then another plane thundered overhead, even closer. Michael would plant his first boat here. This was right. Not directly in the landing pattern. But close enough so that Dan could come to assist if the primary boat got into trouble, close enough so that Dan could take over if the primary boat was lost. He let himself sink again and held up one finger in front of each face. It meant the first boat. They both understood. Both nodded.

Dan sank to the bottom of the bay and the other two followed. It was twenty-five feet down and black. Dan had to switch on his underwater light. Then he drove the anchor into the muck. When he had it started, he pulled the plunger and a small explosive charge drove the anchor deeper into the bottom, then splayed out a spread of metal hooks underneath to hold it in place. Michael pulled on the metal rod holding the anchor in place. It was strong. It would hold. It would anchor a small motor launch in a storm.

The three swimmers tied the first deflated rubber boat to the metal rod, weighing it down with the tank of compressed air. They lashed the sacks of weapons to the same rod. Michael checked the work and was satisfied. Dan would have no trouble cutting all the equipment free with his knife when it was time.

They would need another fifty yards for the second boat. That would keep Dan in range. Michael held his palm down, the signal for Dan to stay, then he and Mick swam off.

He overshot by ten yards, but that was fine. He and Mick sank to the bottom and repeated the procedure, anchoring the second rubber boat to the metal rod of the anchor in the bottom of Jamaica Bay along the landing pattern of John F. Kennedy Airport.

When he had all his equipment set, he sent Mick back to bring up Dan. Then he rose to the surface and waited. When he saw the two swimmers pop to the surface in range, close enough for either boat to do the job, he held up his hands in triumph. Then they marked both spots with homing beacons and headed back to shore.

They changed into street clothing, all breathless. Each one saw it all clearly. Martin stood off to the side, still trembling, holding the signal flare pistol at arm's length. He was glad that he hadn't called Bobby. He'd toyed with the idea, then decided against it. Bobby would have brought down an army to kill Michael. In the process, he would have shot up the pub and killed all the witnesses. No, he trusted Bobby as much as he trusted Michael. Which was not at all. The only thing that Martin wanted was to escape unhurt. He didn't even care about his honor. He'd given up on that as soon as he found out that he had engineered the robbery of a Mafia payroll and decided to turn informer to save his own hide.

When Michael and his men were completely dressed, Martin handed back the pistol, then ran inside the pub. Mick sneered. "I don't like that one at my back."

Dan stood up straight and saluted, addressing Michael by his military rank for the first time. "Commander!" he said. "An honor, sir."

Michael shook his head. "We'll split up now. Be at the number every four hours starting at noon tomorrow. The go sign is 'proceed,' the countersign is 'agreed.' Meet me here ninety minutes later."

They both stood at attention—Dan and Mick—and nodded.

Then Michael was gone. Dan said, "I feel like going to church."

"Why not?" said Mick.

17

Friday, November 6, 4:00 A.M., 53 Hours 45 Minutes and Counting

What could she do now that he had crossed that line, now that he had been to her bed, felt her shudder, heard her wanton moan, seen her wild naked? What could she do? She could not take it back or even change the imprints left upon his memory. She could wear chaste things, button herself up to the neck; she could speak in dainty little powdered evasions, but it wouldn't matter. He had seen her flesh and heard her cry and there was no going back.

And so, with a kind of happy resignation, she let him take her home again, and again she revealed herself to him and he to her, and they sang again like birds in their bliss. It was so much easier now, past the awful, awkward beginning.

"I hope you don't take this as a license to become familiar," she said, lying across Jack's chest.

"I'm surprised at you. How could you think I'd be that presumptuous?"

Her breasts were afloat on his belly.

"There are men who would misinterpret a simple act of friendship," she said merrily.

He reached down and fondled her—soft and yet compact, firm and yet answerable to Jack's tender hand. She drew in a breath, as if he'd reached in under the skin and touched the raw nerve itself.

"Friendship is a wonderful thing," he said. He leaned over, pulled her up a bit and licked on her button-hard nipple. "I personally wouldn't want to sully such a pure relationship with anything dirty."

He took her whole breast in his mouth, and Nora growled at him. "Oh, you wicked, wicked man!" She reached over and touched him, fluttering like a butterfly over the surface of his arousal. He kissed her deep and long and they made ancient sounds in their throats.

Later she made tea, as if to declare the squall over. She held her robe tight against her throat, and he put on clothing as a sign of sympathy. They sat at the kitchen table, sipping the boiling tea, not speaking for a long stretch, afraid to utter the wrong thing, which they were bound to do, no matter what was said.

"I've a child," she said finally. "Did I mention that?"

He looked around. An instinct.

"In Ireland," she said. "Seamus. Just three years old. I intend to bring him here when I get better fixed."

"And the father?"

"There's no father," she said with a hard edge. "He's dead."

They were quiet again. Dead quiet.

"I'm sorry," he said, feeling clumsy, not certain why exactly he was sorry.

"Never mind," she said. "He died for a cause. At least, he thought that he did."

"A rebel."

"A fool."

He let that sit for a moment. "You've no one else?" he asked.

Yes, she did, she thought. She wasn't alone. There was someone to say the mass for her, if it came to that. "I've some aunts," she said. "In Ireland. They're watching Seamus until I can send for him. And I've a brother."

Her voice dropped when she mentioned her brother. He picked up the nuance. He understood it from being a cop. Something hidden behind her back.

"A brother?" he said. "In Ireland?"

"God knows," she replied.

"Another fool?" he asked cautiously.

She looked at him, examining the texture and meaning of the question. Then she shrugged and said, "Worse than a fool."

She got up and swept away his cup. "I didn't tell you about my son to entangle you, Jack Mann."

"I didn't think that you did."

She sighed and turned and ran the water and spoke above the equivocating sound of the hot and cold taps. "It's a complicated life and I'm a complicated woman," she said. "I understand how a man would want to avoid messy complications. I try to avoid messy complications."

He came up behind her and took her face in his hands and kissed her gently on each eye.

"I'm not a young man," he said. "I've been twice around the block and I know the score. As far as complications go." She listened grudgingly, without the signal of commitment either way. "I don't think we complicate things for each other," he continued. "I think we're easy and rub each other like soft cream."

She turned and looked up and kissed him back.

Friday, November 6, 6:45 P.M., 39 Hours and Counting

Johnny DellaCorte hung up the phone, made two motions for his bodyguards and was gone, racing through Queens to the law office of Sally Bones.

A motor patrol squad car saw the blur of the big limousine going down Queens Boulevard, started to give chase—the traffic cop gleeful that he would be able to make some rich guy squirm inside his fancy limousine—but then the policeman recognized the limo and dropped out of the pursuit sheepishly, hoping that no one noticed. The cop knew better than to issue traffic citations to Crazy Johnny DellaCorte or any of his minions. Not only was Crazy Johnny a major figure in the cement business, which is to say organized crime, but Johnny was also a psychopath. It was not impossible that he would—and could—have a New York City policeman whacked out for giving him trouble. There were cops who would stand up to him, but it was always a risk.

At the apartment building, one of the bodyguards went in first. He pushed open the doors and punched the buttons for elevators, giving that preemptive menacing glare to anyone in the lobby. The other bodyguard came behind quietly. He was the one with his hand on the gun. The quiet one. The driver stayed behind in the limo. Only Crazy Johnny was unarmed, oblivious, marching into Sally's office, kicking out the would-be applicant for the dating service.

"Okay, where is he?"

He was standing over Sally, who wanted to get up as a sign of respect, but who was wedged in behind his desk, puffing and sweating and coming up short of breath.

"Take it easy, take it easy," Johnny said, seeing fat Sally's predicament. "Take your time. Just tell me in five seconds or Vito will turn your nuts into silver dollar pancakes."

"He's at a motel by La Guardia," Sally blurted out. He had chest pains, or maybe gas from his tight pants or tight desk.

"What motel is that, Sally?" probed Johnny, as if he were dealing with a slow child, as if he was about to run out of patience.

The trouble was that Sally didn't know. He had known, but he had trouble with names, and he forgot.

"The one, you know, by the highway," he said idiotically, frantically, going completely blank in his panic.

Johnny looked up at the ceiling. "They're all by the fucking highway, you stupid whale! That's why they're fucking motels! What's the actual name of this actual motel, you stupid mook?"

"I forgot," said Sally, who seemed to collapse.

"You better remember," Vito said in that thick Brooklyn accent that always carries a whiff of menace.

"Shut up, Vito," Johnny said. "You should know better than to interrupt me when I am speaking. You piece of wop shit."

Then, to Sally, "You better start remembering."

"It's the one with the red sign, Johnny. Oh, Christ, I got this problem with names. You know that. The red sign." Sally held both hands over his chest, squeezing tears and sweat out of his face.

"I think he means the Traveler's," Vito said.

Johnny turned and smiled. He gave his bodyguard a small, playful slap across the face. Vito tried to smile, tried to pretend it was a joke.

"That's it, that's it!" Sally cried. "It's the Traveler's. I remember now."

They brought along Sally, having pulled out the desk and freed him. The Traveler's motel was across the Grand Central Parkway from La Guardia Airport. Sally had placed two of his men on guard—one at the front and one at the back. The one at the back stiffened to attention at the sight of Crazy Johnny getting out of his limo, as if a three-star chief had walked onto his post.

He came over to the group by the limo.

"How'd you track him down?" asked Johnny.

Former detective Michael Travers said modestly that it had been good, old-fashioned legwork. "We tapped into some old sources," he explained. "You work twenty years on the force and you have outstanding markers. The guys on the desks of motels and hotels all know to give me a holler when I'm out looking for something in particular."

"And you work better than a cop?" suggested Johnny.

Travers smiled. "I don't have to follow so many rules." Johnny nodded. He knew about not following rules.

"Okay, who we got?"

"A kid named Boyle."

Johnny nodded, pushing him along.

"He checked in here the night of the stickup. Couple of hours later. Hasn't come out since. Looks very nervous, according to the floor help."

Johnny bobbed his head. This had all the right sounds, all the right smells—a lead. "What do we know about this Boyle?"

"Well, it adds up. He's an Irisher. Real strong for the IRA. Actually went over there last year. Attended one of their three-week training camps in Lebanon."

"That makes him a soldier," said Johnny.

"I told you," said Sally, beginning to get his legs back now that he had delivered what looked like the goods.

They were standing in the street, all looking up at the window, where the shades and curtains were drawn. You could still see some light seeping out, but whoever was behind the curtain was trying not to be noticed.

"Does he have a weapon?"

"The room service people thought that they saw an automatic." Travers shook his head, bobbed and nodded. "They don't know what kind. But they said there was a clip and some metal. It sounds like an automatic."

"We have to assume that he's armed," said Johnny.

"I guarantee it," said Sally.

Johnny leaned against the highly polished fender of his limousine, looking worried. "Well, we don't want to go crashing in there if he's gonna start blasting," he said finally. "We don't want a major fucking shootout and for this kid to get killed."

"No," said Sally.

"Also, we don't know if he's got the money. It could be with the other guy, it could be stashed, could be anywhere. So we want to take him alive. Am I right?"

"Absolutely," said Vito.

"No question," said Sally.

"Who's his people?" asked Johnny.

Sally shrugged. "Tom Flanagan," he said. "Who else?"

"Grab him," said Johnny. "Tonight. Meanwhile, put six more people on this guy here. We don't want him to get away."

Friday, November 6, 11:00 P.M., 34 Hours 45 Minutes and Counting

Tom Flanagan was a student of power. You didn't get to be a union boss on the docks without knowing how things worked and who got things done. You knew the rough limits of power and force, if you were Tom Flanagan. He was a personal friend of the mayor and the police chief, and he knew Crazy Johnny DellaCorte, although Johnny he did not like. They met, from time to time, on those occasions when their mutual interests overrode their natural competition.

This was like a lot of the other meetings: tense, but moved along by the urgency of practical necessity. It was like the secret meetings between the Israelis and the Jordanians in the Middle East. They arrived at a small, well-protected Chinese restaurant in Manhattan. Neutral ground. The bodyguards and henchmen all remained at separate tables, but in closing distance. Crazy Johnny knew that Flanagan brought along his tough friends. Enforcers. Four armed union men were across the street from the restaurant. Crazy Johnny also knew that they would not act unless Johnny acted crazy.

The two leaders had plum wine and toasted each other formally, but without sincerity.

"You heard about my unfortunate accident at the airport?" asked Crazy Johnny.

"Very sad," said Flanagan. "But I imagine you can make up the loss. What was it, three, four million?"

Johnny waved a hand. "The money doesn't matter. The money is shit. What matters is to set an example. Someone insults your wife, you got to teach them a lesson, am I right? You don't let someone get away with something like that."

Not wanting to answer, Flanagan took another sip of his plum wine.

Crazy Johnny leaned over and whispered. "Listen, I do not want to start a world war, but if I have to . . ." He held up his hands in a helpless gesture.

Flanagan nodded noncommittally. Crazy Johnny looked like a man who wanted to start a world war.

Johnny told him about the Boyle kid and how he was pinned to his motel room by a squad of killers.

"You think I can do something?" asked Flanagan.

Johnny laughed. "Somebody's gonna do something. If not you, then me. Look, I don't know if that kid's got the money or what. But if you don't help us out—and I hear that you have some influence with him—then we are going in. He's not comin' out alive."

Flanagan thought about it. "Suppose I can talk to some people?" he said.

Johnny wanted to clarify a point. "I don't want to make peace," he said. "I want revenge. Do you understand? I want somebody's ass! I want to taste a fucking ear in my mouth. What's wrong with you fucking people? You rob my money and you think I'm gonna take that shit?"

He was getting worked up. Flanagan could see the crazy temper pushing at the seams.

"Hey! I didn't rob the fucking payroll."

Crazy Johnny relaxed in his seat. He knew that he had to get a better grip on himself. He was ready to fly off the handle too quickly. People were always telling him that. And it was true, in part. Sometimes he pretended to be going wild, just to make the other fellow nervous.

"I know you didn't steal my money," he said. "You think I don't know that? You wouldn't be so stupid. But maybe you can help me. You know, with putting this thing right."

Flanagan was in a very tight box. These people were not going to overlook the robbery. They were not going to stop going down a trail full of hot leads. That would mean that sooner or later Michael was going to have to contend with Mafia stalkers. Michael had enough to contend with. Maybe it would be better to make some sort of accommodation.

"Let me talk to some people," said Flanagan. "Let me try and help."

Michael was wide awake. How could he sleep now, with the mission clock ticking? There were so many things to plan, to anticipate. You had to envision the mission. That was what he had learned long ago, when he began doing improbable things. If you envisioned them, they became possible. He had spoken to an athlete once, an American football player, who described how it was that he was able to leap high into the air, way past his limits, and catch a ball. The way he did it was to imagine it. And then he reached for the image.

The phone jarred him out of the mission. "It's Flanagan," said the voice on the other end of the phone.

Michael didn't answer.

"There's a major problem," continued Flanagan. Michael began looking around, mentally assembling his things for a quick escape.

"Michael! Listen to me, Michael."

"How did you find me?"

Michael was slipping on his pants and his shirt and his jacket. He was checking his gun while cradling the phone between his ear and his shoulder.

"Never mind. We got a major problem. The people who were the injured party at the airport the other night, they've been in touch."

"I'm listening."

"They've found one of the missing boys. He's in a hotel near the airport."

"I see."

"The person who found him is in a very testy mood. He wants to raise havoc. I can't seem to convince him that he should be patient and allow the work to continue."

"And you think I could convince him?"

"I can't think of a better man."

"And the kid?"

"Unless someone that he trusts talks to him, he's a dead man."

"Does he have the money?"

"There's no way to tell. No one's been into his hotel. There's only one person who can handle this, Michael."

"Where's the other one?"

"God knows."

"Maybe this one knows."

"Maybe."

Michael knew that Flanagan was right. He would have to talk face-to-face with the Mafia leader. He would have to convince him that the robbery was a blunder, an accidental missile launch. Unauthorized. Then he would have to make good. Not only with the money, but he would also have to deal with the two runaway kids. They were probably just scared. But they would have to be dealt with, all the same. Couldn't leave them loose, not with time so short, not with the prime minister due to arrive in one more day.

"I'll meet with the man," said Michael. "Get a car downstairs in twenty minutes. Have them hold a sign for a Mr. Scott."

Crazy Johnny agreed. He told Flanagan that he would meet this Michael. He didn't have to say that if he didn't get his money back and if he didn't get the skulls of the dogs who insulted and robbed him, then he would take his revenge by killing Michael. This much Flanagan understood.

18

Saturday, November 7, 3:00 A.M., 30 Hours 45 Minutes and Counting

Crazy Johnny was waiting in the backseat of the limousine when Michael looked inside. There were two bodyguards staring bullets straight at Michael from the jump seats. And Flanagan was sunk into the remote corner of the butter-soft leather of the rear seat—pale, holding a drink in his hand. The first thing that Michael thought was, he's made a deal with them.

Michael got in anyway and put his back against the rear panel, ready to shoot it out, take as many down as he could. The car started up, and everyone—with the exception of Flanagan, who was developing a liquor grin—was tense, like a den of cobras, ready to strike.

"Have a drink," said Johnny when they were heading east on Fifty-ninth Street.

"No, thanks." Michael had no intention of letting down his guard.

"Vito, give the man what he wants," said Johnny.

"Nothing," insisted Michael, not taking his hand from his pocket.

"He wants to keep his piece on us," said Vito nonchalantly, indicating Michael's hand inside his pocket.

Johnny laughed. He had intentionally not had Michael searched when he entered the car, despite the fact that his limousine was as sacred as his home. But a man of Michael's rank had to be shown some respect. Johnny understood the trappings of respect.

The windows in the car were smoked. No one could see in. The backseat was soundproofed. No one could be heard. It gave Michael a strange, floating feeling. As if he was separated from the ordinary humanity of life by these cloudy, soundless windows. He looked outside and could see that they were headed for Queens, across the Fifty-ninth Street Bridge.

"You think you scare me with that piece of shit in your pocket?" said Johnny abruptly, smiling. "You think I give a fuck?" Then he flung himself back in the seat, straightening his coat, dismissing his own life with a brush of his hand.

Michael didn't move. Flanagan took another swallow of the drink.

"Let me tell you something," said Johnny, leaning forward again. "I been shot, what? Ten times. Maybe more. You're gonna kill me? So fucking what! I'm a dead man anyway. You go into my business, sooner or later, somebody's gonna get you. So don't think I'm afraid of that." He nodded in the direction of Michael's weapon. "Don't fucking insult me by bringing a pistola into my fucking parlor."

"You want I should take his thing away?" asked Vito.

Johnny ignored him, adjusting his coat, reaching his

hand out in the air. Vito fumbled in his pocket. It could have been anything. A gun. A line of cocaine. It turned out to be only a cigarette. Vito blew his smoke out in the back of the limousine to express his anger.

Michael remained calm. He waited for the right moment, the correct dramatic pause, then spoke.

"I have the same occupational disease," said Michael, smiling, taking his hand out of his pocket, empty.

Johnny smiled, reached over and slapped Michael affectionately on the knee.

"Listen, Mikey, we wanna settle this, am I right? I'm not out to hurt anyone who doesn't have to be hurt."

"That's good. We feel the same way."

"We? You got somebody trailing us?"

The others laughed. All except Flanagan, who turned and looked out of the back window.

"You don't think I'm alone, do you?" asked Michael.

Johnny had a big grin. "Yeah, right now I think you're alone. All alone. Flanagan here is only moral support."

"Don't count us cheap," said Flanagan. "We've got a problem here, but reasonable men can settle problems."

Johnny twisted his mouth into a smile for Michael's benefit, as if they were in on the joke together. "That's labor leader talk." He turned to Flanagan. "The real world is a little more dangerous, pal," he said with some fire. "Sometimes people don't wanna be reasonable."

Michael didn't say a word. He fixed Johnny with a hard, uncompromising look.

"But, hey!" said Johnny. "We got a truce here. We're trying to work our way out without bringing down the whole fucking world, am I right?"

"You are trying to find your money," corrected Michael. "I obviously don't have it. Tom Flanagan here doesn't have it. Maybe this boy in the hotel has it."

"Boyle," said Vito. "Kid's name is Boyle."

Michael nodded. He wondered if there was a joke behind Vito's correction. Looking at the thick, uncomprehending face, he doubted it. He looked out of the window to escape from Vito's face. They were across the bridge and working their way onto Northern Boulevard, heading for the airport.

"I'll do what I can," said Michael. "But there are some things that should be clear between us, since we are in business together, so to speak."

The others flinched at the familiarity. Crazy Johnny quieted them with a look. Let him go on, he seemed to say.

"I am here for a purpose," said Michael. "It is important, to me and to my associates. It is a kind of business. I know how important business is to you. I'm certain that the reason you wish to teach young Boyle a lesson is so that businessmen will recognize and understand that certain trespassing on your property will not be tolerated."

Crazy Johnny smiled brightly. He enjoyed the sound of Michael. "Very good," he said.

"That's understandable and reasonable," continued Michael. "But let me make this point, no insult intended: me and my people will not tolerate any interference with our business. Our main business. You have a claim and it's a legitimate claim and we understand that. We recognize that. It will be settled."

"That's all I ask," said Johnny.

"But if you fuck with my business—if you interfere with the reason I have come here—my people have the capacity to make your business very difficult. Any sort of business at all. We're not just dumb cluck killers—although we are that, too. As you can see, we have some people in key places. Suppose you can't get a ship through the customs or unloaded from the docks? Suppose the cops stop looking the other way when you need a friend? Suppose there are squads of strange killers loose, hunting your men? Your business will suffer, I daresay."

Vito almost lunged. "Let me take out his fucking eyes!" he cried.

Michael held up his hand. "I'm not making threats. I'm telling you, one businessman to another, what will happen if something bad happens to me and my business. As you say, you're a dead man. So am I. And as dead men we both know that we speak with a kind of deathbed truth."

Johnny was bent forward, wearing a deep frown of concentration. Compelled by what he had heard. He held out his hand and Michael held out his. "We will settle this," he said, folding his second hand over Michael's.

Outside of the motel, former detective Travers was waiting to meet the limousine.

"He's still inside," said Travers, reading from a notepad. "Hasn't budged."

"I'll go up," said Michael. "I'll handle it."

"Vito will go with you," insisted Johnny. "You don't mind? It's not that I don't trust you."

"Fine. Just tell him to keep quiet."

Damian didn't answer the door at first. But Michael kept calling. "It's Michael, Damian. I want you to let me in. Do you hear me?" The hallway was empty. "Damian. Let me in."

Finally the door opened just enough to let Michael

and Vito squeeze in. They were unarmed. Damian kept them both covered. When he recognized Michael, he relaxed.

"Oh, Christ!" he cried, folding up on the bed, sobbing like a child. "We screwed it up! We screwed up everything!"

Vito tried to position himself so that he could eventually make a grab for the gun. Michael motioned him away. He took a chair and sat across from Damian.

"Tell me what happened."

"I don't know." He kept sobbing. "I swear. I don't know."

"Stop that, man! Tell me what happened. We have to know."

Damian tried to pull himself together. "It was a mess. All of a sudden, these guys in the truck opened up. Started shooting, and the two others from the other side started firing back. Matty got into a crouch and returned fire. One, two went down. I didn't see it too clearly. I was scared, Michael. I never even fired my weapon. I was ducking away from the bullets, thick as rain."

"Fine. Fine. Now, what happened to Matty?"

"He was supposed to meet me here. That was the plan. But he never showed up. The other two are dead. I heard that on the news. God help us."

Michael stood and paced. He studied the layout. Looked inside the bathroom.

"Damian, what happened to the money?"

The dark young man blinked. He was a good-looking boy, thought Michael. The kind that girls liked to suffer. He had no business with a gun in his hand. Too soft. Too close to his own skin.

"I don't know, Michael. I swear."

Michael rubbed his head. "Look, boyo, somebody took the money. We're all in a desperate situation here, and it calls for complete honesty. This is not the time to be tactful. Did you take it? Did you put it someplace?"

"No! I swear on my mother's grave!"

"So where did it get to? You didn't take it. The two dead fellas didn't take it, that's for certain. That only leaves Matty. Did he take it?"

Damian looked at Vito before answering. "I think so. At least, I think I remember seeing him grab the sacks of cash and stuffing them into a duffel."

"You think so."

He looked at Vito again.

"Tell me. It's all right," said Michael.

"I saw him."

"And he never made the rendezvous?"

"I'm still waiting, Michael."

"In other words, he took the money and took off," said Vito.

"Not Matty," said Damian, clenching his gun tighter. "Never. He was a believer. A true believer. More than me."

Michael nodded.

"Yeah, sure," said Vito.

"He wouldn't," pleaded Damian.

Saturday, November 7, 8:45 A.M., 25 Hours and Counting

Nora took the call, and Jack could tell that she didn't want him to hear the conversation. "Excuse me," he said, ducking into the bathroom. When he came out the phone was on the cradle and Nora was half dressed. "I have to go out," she said coldly.

It was then that Jack knew that she was involved with some IRA plot. It was not another man—the emotions for him were too strong and too obvious. She was not a criminal. This was a woman of strict moral and ethical accounting. The mysterious brother, the dead father, the phantom business at the Shebeen, it could only mean the IRA, which, in the old country, was a family business.

"Do you want me to drop you someplace?" asked Jack.

"No. You can stay. Just don't answer the phone, if you don't mind."

She was looking off into some middle distance, not even paying attention.

He was amazed to watch her dress so quickly, so efficiently, without the elaborate displays of vanity he had seen when he had watched other women dress. She checked her dress to see if it was straight, not to see if it was lovely. She put on lipstick to blend in, to attract less attention.

When she was done she looked around, noticed Jack sitting at the kitchen table, and went over and kissed him on the forehead. Like a dutiful but distracted husband going off to work, thought Jack.

She stood there for a second and almost said something, but she changed her mind and left.

Jack watched from the window. She walked quickly, heading to the subway. God, he thought with admiration, I wouldn't like to be the mugger to take that one on.

He was dressing as he watched. It didn't take him long. He guessed that she was heading for the Astoria subway station, and he took a parallel course, one block away. He ran and was out of breath when he got there, but he saw her passing through the automatic toll revolving door. He realized that he didn't have a token and there was no token booth. So he stood there for a moment until a stranger came along.

"Excuse me," he began, and the man flinched, thinking Jack one of the street people who beg for a living. He didn't notice that Jack's clothing was fresh.

A nurse came off the inbound train, and Jack began his appeal before she could duck and run. He held up two dollar bills. "Two dollars for a token," he pleaded.

She was one of those no-nonsense ward nurses who get things done without the interference of doctors.

"A dollar will do," she said, grabbing one and handing Jack the token.

"Thanks, thanks a million," said Jack.

"Next time keep a spare in your wallet," she scolded over her shoulder.

Damn Nurse Ratchet, he muttered as he raced up the stairs, hearing the Manhattan-bound train arriving.

Nora was in one of the front cars. He could see her as he found a seat one car back, half hidden behind a large, sleeping man.

She did not look around. She was tired. And annoyed. Pulled out of bed, pulled away from a warm man on a cold night to chase Michael's wild goose. She took no precautions. The old training was gone. She would have spotted Jack back there in the old days. Without even looking, she would have seen the familiar coat peeking out from the slumbering belly of the tired worker. And she would have lost him. No one was better at losing a tail than Nora Byrnes. Duck in one doorway and out the next. She had an instinct for an alley with an exit. It was uncanny, they said.

She didn't feel much like a soldier right now. She was still aglow from Jack's arms. A nice warm man with a good job in the telephone company. A house to bring Seamus home to, and a place to fuss over cupboards and hutches and linen.

These were her thoughts as she rode the subway into Manhattan, trailed by her lover.

Martin was waiting in the coffee shop on Forty-third Street and Third Avenue. From across the street Jack recognized him. Christ, he thought, she's in it up to her neck!

"We've lost him," said Martin with some panic.

"I thought you said he needed me?" said Nora.

Martin shook his head. "We need you," he said. Two men came up behind her. "Don't make a fuss," said Martin, who seemed in command.

Across the street, Jack witnessed the abduction through the window. When he saw the struggle and started to come to Nora's rescue, two men came up and grabbed him, one under each arm.

"Hey!" he said.

"Don't make any noise whatsoever," ordered police sergeant Bobby Palleo, snapping on handcuffs and stuffing Jack in the backseat of the police cruiser. Nora was coming in the other side, and Jack couldn't help but smile.

Crazy Johnny was sitting in the back of the limousine, smoking. He looked at Michael. He looked at Vito. "You searched the whole fucking room?"

They both nodded.

"There's no fucking key? No deposit slip? Nothing?"

Both nodded again.

"That guy is waitin' for his partner?"

"That's what he says," said Vito.

"Balls."

"I believe him, Johnny," said Vito.

"So it's this other fuckin' creep what has the money, am I right?"

"That is what it looks like," said Vito.

Johnny sat there, pulling away at the cigarette.

"What about him?" he said, indicating Michael.

Vito shrugged.

"Michael, step outside for a minute, I wanna talk to my gumbah, here. Okay? No insult, right?"

Michael got out of the car and took in the air.

"I believe him," said Vito when they were alone.

"Fuckin' cold," said Johnny, annoyed, pulling his coat tighter. "You believe him? How do I believe you?"

"Johnny! C'mon. You can't believe me? I'm your fuckin' cousin!"

"So? You think a cousin can't pull something?"

They sat there. Vito knew that Johnny didn't mean it. He knew that Johnny trusted him. He just didn't know what to do about Boyle or the question of Michael—the fuckin' Irish legend.

"I say we put them both on ice," said Vito.

There was a tap on the window. It was Michael. He motioned to Vito. "I understand your problem," he said. "Come with me."

Vito shrugged; at Johnny's nod, he got out of the car and went with Michael back to the room. Damian was on the bed, bracketed by two of Sally's thugs. Michael chased them out. Then he took the gun off the bed, checked the chamber, and went into the bathroom. He came out with his hand wrapped in a towel.

"Damian, this is the last time that I am going to ask. Where's Matty; where's the money?"

Damian saw the towel, understood what was about to happen and began to weep. "I don't know, Michael. Jesus have mercy."

Michael put the hand wrapped with the towel up to Damian's head, fired once and splattered blood and brains and bone over the table and the bed and the walls. There was a large chunk of brain stuck to the television screen. The shot was muffled by the towel, but they still hurried out of the room.

As the limousine was pulling away, Vito told Johnny what had taken place in the room.

"I know that this does not even the score," said Michael, looking out of the window, feeling just a pang of remorse about the handsome dark face that was smeared like a science slide over the dusty surfaces of a room inside a dingy airport motel. "I know that we still owe you some money. The amount will be refunded. Flanagan will see to that."

Flanagan nodded.

"As for the original money—the money that was stolen and the man who stole it—he, too, will be killed and the money will be returned as interest. Use it for the welfare of the dead guards."

Crazy Johnny didn't say a word. He stubbed out his cigarette and dropped Michael at a Manhattan street corner.

When Michael had left, Johnny leaned over and said to Flanagan, "He's crazier than me."

19

Saturday, November 7, 9:45 A.M., 24 Hours and Counting

They drove to a house in the heights of Manhattan, an enclave of Irish immigrants overlooking the Hudson River. The house was old—a last gasp of nineteenth-century urban architecture—but it was kept polished and bright by the working-class sweat of its owner. Tommy Keough was a supporter of long-lost causes and romantic wars. When Martin told him that they needed a house to host a meeting of the leaders of the Red Hand Society, Tommy packed a bag, left a key under the mat and went off to spend the week with relatives on Long Island. He would do anything to break the English yoke, including spending a few days with a bad-tempered aunt and her lazy son. Take it, he told Martin, feeling as if his was a blood sacrifice.

Jack and Nora were ushered through the parlor and put in a bare room with two chairs and one table. A pair of meaty guards stood by the door. Cops, decided Jack, noting the shoes and the slouch. What were cops doing here? he wondered. How come they were snatched by cops?

No one else came in.

Finally, when he could stand the silence no longer, he said, "So, Nora, what brings you to this neck of the woods?"

She smiled. She couldn't help it. The man made her laugh. Even when he acted like a fool. "I'm sorry I got you into this," she said. "But it should teach you to follow people. Did you think I was meeting a man? Were you jealous?"

"You *were* meeting a man," he said.

"Martin? A man? Oh, Lord!"

The door opened and in marched three nasty-looking characters—and Martin. Only he didn't look like the frightened buffoon who chased Nora around the bar at the Shebeen. He had a coiled, cunning look now. Martin looked dangerous.

Jack knew two of the other three slabs of beef. One was Sergeant Palleo from Citywide Anticrime. Jack remembered him as cruel. One of those cops who liked to put the cuffs on extra tight to make the suspect suffer. There was his plainclothes sidekick, Sonny Federicci. Jack recognized him from the night Barry was killed. It was probably Federicci who had burned down his home. The other one was also a cop, by the look of him—a massive man with dead eyes. The type of brute they had on every force, a man who would run through a wall on command.

"Jack," said Palleo, smiling.

"How are you, Sarge?" replied Jack, grinning.

"He remembers you," said Federicci.

"I never forget a brother cop."

Nora looked baffled. "What's going on here?" she asked.

"Oh, just some old friends," said Palleo. "Kind of like a reunion. Right?"

"You don't work for the telephone company?" asked Nora. Jack looked embarrassed.

"The phone company!" said Palleo. "Did you hear that? Nah, lady, you are looking at one tough cop."

"Not anymore," said Jack.

"Oh, yeah, that's right," said Palleo, leaning closer.

"You're off the job now. I heard that." Then, turning and looking flush into Jack's face, "So what the fuck did you do with the money?"

"You wanna tell me what you're talking about?" said Jack.

"Oh, he knows," Palleo assured the others. "You can see it in the eyes. I'm tellin' you, we got the right guy."

"You could tell," said Federicci.

"You're a policeman?" said Nora, still unable to absorb the shocks.

"I was a policeman," said Jack. "I'm retired. No longer a cop."

"What about the money?" insisted Palleo.

"What money?" asked Nora.

They ignored her.

"Look, Jack, we gotta get the money back," said Palleo. "It's our ass."

Jack nodded. Maybe these guys were moonlighting, protecting the payroll. If they lost it, it made sense that their asses would be on the line. Maybe they were cop/hoods hired to bring it back to its rightful owner. That sometimes happened. Or maybe they were freelancing, out to score the money for themselves. Maybe that was the truth. He had no idea what they knew, how much they knew, or even if they knew of his involvement. They knew about Barry, but maybe that's all they knew. Right now, his only chance was to be vague and play it by ear.

"I'm sorry, Sarge, but really, I don't know how to help you," said Jack.

"Will someone please tell me—" began Nora.

Martin broke in. Even his voice sounded different, more in command. "Nora, dear, you were cruelly misused as an accessory to our greedy schemes. I am afraid, child, that the money we are talking about was the cash stolen at the airport the other night."

"What's that to do with Jack?"

Martin said nothing.

Palleo continued. "See, we know that the money was stolen, right? I mean, it did not just get up and walk out of the airport. So we got four, maybe five million missing."

Jack almost gave himself away; he was about to say that there had been only two plus million, then caught himself.

"What's it to do with Jack?" asked Nora.

Palleo shook his head. "We don't know. Not for certain. See, the money was stolen. Four guys took it. Two of them are dead on the spot. We know that they're innocent. Two guys and a bag full of money are missing."

Nora still looked confused.

"Well, nobody knows what to think until the next day," said Palleo. "That's when this kid shows up at a chop shop looking to buy a hot car. Kid has deep pockets. Lots of cash. He pays off a lot of old debts. And this is not a kid who comes into sudden windfalls."

"I still don't understand," said Nora.

"See, the money this kid is waving around comes from the airport. The kid's name is Barry, and his uncle is an ex-cop named Jack."

"So you killed him," said Jack coldly. "He could have found the money. He could have been passing it for someone else."

"He killed himself," said Palleo, dismissing Jack's complaint. "Besides, that kid killed two of Iennello's hoods. That made him a dead man, no matter what."

"The point is, where's the rest of the money?" pressed Martin. "You see, if I don't find it, I'll have to pay with my life."

Jack was playing for time, looking for an opportunity. All he saw here was his own destruction. He had to find a way to get him and Nora out of that house.

"You didn't think that it was a romantic accident that Jack here began a courtship?" said Martin. For the first time, Nora was beginning to see the ugly implications.

"I was trying to find out who killed my nephew," Jack told Nora.

"Let me tell you the way it looks to us," said Martin. "First, we see Barry with proceeds from the robbery. Then we see Nora here and Jack—an item. Can Michael be far behind?"

"Who's Michael?" asked Jack.

"My brother," said Nora.

"And now Michael's gone," said Palleo. "Thin air. He was stayin' at a hotel in Manhattan and now he's vanished."

Martin continued. "The connection is all there. Michael. Nora. Jack. Barry. We just don't have the pieces in the right spots."

"You think that Michael has this money?" asked Nora.

"I'm certain of it," said Martin.

"Then what's the problem?" she asked. "Isn't that where you wanted it to go in the first place?"

Jack saw the fallacy of that line of reasoning first. Bobby Palleo had to spell it out. "A year ago, Martin here got it into his head to pull the perfect crime. A lot of money. A chance to help Michael. Kill two birds with one stone. Trouble was that he didn't do his homework. The people he was planning on sticking up were Mafioso. They are very sensitive about their property. Well, once the job went down, all hell broke loose. Shots. Killing. Stealing. The whole schmear. And the money is nowhere to be found. Michael didn't have it. He had to go to some big shot to finance his mission, whatever that is. By the way, do you happen to know what it is?"

Nora shook her head, and Palleo went on, "Martin gets very nervous and calls us, because he knows us. He knows that we will make a deal; we have certain contacts with the aggrieved parties and can maybe arrange for him to live. Because the truth is that his life is hanging by a thread. The problem is, we gotta find the money. Without the money, we can't arrange dink. So, we put a tail on Michael, figuring if he does not have the money, sooner or later, one of these brave soldiers is gonna try to make contact with him."

Jack could see that they didn't really know where to look. They were groping for some handle on the mystery. Why so rash? Why not sit back and wait until the answer revealed itself? The answer had to be time pressure. Something was about to happen and they could not sit back and wait. Michael's plan was about to hatch.

Saturday, November 7, 11:45 A.M., 22 Hours and Counting

He could not go back to the hotel. That would be too great a risk. He didn't want to expose himself by checking into another hotel. So Michael went back to Sarah's house. He rang the downstairs bell, and when her sleepy voice came on the intercom he said, "It's me." Before he could even finish, she was buzzing him in. Obviously, he thought, she is alone. If there was another man there it would have taken a lot more time.

She was standing in the hallway in her nightgown, shivering. "You shouldn't leave your door open," he said tenderly, but already she was crushing herself against him, pulling him into the apartment, burying her face in his neck. "I knew you'd be back," she said, breathing in his smells. She held him away to look. "Oh," she said, looking at the gray blob on his coat. "What's that?"

"Some guy, in the street," he said, cleaning it off with a handkerchief.

He was too tired for the exertion that she put him through, but it was the price of the lodging, and the truth was that, after a while, he got into it. "I thought about you," she said afterward, then turned and saw that he was asleep. That was, in a way, better. She felt protective and safe, watching Michael's worried face soften in sleep.

Then she began to plan breakfast. It was an amazing thing, and she was struck by it herself, but here she was, a woman of feminist inclinations, dreaming about a menu and place settings to please a man. And she wanted to please Michael, so quiet now. She might not have had the same opinion about his gentleness if she had known that the gray blob that he cleaned off his coat was part of the brain of a man he had murdered. It might even have disturbed her plans for breakfast.

They were left alone. Nora was furious with Jack. Her pride was hurt. She sat there in her cold silence while Jack tried to think of some way to tell her that the others were listening, that she had to be careful in what she said.

"Does Martin know Michael's plan?" he asked.

She sent back fire from her eyes.

"I know that you're angry and hurt . . ." he began.

"Oh, you do, do you? Do you also know that I think we should speak?" She was looking at the light fixture on the wall. She was telling him that the others were listening.

He was proud and more than a little impressed. And so they didn't speak. Finally Martin came back into the room, trailed by his police friends. They were standing behind him, exerting pressure. He spoke on their behalf.

"I want to know about Michael's plan," he said. "The mission."

"You know more than I do," she said stiffly. "I know that it's soon and I know that he has a lot of equipment stored in a lot of places. But I have no idea about the target or the exact date, or any of the other details.

"Do you think he'd tell me?" she asked. "You know

that he is closed-mouthed. He isn't likely to shoot off his mouth to me."

Martin considered this. "He might have left some clues. He might have said something."

"The only thing that he ever said was that he was tired."

"Me, too," said Jack.

Palleo wanted to know about Barry. Jack didn't know what to tell him.

"I think I locked him up once," said the sergeant, and Jack wanted to come to his nephew's defense and break the sergeant's nose.

"What was it, a fag thing?" asked Federicci, trying to provoke Jack into a reaction.

They came in and out during the day. Martin fed them dry tuna fish sandwiches and orange juice. "It's all that this man keeps in his refrigerator," he apologized.

It was not possible to tell what Martin and Palleo had in mind. Nora and Jack exchanged looks, but it was hard to tell what they meant, beyond the simple fact of sympathy. That was some comfort, that they each felt some sympathy for the other.

Sarah was humming, setting the table, arranging and rearranging the flowers. Placing the bacon strips carefully on their plates. When she turned, Michael was standing there, watching her, smiling. "I thought you didn't believe in such things," he said.

"What things?" she asked coyly.

"Being domestic."

"Oh, well"—and she waved her hand, dismissing the evidence on the table—"this is just breakfast. This isn't domestic."

"Breakfast in the afternoon. I like it. I like the fact

that you ran out and bought flowers and fresh rolls," he teased, and she laughed and ran into his arms again, and the breakfast got cold while they lay in bed.

"I thought you could use a good meal," she said. "If you don't have anything to do, that is. We could see some movies . . ."

"You Americans and your movie days!"

"Just like you like your tea."

"A man could get used to this," he said wistfully.

20

Saturday, November 7, 6:45 P.M., 15 Hours and Counting

The sun had turned cold, and Sarah walked close, clutching Michael's arm as they came out of the theater.

"Did you like it?" she asked.

He didn't know. He hadn't even seen it. He was lost in thoughts of the mission. It was only a matter of a few hours.

"It had moments," he said gravely. He was thinking about Dan and Mick. The boys in Queens would feel the tingle by now. They knew. They were not fools. The British delegation was due, the prime minister included. It was a prominent part of the story. The newspapers were full of it. Mick and Dan would be hovering near the phone, waiting for his call.

"I thought it was touching," she said. "The business with the boys and how they live together in a dormitory. I usually hate subtitles, but I thought this movie was touching."

"Very touching."

"Actually," she said soberly, "I didn't pay that much attention, either. I was just so happy you came back."

He smiled and leaned over and kissed her. "Let's get some Chinese food," he said. "I'm in the mood for a real feast."

"Chinese food. Yum. That's what I'd want for my last meal," she said. "Chinese food. No question."

"On second thought, could we eat at home?"

Sunday, November 8, 6:45 A.M., 3 Hours and Counting

Jack had an idea. He couldn't tell Nora, except by some eye movement, that something was up. She indicated by the same silent method that she understood. "Could I use the bathroom?" he asked one of the men standing outside watching through the peephole.

It was a fancy toilet, or what passed for a fancy toilet by someone driven to turning the functional imperative of a toilet into something cute. The toilet paper was dispensed from a little homemade house. The cabinets and walls were dotted with depictions of bright, sunny flowers. The room itself was a riot of artificial scents—pine, rose, lemon—all collecting in one unbearable, sweet, unseen cloud. Jack took the matchbook from the Shebeen and curled the cover into a circle. He stuck one of the matches behind the rest, leaving about an inch between the tip and the heads of the rest. The fuse would burn for ten seconds before hitting the others, causing an eruption of flame. It was a classic, homemade bomb.

Jack loaded up the bathtub with unwound sheets of toilet paper. He stuck in anything else that was flammable, including the towels. It would make an intense oven. Then he made a trail leading up to the curtains. He sank all of the aerosol cans that he could find—cleaners, hair mousse—into the bathtub full of paper. Then he placed his homemade bomb near the edge of the flammables and lit the single match, setting off the fuse. Ten seconds to get back to the room. The timing was important. There were two guards. He had listened for the footsteps (thanks to Mo's training) and come to recognize the tread of two separate and distinct men.

"I thought of something," he told the guard as he emerged from the bathroom, closing the door behind him. "Is Martin here?"

"Nah, they went out to breakfast."

As the guard spoke there was a whoosh and a crackle and some pops from the bathroom. Smoke began crawling out from under the door. They both turned at the same instant. Jack turned into the closest guard, hitting him solidly in the gut with an elbow, knocking him down. He pulled the .38 out of the holster, aimed it at him, but he couldn't fire. "What's that?" called the other guard, who ran into Jack, holding the gun at his head. Jack sapped them both, tying them up with linen. Then he kicked open the door and freed Nora and made for the street.

She kept looking over her shoulder as they ran for three blocks. "Too easy," she said.

Jack noticed that he was breathing harder than she was.

"Yeah, well, we caught 'em off guard," he said, sucking in as much air as he could get.

"Walk," she said, and he nodded. The running would attract attention, as well as wear him out. She kept glancing into store windows, looking over her shoulder, checking out the trailing cars. "Too damn easy!" she said.

When they hit Broadway, which was crowded even that early in Manhattan, they were able to flag down a cab.

"Thirty-fifth Avenue in Astoria," said Jack. Then, to Nora, "I want to pick up my car."

The driver began to complain.

"Hey, listen, pal, I ain't goin' to Queens. Catch another cab over by the subway."

The driver started to pull over to the curb, but Jack reached around the bulletproof partition, which was, as in most cabs, only half engaged, and put the guard's .38-caliber pistol at the driver's head.

"We're goin' to Queens and I don't want any more shit," he said. "This is police business."

"You a cop?" challenged the driver. "Cops don't stick guns in your ear. You ain't no fuckin' cop."

"They do when you talk too much. Now cut it out and drive and let's not take the Triboro Bridge."

"Sure, you don't want the real cops at the toll booth to spot you."

The traffic was lighter than usual, and Nora spoke as Jack kept one eye on the driver. "I think I know what Michael's up to," she said.

Jack turned quickly. He faced her. "It's the prime minister," she said.

In the unmarked cruiser behind them, Palleo and Martin fell in line.

"I think you're right," said Palleo.

"It's got to be the prime minister," said Martin. "He wouldn't risk all this for anything less."

In the cab, Jack was reading the paper. "She's arriving today."

Nora was angry. "You were not honest," she said.

Jack shrugged. "Were you?" he asked.

"I suppose not."

Jack was frantically trying to understand what had happened, but the facts were so full of deceit and treachery that he kept getting confused.

"So Martin was trying to save his skin," Jack said. "I understand that. But why Palleo? Why bring him in?"

"I don't understand these things," said Nora.

"I don't know what Palleo's game is."

"The money."

"Maybe. Well, it doesn't really matter, does it?"

"What do you mean?"

"Unless there's something wrong with my capacity to reason, your brother is a terrorist."

"He performs missions for the Irish Republican Army," she said. "All loyal Irishmen do that much."

"You, too?"

"Michael has control of my child. I cooperate."

"I see."

"No, you don't. Right now, I just want to get back to Ireland. I want to find a quiet spot in Galway and bring up my Seamus in peace."

"There's something else we have to do first."

She looked at him. "We've got to try and stop Michael," he said. Her eyes widened, as if to ask, Why? "I'm an old cop," he explained. "It's in my blood. I can't just let him kill the prime minister, can I?"

She didn't say anything. The cabdriver strained to overhear, but they whispered.

Then they fell silent, save for issuing directions to the driver, who had by then decided that he was not going to be shot and was worried about a tip. The meter said $15.75 when they arrived outside of Nora's house. Jack's car was still there.

"I don't have any money," Jack said to Nora. "I forgot." He held out two dollars and some change in his palm.

"I left my purse," said Nora.

The driver was now turned around in the seat, giving them one of those are-you-going-to-try-to-beat-me-out-a-fare-in-addition-to-everything-else? looks.

They sat there for a moment, then Jack said, "Hold it, wait here a minute."

He leaped out of the cab and ran across the street. He opened the trunk of his car and bent inside. Nora could see his backside and him reaching into something, and then it dawned on her what he was doing. He closed the trunk, came running back across the street and handed the driver a fifty-dollar bill.

"I can't change this! What's wrong with you? First you pull a gun on me, then you drag me out to Queens from all the way across Manhattan, then you ain't got no money, then you got money, only it's a fifty. What's the matter, don't you know how to ride a cab in New York, pal?"

"Keep the change," said Jack.

As the cab pulled away, the driver rolled down his window. "Forget what I said. You're my kind of passenger."

When they were alone, Nora turned to him. "You

mean to say it's been in the trunk of your car all this time?"

Jack grinned, shrugged. "I forgot," he said.

Jack turned on the heater and they sat in the car for a moment enjoying the flood of warm air. Jack explained what had happened. How he had stumbled into the robbery and how he had killed a man who was going to kill him. How he found himself stuck with all that cash and decided to give it back, only there didn't seem to be any convenient way of doing it.

"If I was smarter or quicker, Barry wouldn't have gotten killed," he said. "That's what really bothers me."

"What are we going to do now?" asked Nora.

"Well, after we do something about Michael, we have to give the money back. Find some way of doing it discreetly. But let me ask you something. Doesn't it bother you that he is going to try to kill the prime minister and maybe a lot of other innocent people? Doesn't that disturb you a little?"

"Frankly, it doesn't."

He looked shocked.

"They have a shoot-to-kill order out on Michael. He's a soldier. They have their soldiers. We have ours. Besides, I have Seamus to worry about. You're a good man, Jack. But I don't think you know the first thing about war."

"Is that what this is, war?"

"What did you think it was?"

He rubbed his hands and stared down at the heating vents. "I'm a cop," he said.

The cruiser had slid into a spot down the block that was shielded by some trees from a clear view of Jack's Buick.

"He's going into the trunk for something," Martin had said, squinting through the windshield.

"What's he goin' after?" Palleo had asked.

"Can't tell," Martin had replied.

Then: "Oh, God, it's the fuckin' money!"

"Okay. He's got the money. Keep an eye on him."

Martin was stunned. "He's got the money," he said. "Why don't we just grab it?"

Bobby Palleo turned and fixed Martin with a sick smile. "It was never the money we were after, you stupid old fuck."

"You're after Michael!" were the last words Martin ever spoke. The cop in the backseat, on a signal from Bobby Palleo, put two bullets into Martin's back. The silencer muffled the sound, and the cop held Martin's corpse in place so that he looked like a sleepy passenger.

Sunday, November 8, 7:45 A.M., 2 Hours and Counting

Sarah was restless and couldn't sleep. She was planning breakfast and lunch and dinner.

"Real shepherd's pie requires lamb," she said, seeing Michael watching her. "But in a pinch, or in America, substitutes are acceptable."

Michael nodded his agreement. Then, "I have a call to make," he said.

"Make it here." But as she said it, she knew that the whole point was that he had to go out to make the call. God, she thought, was she becoming that cloying overnight? Was it possible to just slip back into retrocultural evolution with the right man? Was that all it took?

"Sure, of course," she said. She wanted to ask if he'd be back. But she didn't. She watched him put on his coat and his peaked cap and go out. And then she waited for him to return. She would wait a long time.

Michael was in a phone booth on a street corner ten blocks away from Sarah's house. "Where've you been?" demanded Flanagan. He sounded very frightened.

"Why?" asked Michael.

"Shit is hitting the fan."

"I thought that we were all straight with DellaCorte and his people?"

"Something's gone wrong; it's not DellaCorte. Somebody's out hunting for you."

"Is it police?"

"No. Not strictly police."

"Maybe federal?"

"No. Maybe. I can't tell."

"Then what do you know?"

"A lot of questions. My friends in the department have become very wary, very cautious. There's a sense of something. And your sister has disappeared. I'm telling you, there's some frantic shit going down."

Michael thought about it. "What do you recommend?"

"This whole thing has turned sour," said Flanagan. "Break off the mission. Get out of the country. Go to ground. Find those two boys who were to help and warn them. But for God's sake, call it off."

"Okay," said Michael finally. "It's ended. I'm canceling the mission and pulling my people out. I'm going home."

"Thank God," said Flanagan, who hadn't expected reasonable behavior from Michael.

Michael hung up the phone, thought of calling Sarah, decided against it, and walked fifteen blocks to another phone and waited. It was almost eight. She was a nice girl. She had a nice life. He reached into his pocket and found a strange piece of paper.

"I know that we don't know each other that well, but I feel the stirring of something," he read.

Lucky man who would get her, Michael thought. Little notes. A sweet nature. Lucky man. Not him, of course. He had no intention of giving up the mission.

21

Sunday, November 8, 8:30 A.M., 1 Hour 15 Minutes and Counting

Michael was waiting for them down the road from the Shebeen. It was a risk, exposing himself, but he had no choice. They showed up in forty minutes. Michael got into the pickup and told Mick and Dan what had happened.

"From now on, we are in quarantine. We are on the mission," he said.

The two young IRA soldiers were impressed by the great sweep and drama of the moment. They slipped the truck into a parking lot two hundred feet away from the entrance to the pub. Then they crept down to the shed and emptied out the necessary equipment so they would not have to come back. It took four trips to carry it all back to the truck, and they were winded when it was done.

"I don't suppose we could stop in for a pint," said

Mick, and Michael looked up quickly to make certain that he was joking.

Sonny Federicci watched Michael from the mall across the highway. He put in a quick call to Bobby. "It's him. At the Shebeen. This looks like it."

"Hang on him till we get there," said Sergeant Palleo into the radio. "If they look like they're making a move, stop them."

"Right," said Detective Federicci. "Out."

Jack and Nora had been too tired to sleep. They lay in her bed for a while, staring at the ceiling. "How can you just leave it down there?" she had said.

"It's as safe there as anywhere else," he had shrugged. There were shadows on the ceiling, and she had laughed. "God, what I could do with that money."

"What could you do?"

"Go back to Ireland. Take care of my child. Feed a lot of children, for that matter," she said. "There's a lot of hungry children in Ireland. There's a spot in Galway where there is no war. Just peace and beauty. A true sanctuary."

"It's stolen money," he had said. "It doesn't belong to you."

"Who does it belong to, then? To greedy little Martin, who'd use it to drink himself into an early grave? Is that the proper owner? To those villains who wanted to kill us today?"

He had sighed and gone into the bathroom. Then he came back and stood at the foot of the bed.

"Look, there are a few really strict rules in life," he had said. "You're not supposed to lie and you're not supposed to cheat and you're not supposed to kill and you're not supposed to steal. So it says in the Bible. So I believe. I've broken a few of those rules, but I'll tell you something, Nora, I still believe in them. I still believe that it's wrong to take money that does not belong to you."

She sat up and took his face in her hands and kissed him. "You're a good person, Jack Mann. I have to tell you that. And good men are rare indeed. But this money does not belong to anyone that matters. These are Mafia people. They will use this money to buy drugs and slaughter black children. This is not money that should be returned to its owner. There is no rightful owner.

"What would you do with a lot of money?" Nora had asked.

"Return it," he had said.

"No, really, what would you do?"

He had thought about it. "Take it easy, I guess. Give some away. Just take it easy."

"I'd have too many things to do with it. There's not enough money for all the things. Oh, you're right, money is a terrible curse. It's like flypaper on your soul."

"What would Michael do with it?" Jack had asked.

She had laughed. "Michael? What he always does. Buy some guns and bombs."

"What would he do if he were buying something personal?"

"He doesn't have anything personal."

"Yes he does. Everybody does. Make believe."

"Pretend? That's not easy with Michael. If he bought something personal it would be an island. His own private island. Mined, of course. He's a lone wolf."

"Not an island. Wolves don't like water."

"That one does," said Nora. "When he was in the British Commandos he specialized in underwater demolition. He's like a fish when it comes to water. They say it was him that got Mountbatten. Swam two miles underwater and planted a limpet mine on the boat."

"Do you believe it?"

"I don't like to, but, yes, I believe it."

"Pretty cold-blooded, that."

"He likes the technical challenge. He likes to take on an impossible job and get it done."

"We have to stop Michael's mission. Get dressed."

He stood on shore and studied the chop. The boats would be hard to hold steady, thought Michael. But it would keep surveillance down. Bad weather had a tendency to make security people sloppy. They had the irrational notion that an attack could not develop in inclement weather. This was how the Allies got ashore on D day in World War II. The silly Germans thought it was a day off when it rained.

"When do we go in?" asked Dan, standing next to him. They were between two houses clamped shut by sheriff's notices. A good spot to enter the water. A little off from the point they would have entered if they used the Shebeen. But not far enough off to endanger the mission.

"Now," said Michael.

"Hold it!" cried Sonny Federicci, holding up his badge, his gun out. He couldn't wait anymore for Bobby. He saw that they were about to go into the water. "Police! Freeze!"

The three of them froze. "Steady," said Michael under his breath.

Detective Sonny Federicci thought that he could contain the three of them, but he miscalculated. He couldn't keep them all in his vision. And in an instant Mick had a pistol in his hand and was in a combat crouch and firing at Federicci. Sonny tried to return fire, but by the time he lowered his pistol to line up a shot, Michael had also dropped into a crouch and had taken the detective in a crossfire. Federicci didn't have a chance. Mick caught him once in the throat. Michael had him three times in the chest. He was dead before he could even fire his weapon.

"Okay!" said Michael. "Let's get going! Quick! Quick! Quick!"

Mo was still asleep when Jack called. "Yes," he said. "Of course I know about the prime minister. She's visiting the United Nations. Today."

"And she's flying into Kennedy, right?" asked Jack.

"You know, there are a lot of people who would like to talk to you, fella."

"Mo, please, just bear with me. The prime minister is coming to the United Nations. She is going to land at Kennedy Airport and someone—an IRA terrorist—is going to try to kill her."

"How good is this tip?"

"It is a very educated guess. Mo, get them to change the airport. Let her land at Newark. Washington. Anyplace but Kennedy."

"C'mon, Jack, you know it's not that easy. This is State Department. Besides, how am I gonna justify it? Say I got a tip from a slightly disreputable friend?"

"Mo, this is not some bullshit tip. This is for real."

"I hear you. The question is, What do I do?"

"Something. Call emergency fucking services. Call

nine-one-one. Make it a fucking ten-thirteen. I don't give a shit."

"Jack, Jack, Jack! Listen to me. I'm your friend. You need help. You need a friend."

When he hung up, after fruitlessly pleading with Mo, Jack knew that no one else was going to stop Michael.

"I've got to go out to the airport and try to stop this."

"How can you? You're a wanted man yourself."

"I know."

"You don't even know what Michael looks like."

"You wouldn't happen to have a picture?"

"I'm going with you," said Nora. "At least I know what he looks like."

They changed close to the water, out in the open. They put Federicci's body behind the shed and went to work. No one noticed, or if they did, they assumed that the three men were police divers going out on the job. They took their weapons out of the van and encased them in waterproof plastic, checked the equipment and turned on the homing beeper. Michael heard the answering beep. All three smiled.

Michael looked up at the darkening sky. It wouldn't prevent the prime minister's jet from landing. Not the thunderheads. Not the cloud cover. Not all the heavens. But maybe he would. It was 9:10. The plane was due at 9:45. Plenty of time.

Mick came over and shook Michael's hand. Dan had tears in his eyes. It's understandable, Michael thought. They'd never been out on a job of this size. No one had.

Then they walked out into the bay, squishing mud under their feet, keeping a low silhouette. No one felt cold. They were warmed by that inner fire.

* * *

"The plane's due at nine forty-five," said Jack.

"You're repeating yourself," said Nora.

Behind them the cruiser followed the Buick along Cross Bay Boulevard, skirting the airport.

"They're going for it now," said Palleo. "Where's Sonny?"

"I can't tell," replied Detective Schultz in the backseat. "I can't see him."

"He should be here," said Palleo.

Jack pulled onto the Belt Parkway and headed west, away from the airport.

"Where're we going?" asked Nora.

"I have an idea," said Jack. "Trust me."

"Have I ever let you down?"

He turned off the highway at the Flatbush Avenue Extension, then swung into the old Navy Gate leading to Floyd Bennett Naval Air Station.

"They're trying to lose us," said Palleo.

"Traffic should start to get thick about now," said Schultz.

Michael's sense of tranquillity returned underwater. It was a soothing element, even with the debris that floated in the harbors around New York City.

There were landmarks that he recognized. An old car. How did it get out here, in the middle of the bay? he wondered. Fell off a barge, probably. The homing sound was getting stronger. He checked his watch: 9:25. Ahead he could see the faint blink of the underwater beacon. He began to imagine the act itself.

"Here we are," said Jack as they pulled into the police department's helicopter squadron area. The air policemen were getting ready to take off, a routine mission to seal off Kennedy Airport before the arrival of the jetliner. They would form a four-helicopter box, keeping private aircraft away. Air force fighters were scrambled at a much higher altitude. The choppers would also shoo away the small fishing craft that wandered, as they always did, into the forbidden zone.

There was only one man, and one helicopter, left on the pad when Jack and Nora pulled up. The others had already left for their stations.

Jack jumped out of the car. "I forgot to ask—can you drive?"

"Better than you," said Nora, sliding over behind the wheel.

"Look, this may not work," he said. "I just wanted you to know . . ."

"I'll wait for you," she said. "I'll be at the pub."

The men in the trailing car didn't know what to make of it. They were confused and expected Jack to lead them to Michael. By the time Nora took off in the Buick, they didn't know who to follow. So they followed her. She would lead them to Michael.

Jack had his old badge flapping out of his pocket, and the maintenance crew paid no attention. Another cop on assignment. He went walking up to the man in the flight suit, reached behind as if he had some kind of paper or set of orders, then pulled out a gun.

"What's going on?" asked the cop.

"I'm on the job," said Jack. "You gotta believe me."

"I know you," said the cop. "I've seen you at headquarters. I know you're a cop. So why the fucking gun?"

"Somebody's gonna try and kill the British prime

minister. I'm the only one who can stop it. And I can't do it without you."

"You ain't gonna do it with me," said the pilot.

"I'm gonna have to kill you if you don't help me. Believe it."

The cop considered it.

"I'm really trying to prevent a tragedy," said Jack.

"You know, if we go into that restricted zone, we'll be shot down."

"It's a chance I gotta take."

"We."

"What?"

"If we go, I'll be in the craft. So it's a chance *we* have to take."

The first rubber boat was intact. Michael nodded, and Dan dropped out of the formation. It was good that they had had the rehearsal, Michael thought. Always better to know what to expect.

Time was close. They swam quickly and found the second boat. It was 9:35. Michael unlimbered the boat while Mick attached the nozzle for the compressed air tank. Michael's pulse was thundering.

There was a rifle inside the cockpit of the helicopter. Jack took it off the rack. The pilot, meanwhile, was wigwagging, trying to signal his buddies that he was in trouble. Jack shook his head and yelled above the engine. "Quit it!" He showed him the gun. The other choppers stayed out of the dead zone.

Suddenly Jack heard a jet engine somewhere behind him. Oh, Christ, he thought, it's happening too fast. He was right over the incoming lane of landing traffic.

Loudspeakers were calling, telling the pilot to move out of the landing pattern. Two other helicopters—one Coast Guard, the other Marine—were closing in, lining him up, confused by the police department markings. Radios and loudspeakers were squawking, ordering the chopper out of the area, asking for identification.

Just then Jack saw the first boat pop out of the water. It broke water fifty yards off to Jack's port side. A man in a wet suit was climbing out of the water and into the boat. The man had a bundle. He ripped it open and out came an automatic rifle with the clip already loaded.

It was 9:41. A streak of bullets from the boat tore into the Marine helicopter coming in alongside the Coast Guard chopper. The Marine helicopter wavered, started to fall, then exploded. The Coast Guard chopper hesitated, trying to rearrange its targeting computers. But the man in the first boat was too quick. He fired off a heat-seeking missile, which exploded with devastating impact. The force sent Jack's helicopter reeling. The pilot was radioing: "Mayday! Mayday! We got every kind of shit going down."

He turned the chopper back to the target, and Jack put a burst of automatic fire across the assassin's chest.

The prime minister's jet was a tiny dot growing bigger in the south over Manhattan. It was safe now. Jack indicated that they could head in for shore. The helicopter pilot looked relieved.

Then Jack saw the second boat blown onto the surface. He slammed the shoulder of the pilot, who didn't see what was happening. Pointing down.

Two men had climbed out of the water and onto the second boat. One had a rifle and another was ripping the covering off something. With a jolt, Jack realized that these were the real assassins. The first boat had been a decoy!

He could not actually hear the sound of the firefight, but Michael could feel the shock waves. He could feel the sea growing turbulent. He signaled Mick. Blow the compressed air.

They came out of the water to see the sky abloom with little bouquets of fire. When he turned, he saw Dan catch a stitch of automatic fire across his chest. Done for, he noted.

He climbed out of the water while Mick held the boat steady. He held it for Mick. In fifteen seconds they were up and crouched and at work on the platform. That one helicopter was still there—rocking, but still there. The jet was committed, closing in on the landing approach. Michael tore the wrapping off the missile and got it locked and loaded. He turned to aim at the incoming jet. He could not miss. Not at this range.

The gun jammed, and Jack saw that there was no more time. He motioned the pilot closer to the raft and then he dove, fifty feet above the surface. He heard his arm crack just as he hit the man with the missile. But he was satisfied. The heat-seeking missile fizzled harmlessly into the bay.

Mo was waiting when the Coast Guard launch dropped Jack on the shore. There was a cluster of police brass with him. The members of the media were roped off in the distance, clamoring for an interview. While the paramedics were stopping the blood and patching the fractured arm, Jack asked Mo to bring Nora and his car back from the Shebeen.

The mayor arrived and congratulated Jack on his quick thinking and his bravery.

"We got one prisoner," said the deputy chief in charge of Queens detectives.

"One?" asked Jack.

"Yeah, that third guy, the one you landed on, he's drowned."

"Are you certain?"

"He took a pretty bad shot. Where else could he be?"

They never did find the body. And they didn't find Nora. A woman matching her description had left the airport, when it was reopened, on a flight to Canada, with connections to Ireland.

"Well," said Mo, philosophically, seeing Jack crestfallen, "she stole your car, but she left it at the airport."

"Yeah," said Jack. "I guess I'm lucky. I came out even."

Epilogue

It was spring in Ireland, and the man who got off the plane in Dublin felt the sunshine and stood for a moment, basking in the warmth. He waited for a cab that drove him through the city to the train station. He stepped across the street and had a coffee. There was some time until his train was due. The woman behind the bar noticed that he winced when he lifted the cup.

"Hurt yourself?" she asked.

"I guess I did," said the man.

The train ran due west across Ireland, and the man sat by the window for six hours, drinking in the green. "Lovely," he said. The people around him on the train thought him "queer," but then Ireland was famous for drawing the queer ones.

When he got to Galway he had a porter check his bags into the Great Southern Hotel. Then he got into a cab and asked the driver some questions. They took off past the town square with its old cannon and drove down past the jetties. They could see the spot where the men of Aran landed with their catches. And the old houses where the wives waited for the fishermen.

Finally they pulled into an old house. It had been a fine house and had run down. But it was rebuilt now, and the lady of the house was famous locally for her great charity.

She was in the yard when the man came along the path, having released the cab to go back to town. They walked to each other slowly, Nora and Jack. They had time. "I was expecting you," she said as she walked into his arms. "Welcome to my sanctuary."

Detroit City Ordinance 29-85, Section 29-2-2(b) provides: "Any person who retains any library material or any part thereof for more than fifty (50) calendar days beyond the due date shall be guilty of a misdemeanor."

The number of books that may be drawn at one time by the card holder is governed by the reasonable needs of the reader and the material on hand.

Books for junior readers are subject to special rules.